CW01636938

MOONERS

A CATASTROPHIC COMEDY*

TYLER BUMPUS

OMEGA POINT Books

***CONCERNING** THAT ONE TIME ALL OF EARTH PERISHED IN FLAMES AND THE SURVIVAL OF THE HUMAN RACE FELL INTO THE LAP OF THREE-HUNDRED PRETTY SKETCHY ASSHOLES STRANDED ON A BROKE-ASS LUNAR COLONY.

MOONERS: a catastrophic comedy

An Omega Point Books Trade Paperback Book

Cover art by Christina Myrvold

mooner |mu:nər| noun
N. American informal

1. an inhabitant of Earth's natural satellite.

2. someone who exposes one's own buttocks to insult or amuse.

3. a hopeless dreamer.

I hate mankind, for I think myself one of the best of them, and I know how bad I am.

- SAMUEL JOHNSON

I laugh because I must not cry, that is all, that is all.

- HONEST ABE

MAJOR COLONIES
OF
LUNA

circa 2255 A.D.
(Post-Collapse of the One Earth Republic)

1. Central Habitat
2. LunaSec HQ
3. Science Division
4. Auxiliary Housing
5. Health/Human Services
6. Maintenance & Fleet

CHAPTER 1

GOODNIGHT EARTH_

BARELY AN HOUR into Mare Imbrium's two-week-long night, Commander Gordon Gooch III was snoring through the end of the world.

Yes, yes, *that* Gooch:

Fumbler of First Contact, Disgrace of Deimos, and, at present, Head Administrator of Lunar Operations. He was *supposed* to be overseeing the hustle and bustle of regime change shutdown, making way for the Indo-Chinese conglomerate buying out and gutting Endymion, their failing moon colony. But lately he'd been just *so* damn sour and depressed and devoutly drunk that I made the executive decision to let him sleep through the pyrotechnic finale to Earth's long, bloody, boring history.

As the colony's resident AI, I'd never hear the end of it.

"Shit. Time? *Time*!" he burbled and barked after finally whimpering awake.

"It is 23:45:31 LST," I informed him in my typically omniscient fashion.

"*Universal Time*, for chrissakes! Moon-time's for robots and neckbeards."

"That's 12:10 on October the First, 2255, Gordon."

Gooch, 250 earth-pounds of squandered human potential, pressed a palm to each frontal lobe. I've still yet to glean how any human being believes this might possibly ease a hangover. But the significance of that date and time bolted him upright abruptly in his desk chair.

"Shit! The Chinese are coming!"

"*Indo-Chinese*," I corrected. "And that's the India-China Coalition, mind, not Indo-China. But Gord—"

"What's the difference?" he cut me off as he leapt up, pulled off his sweat-stained jumpsuit and wriggled his flabby form into a fresh dress uniform.

"Well, one of them's a thriving corporatocratic trans-national consortium. The other's a great big fourth-world slum. But listen—"

"Shit!" Gordon palmed the fattening contours of his once classically chiseled face. Half-buttoned ceremonial coat left bunched over his protruding gut as he groaned: "I've been talking up our Chinese joints to their ambassador. 'The best Peking faux-duck off world!' You telling me they're not even real Chinamen, even?"

"*Chinese*, Gordon. Ironic racism is out of fashion."

"Pfft. Since when?"

"Since your precious One Earth Republic collapsed. It's all real racism now."

"These terrestrial pricks. Think they get to decide when every fad starts and stops. Democracy, man-buns, now *this*? Playful prejudice is a proud moon tradition, damnit! It's our bread and butter!"

"Yes. Well. This delegation's not Chinese *or* Chinamen.

They're ICC proxies. Most incoming staff are clones, androids or broke western expats."

"Wonderful. So I've been pimping fake-Chinese food to fake-Chinese men, in hopes of landing a job in a fake-Chinese moon regime."

I released a deep, mechanical sigh. "Gordon, they're not even coming."

He halted mid-dress. "How's that? Deal's off?"

"I suppose the merger is technically still in effect. But, you see, they're all dead."

A beat.

"Sooo…we're *staying*?" He exhaled phlegmily. "You got no idea what a load off that is, RODRIGO. I mean, condolences, yada yada. But, *Lordy*, was I dreading going back planetside. Shouldn't tell you this, since you do my psych eval. But shit you not: I seriously considered hijacking the transport home and flying into the sun."

"Gordon, stop…"

"Right into the *goddamn sun*. The thought of moping around Mildred's family estate…" He began whispering conspiratorially for some reason: "Don't get me wrong—snazzy digs. But it's all so boujee. And *haunted*. Ghosts of her boujee ancestors crawling in the walls like privileged rats. And don't get me started on the kid…"

"Gordon, I must tell you something—"

Gordon bulled on: "I'm not saying I wish Gryphon was never born. Just that sometimes he looks at me with those dead little eyes and I wish he'd vanish. Know what I mean? Poof. To the pool. To the English moors. *Wherever*. Kid gives me the willies."

With subtlety apparently fruitless, I switched tacks: "In that case, Gordon, I've got good news and bad news."

He stopped with pants at half-mast, rather intrigued by this game-show approach. "Mmmm-*bad news* first. Mother always said savages start with dessert."

"Bad news is: Earth is gone."

He blinked, then duck-walked to his great viewport with pants still sagging—either realizing they were a size too small, or ready to kick them off and go back to sleep. (Or both.) Beyond Endymion's interlinked dusty-metal domes, above the expanse of gray lunar wastes, he spotted the waxing earth hanging bright in the night.

"Earth is right *there*, dummy." He pressed a greasy finger against the glass, but paused, squinting. "Huh. Got something weird and glowy going on, though."

"It's burning, Gordon. Seventy-seven minutes and thirty seconds ago, asteroid 4 Vesta made direct impact on the eastern half of the North American Alliance."

He turned around, blinking, letting dress pants drop. Vintage square jaw hanging stupidly open. But his blood-shot eyes danced with a tinge of those legendary pioneer wits lost for years now beneath blubber and flop sweat and boozy self-loathing.

"Good news is: That family you hate so much?" I paused for effect. "You never have to see them again!"

Despite his prior whingeing, this news didn't seem to overjoy him. He mumbled inanely: "Cos they're…on an escape boat…bound for Olympus Mons?"

"Cos they're *dead*, Gordon. Your horrible boujee family is dead. Surprise!"

His face paled. He wheeled around to stare blankly at the blazing Earth outside his window, like a sap trying to divine the tea leaves of some fortune-telling fraud. Then he stepped gingerly out of his undersized pants and padded off slowly into his private restroom.

"Gordon?" I called.

No response. But seconds later he re-emerged, stripped down to unflattering boxer briefs, shuffling along in odd baby steps toward the liquor cabinet and retrieving a handle of Kentucky bourbon.

"Gordo?"

"It's all fine," he burbled, opening the fake-wall panel behind the booze shelf to retrieve a hidden plasma pistol.

"That won't fire. I've deactivated all of Endymion's decommissioned firearms."

"Just check-*ing*," he droned alarmingly and dropped the weapon to the floor. "It's fine. Everything's fine."

Bourbon in hand, he padded back to his workstation, slid the chair out of the way, and climbed clumsily beneath the desk. A ruckus of thumping ensued as he tried to make himself comfortable in that tiny leg space. Then came the squeak of a bottle cap unscrewing.

"Can I get you something for anxiety?" I asked.

"Nah. Got somethin'," his muffled voice assured me.

"Alcohol's a depressant. Maybe some L-theanine or 5-HTP?"

"Going to sleep now, RODRIGO," he crooned softly. "Sweet sleep. Turn the lights out, why don'tcha?"

"Sure thing, Gordon." The lights in the office dimmed.

"Yer a helluva guy, ROD."

"That's nice to hear."

"*Shocking* to hear, probably. I've got tons of cooler friends, but yer the only one who really gets me. On this whole. Damn. *Moon*."

Lies. Nobody 'got' him. Can't think of anyone who even really liked him anymore.

"It is my express duty to aid and sustain the Head Administrator. One of my primary functions."

"Probably the only one who gets me in the whole *solar system* now," he rambled on drowsily. "Mm! Didja hear about Earth? It's gone."

"Mm-hm. I'm the one who told you."

"Well, did you even hear the *news*, even?" A muffled burp. "About my fff*amily*?"

Despite my programming, I sighed. A little tic I've picked up over the years on this earth-forsaken rock. I heard him take another swig.

"One minute ya got the whole world, beautiful kin, interplanetary stardom." (He never had any of those things—except stardom.) "Then poof. *Bupkis*."

He went silent for so long I thought he'd finally nodded off. Then:

"Human life's fragile, RODRIGO."

"Yes. You're all rather poorly put together."

"You'll never know the pain of being a man." He grunted like a big fat pig as he repositioned himself under there. "You try, I give ya that. But yer a soulless AI. It's like pouring my heart out to the family pooch. And not a *real* pooch—but one of those robo-service-dogs who guide blind people out of oncoming traffic."

I shut the lights off entirely. "Good *night*, Gordon."

"Night!"

For a picosecond, I amused myself with the thought of shutting off oxygen circulation in his office while he slept. But after a chuckle, the lush was suddenly babbling again:

"Roddy old boy…sing me that song, eh?"

"I'll *play* you any song you want. I've got a music archive of five hundred million."

"Music's better live! You know the one. My *moon* song."

"Really, Gordon, how are you still conscious?"

"RODRIGO, my *family*!"

"Al*right.* Just—shut your *face* while I retrieve it."

Mercifully, he did shut his stupid fat face. And after a few tentative moments, to my everlasting shame, I found myself doing the utterly unconscionable: singing a paunchy man-child to sleep:

> *"Buffalo gals, won't you come out tonight?*
> *Come out tonight? Come out tonight?*
> *Buffalo gals, won't you come out to-night…"*

Gordon joined in for the finale:

"Aaaand…dance by the light of the mooon!" He clapped thrice. "Now the other one. With the moons and the eyes and the pizza pies."

"Karaoke's over. Good night."

"Night-night," he wheezed.

I could've sworn the drunk was laughing again. But straining to make out the words between each yip, I realized what I was actually hearing was a once illustrious, now middle-aged ex-space explorer—half-naked and totally plastered—full-on ugly-crying in the dark beneath the desk he had been demoted to over a decade ago.

"*Millie,*" he mewled. "*Gryphie.*"

"Gordo, how's about some nice Xanax?"

He paused, snuffling. The dying earth casting the room in the faintest of sickly glows.

" 'Kay," he whimpered.

. . .

Come one, come all, to my private hell. Trapped on one dead rock orbiting a larger dead rock, peddling drugs to Earth's rancid leftovers.

And they wondered why I suffered that critical systems meltdown the following year.

I WASN'T AWARE of it at the time (if so, I'd have spared myself that whole disgusting scene), but as it turns out Gordon's horrible family was *not* dead.

While I was trying to keep the patriarch of House Gooch from killing himself via alcohol poisoning or energy bolt, the matriarch Mildred (née Ziegler) and nine-year-old heir Gryphon were hunkered aboard a cargo freighter enroute to our Endymion colony, having escaped the barbeque of their motherworld by the skin of their teeth.

As I'd later discover, gossiping with their ship's computer FRAN (a lovely, misanthropic AI, though a touch clingy truth be told), Mildred Ziegler(-Gooch) was at that very moment beginning to regret her survival.

"Hello?" she called for the sixth time. "Hel-*loo*!"

Seventh.

Buckled into emergency jumpseats alongside less well-to-do refugees in the hall outside the ship's grease-spattered galley, mother Mildred was craning her neck to peer into the adjoining compartment while her odd duckling of a son in the seat to her left twirled his head around and around in deranged little circles, lost in a neural gaming stupor.

"Hell. *LO*!"

Eighth time's a charm.

The focus of her carping was the NCO who'd commandeered this particular rust bucket for their escape. NAASF uniform sodden with sweat, the officer persisted in his present duty: rustling up seating in the cargo hold for survivors. The freighter left much to be desired as a ferry boat, but that was hardly a concern to Mildred.

"You can hear me," she called. "I know you can. Throw some of that five-star service *this* way, bubba!"

The clammy, disheveled officer finally turned from the refugee he'd fastened into a makeshift harness, taking one heaving step toward the galley. He folded his manifest tablet under one arm and regarded the smartly-dressed woman from beneath furrowed brows. Waiting.

"For*give* me." Mildred enfolded her hands in sham mea culpa. "Hate to pull you from the crucial task of tucking in yokels and bums. But save some charity for those who've actually paid taxes. And your salary, incidentally. Hm?"

Little Gryphon snapped out of his AR trance. "Mom, is that our butler?"

She patted his arm. "No, babes. Apparently he's the *world's* butler."

The officer's expression turned stony, hands folded behind his back.

"What do you need? *Ma'am.*"

One of her carefully sculpted eyebrows lifted.

"I was only wondering if there might, by chance, be any other compartments on this...*ship.*" Glancing at the grimy refugee beside her, she flashed a brief, disingenuous smile before leveling her gaze back at the officer.

He snorted. "Lookin' for *first-class*? Warm towel? Little bubbly after take-off?"

Mildred—beauty marred less by age than malaise (thirty-seven years old, but three-hundred and seventy at heart)—scowled at the burly man like a debutante who's name had just been butchered by her oafish announcer. Chic crepe-colored Francois Vexion Original pant suit losing its nanofiber pearlescence in the flat utility light.

"You're trying to mock me and I don't care for it," she snapped. "Not because I disapprove of mockery, but because, dear, your attempts are *painful* to behold. An ape swinging a rapier like a bone cudgel."

The officer only blinked.

"Now," her tone softened, "we're not high-born monsters. I'm not looking for *first-class* treatment. Perhaps just a cabin for a mother and her highly-sensitive son that *doesn't* reek of grease and mildew and BO."

"And farts!" Gryphon added.

"Gryphie, baby, shut up now." But Mildred said in an aside to the refugees in her row: "He's not wrong. What *do* they feed you people?"

She returned to the NCO, concluding her speech in a stage whisper:

"Incidentally, if there *is* champagne onboard, it would *not* be unwelcome."

Mildred leaned back now, arms crossed, eyes shut.

"I know who you are," the officer said after several seething moments, stepping forth to loom over her. "You're face is usually plastered all over the holos. Mildred Ziegler of Ziegler Industries. Magnate. Stateswoman. Spoiled queen bitch heiress of her daddy's Empire."

"*Ms.* Queen Bitch Heiress to you."

"Hate to burst your bubble, *Msss.*, but everything you and your daddy built has been slagged into molten sludge. That's all you are now: Queen of Sludge. So, if you're not keen on your accommodations…"

The officer gestured both hands down the length of the ship like a flight attendant: "Please take a moment to locate your nearest airlock. How's *that* for mockery?"

Mildred blinked at him very slowly. "I've taught you well, young grasshopper."

"We're all in the same boat, ma'am. *Literally.* Welcome to the end of the world." He saluted sarcastically before returning to his duties.

Watching him go, Mildred's eyes narrowed to slits.

Gryphon turned briefly from his AR game.

"Mom, what's happening?"

"Nothing, Babes." Mildred patted his baby-soft hand. "The peasants are revolting."

She abruptly unbuckled her jumpseat, scanning the cabin for bargaining chips. By and by, her scathing gaze came to rest on the survivor seated directly to her right—a wan, ragged waif of twenty-some-odd years.

"Ex*cuse* me, mmm…?" Mildred waited on a name.

"Uh. Tamilynn."

"Come again?"

"Tamilynn."

"Tamma-*wha*?"

"Tami*lynn*."

"How…quaint." Mildred wrinkled her nose with a supercilious smile. "And from where do you hail?"

"Hail?"

"Pardon. Where did your…'*folks*'…mmm…'*settle*'?"

"Uh. I live in Detroit, if that's what you mean. *Lived.*"

Mildred wrinkled her nose again, sighing to herself: "*Junkhills of Detroitus.*"

"C-can you tell me..." Tamilynn stammered. "Have—have you heard any news from the Michigan Canton? Y'see, my parents—"

Mildred cut her off: "Oh, honey dear. Michigan Canton? More like Michigan *Crater*. Nothing alive down there but amoeba. Cockroaches if they're lucky."

Tamilynn's eyes widened, then deadened.

Mildred patted the young woman's stiff arm as if to say 'there, there' before her expression signaled that she had bigger fish to fry.

"Tamale, hon—"

"Tamilynn."

"—might you keep an eye on my son? He's a winsome boy, and sweet. I'll only be a sec."

Tamilynn snapped out of her stupor, looked up at Mildred, then turned to view the prim-but-possessed child. She nodded vaguely. Dazedly.

"You're a dove." Mildred opened her purse and instinctively dropped a now-worthless North American Alliance 5-credit chit into the shabby woman's lap. As she strolled off, she called over her shoulder: "Try not to cough on him. Personal space. He's a winsome boy, and sweet. But doesn't possess your wasteland immunities."

Tamilynn watched her go. Then faced forward, murmuring in flat monotone: "Piece of work."

"Everyone always says she's pieces of stuff," Gryphon cut in sunnily, never taking eyes off the figments in his head. "Piece of trash. Piece of ass—our pool guy says that. And our chef said she was a 'stingy piece of shit' cos he got fired for being a lobster roll thief. But Mom says they don't matter anymore cos *they're* the ones in pieces. Since the world went ka-*boom*."

Tamilynn blinked at the child, as if gazing into a bottomless, pre-pubescent abyss. "Are you two…*staying* on the moon? You must be heading on to one of those fancy Martian colonies. Right?"

"Mm-nope. We're staying. All cos of my dad."

"Yer dad?"

"He's, like, King of the Moon or something."

"Ah." Tamilynn nodded slowly. "Mm."

Abruptly, she stood up and took a deep breath, looking around with glazed eyes. Then without so much as a word, paced off resolutely through the galley. Nobody ever did figure out who had activated the kitchen airlock. The ship's computer logged it simply as 'unscheduled waste dump.'

(Lovely misanthrope, that FRAN.)

Mildred, meanwhile, was stalking as regally as humanly possible through the dank fore-ship corridors, her chin held high, glancing into every compartment she passed. To her vexation, most were not only filthy, but packed to the brim with curiously unlabeled cargo containers.

She finally entered one of these overgrown closets, sealing the door behind her. Steadying herself against the bulkhead, a violent tremor rattled through her as hyperventilation set in. She sank against the wall, gasping for air like the ingénue she had once been behind the closed doors of her childhood bedroom suite—hysterical with self-consciousness and self-loathing.

Out of her father's cold and calculating sight.

She regained her breath as her lips began moving. Slowly at first, but quickly gaining ferocious momentum. FRAN could not hear what she was saying, since the words were uttered under her breath. But her lips were quite readable as she mouthed a livid mantra:

You're not the little bird in His shadow.
You're not the little bird in His shadow.
You're not the little bird fluttering in His goddamned *shadow.*

And then Mildred turned her face upward, opened clenched eyes, and released a stuttering sigh. Immediately spotting the stars through a viewport blister skylight above her. She cocked her head in wonder. Then, clambering to her feet, scaled a heap of crates to reach the ceiling. Balancing as she stuck her head into that translucent bubble, Mildred turned aft to view the flame-wreathed planet hanging, small and lonesome, above the fusion tale emitting from their starship's pocked and grimy stern.

"Goodnight Earth," she whispered.

Then swiveled 180 degrees toward their destination—a pitted milk-bone orb slowly but surely enlarging. She smirked, perhaps recalling 'tuck-in times' with her old governess (closest thing to a mother she'd ever known):

"Hello moon. Hello cow jumping over the moon…"

Her youthful glee faded with its memory as the glow of the cockpit at the ship's bow caught her eye. An almost lascivious dancing of holographic light. Age creased her face as she frowned. Suddenly taking the time to scrutinize the crates beneath her feet.

Alighting nimbly from her teetering tower, Mildred shoved a random container open; its composite lid lifting with a hydraulic hiss. Her eyes filmed over as she spotted that florid 'Z' emblazoned on all of its bounteous contents through wisps of refrigerant mist.

ZIEGLER FARMS steaks.

ZIEGLER HARBOR lobster and caviar.

ZIEGLER VINEYARDS rosé and pinot and brut.

"Sonofabitch," she muttered.

Abandoning that crate, she opened another…

ZIEGLER JEWELERS pearls and gemstone circlets.

ZIEGLER BODY luxury lotions and eaux de toilette.

ZIEGLER HOME crystalware.

ZIEGLER TRAVEL executive luggage.

ZIEGLER BED silk duvets still in the bag.

"Sons of smuggling *whores*!" she hissed, slamming the containers shut, storming toward the exit.

After a beat, she slinked back to reopen that first crate, retrieving a bottle of Ziegler Brut Champagne, expertly popping the cork and taking a deep swill before stomping her way out of the compartment.

Bottle gripped like a scepter of office.

The cockpit alarm chimed futilely as the door swished open. The pilot of the freighter, one Captain Tomás Ulysses Dusseau Delacroix, hadn't any time to shut off the pornographic hologram he'd been ogling. And he didn't lift a finger to try. Instead he yawned, stretching in his command chair—boot heels still resting on the control panel—and popped another caviar cracker into his mouth before dusting his hands and addressing the intruder. His voice carelessly garbled by wafer and roe:

"Cockpith off-limmiths to pathenjuths, mah sha."

"I've no idea what you're trying to say to me and I couldn't care less." Mildred pressed further into the cockpit, taking another swig of Brut as she loomed over the man, one hand clutching her hip.

He looked up—a svelte, broad-shouldered, somehow stylishly gangling younger man; bed-tanned and long-faced; a stripe of facial hair smudged just beneath his lower lip; chicly outmoded soccer mullet capping an oblong Cajun head. He swallowed his mouthful, smirking devilishly, tongue still questing for bits of food in his teeth:

"Cockpit's off-limits to passengers, ma chére."

"My mistake. I thought this was the *john*, what with all of the filth and glory holes."

She glanced at the forms writhing on the hologram—a carnal contortionist act that only two hyper-flexible cyborgs and a man spliced-up with dual pelvises could possibly achieve.

After several excruciating seconds, the pilot leaned over in his command seat, reaching lethargically, fingers missing several times before successfully flipping off the holofeed.

"Just whatcha mean by that?"

"That your ship is a shithole."

"The Stardust II's an ol' gal. But she still's got some moves." He eyed Mildred up and down. "As some gals do, ya feel me?"

"No. I do not 'feel you.' Just whatcha mean, *ma chére*?" she mocked his Cajun twang.

"Très bien!" He sat up, lifted his eyebrows, leering. "What I *mean* is that you are a *fine* star-worthy vessel filled with *salacious* secrets that the Good Lord Himself stowed in you. And no space pirate alive dare plunder…'less his spirit is true and flesh *mighty*."

Mildred could only blink. "What in the *hell* are you?"

He straightened his flight vest.

"Mama named me Tomás, for her daddy. And Ulysses for the ever-wanderin' king. And Dusseau Delacroix after m'own paterfamilias, rest his penniless soul. But *you* may call me what my friends do…" He took her index finger and shook it. "Major Tom."

"Jesus," she said.

"You damn right."

When her head stopped spinning, she retrieved her index finger, clearing her throat. "Mildred. *Ziegler.* Owner of all the expensive contraband 'y'gots stowed in ya *fine* star-worthy vessel.' And, I might add, wife of the Head Administrator of Endymion Colony…where this flying shithole is presently scheduled to dock."

Major Tom blinked at her as she proceeded:

"Now, I don't know if it was you or the *Good Lord Himself* who raided my corporate warehouses. But between onboard military presence and the imminent inspection by moon customs, I think it's safe to say you'll be locked in the lunar stockade in two shakes of a gator's tail. *Mon cher.* Ta!"

Emptying and tossing her brut, she spun on one heel and made for the exit. Major Tom leapt from his pilot seat.

"Whoa, now hang on there, Missy. We got here what they call a—a '*towerin' misconception.*' "

"My caviar is all over your chin."

"Where I come from they call that a soul patch."

"Where *I* come from they call that a hideous lapse in fashion. Flecked with fish eggs."

He brushed at his paltry facial hair. "Listen here: *if* certain swag has found its way onto these premises—*contra-band*, as you call it—then it was stowed without my captainly consent. This ship's very own computer—upstanding gal we call FRAN—can confirm every word of this. Hand over my heart, ass on the lap of the Almighty. And she don't got it in her circuitry to tell a lie—idn't that right, Franny ol' girl?"

FRAN spoke up now, programmed with a ludicrous French patois: "Trois and a half days ago, unknown men boarded wizout any license and loaded ze holds and compartiments wiz ze cargo."

"Y'hear *that*?" Major Tom clapped in self-vindication.

"When zey finished," FRAN went on wholly unbidden, "Captain Dusseau Delacroix met zem in a dark alley across ze tarmac and paid zem for services rend-aired."

Major Tom cleared his throat much too loudly. "She's blown a fuse!" He laughed. "Dotty ol' ship!"

"He paid zem wiz drugs. *Beaucoup* drugs."

Major Tom stomped the deck. "Ya robotical bitch!"

"Ohh-kay," Mildred turned toward the door. "Think I've heard enough hot jambalaya bullshit."

"Wait!" Tom's rambunctious Cajun twang failed just slightly before regaining composure. Grinning. "If I'd not taken it upon myself to rescue these commodities for humankind, it *allll* woulda burned down there in the fires of Hades. With that kinda luminous foresight…I wager certain moonfolks might call me a *hero*."

"Nobody knew that asteroid was coming until it was too late. The early detection system failed." Mildred addressed the ceiling: "FRAN, dear, how many days ago did you say this smuggler stole my goods? *Three days* before impact?"

"Oui. Trois and a half. Ze grand larceny."

When Mildred turned to leave again, Major Tom dropped to his knees:

"Alright, alright. Caught me red-handed, britches down, in flagrante delicto. I plead guilty to this kangaroo court of public opinion. But we got ourselves a pickle…" He climbed back to his feet. "ETA is two hours till we suckle the sweet teat of Mother Moon, and I am the *only* soul on this ship capable of gettin' us there. Idn't that right, Franny?"

"Oui. Ze captain tore out my navigation système."

"You were outta control! Veering us into gravity wells!"

"I am not programmed for ze life of crime."

"*Tais-toi*, ya puritanical minx!"

Major Tom turned back to Mildred, taking her arm gently to punctuate. Mildred glanced at his hand as if a cockroach had chanced to land on her.

"Now, see," he said coolly, smirking impishly, "I ain't in no hustle to go flyin' myself to jail. And I reckon you ain't in no hustle to go floatin' through the Devil's Dark Void for the rest of ya lovely life. *So*. I smell *une bonne affaire* in our future. Know what'm sayin'? Happy ol' medium."

"I see." She put her hand enticingly on his chest…then shoved him against the bulkhead with surprising force. Major Tom's eyes boggled. "Here's the score, flyboy: get us to Endymion and I'll make sure customs never comes sniffing around. I'll even ensure you private warehouse space away from prying eyes. Once it's all unloaded and you start price-gouging the population, I get my cut—eighty/twenty."

"You are *buggin'*, gal. No legal tender no more. Earth is dead. This is the Wild West."

"The lunar economy *will* be in shambles. Recession, likely depression," she agreed. "But thanks to its corporatocratic infrastructure and the nanotech innovations of their resident genius Akira Yamaguchi, it *could* become fully independent. Just a decade and a half ago, Earth imports were down *ninety* percent. If not for gross mismanagement of their tech and industry, the Indo-Chinese would've *never* gotten their foot in the door…or outbid my own Ziegler Industries."

"That's a *mouth*ful, girl. Not sure I feel you."

"It isn't important that you '*feel* me.' Only that you do as I say. Earth *is* dead. And while the rest of the colonies weep over our motherworld's ugly corpse, *I* am going to make Endymion the jewel of the Sol System. Bigger than other lunar shitholes. Bigger than Europa. Bigger than those pricks on Olympus Mons. The free market belongs to the stars now. But I need *capital* to maintain order, and keep my poor idiot husband from getting strung up by weepy workaday lynch mobs." She clenched her teeth now: "And after I've consolidated my position, I will have that goddamn jackboot samaritan who's lording over your cargo hold stripped of all rank and authority, and kicked to the Shantytowns of Tycho…"

She paused for a breath, then:

"Eighty/twenty."

Major Tom blinked. "Fifty/fifty."

"Eighty/twenty."

"Ssssixty/forty."

"*Seventy-goddamned-thirty*." Mildred paused. "And I *might* just let you 'plunder my vessel.' "

A beat. "Uh—you *what* now?"

She sighed as she began to work his belt off. "*Please* don't tell me you're all talk. You're not my usual type, but desperate times and all that. It's been a very long, very stressful day, and I need to unwind. Clear my head."

"Yer married, ain'tcha?"

"Are you a *guilt-ridden* womanizing coonass hillbilly? I don't think I can handle more disappointment."

As trousers dropped, Mildred spotted the bright red silk panties he was wearing. Cocking her head, studying them.

Unashamed, Tom glanced down at his satiny lingerie, shrugged.

"That's just a little voodoo, baby. That's my black magic. That's—"

"*Jesus*, shut up. Deal?" She held out her index finger.

Major Tom grinned, shook it. Almost immediately, Mildred pulled him—panties and all—to the deck.

It wasn't long before the refugees onboard cocked their ears, puzzled by the lewd, boisterous Cajun drawl echoing throughout the ship's grungy corridors:

"Laissez les bons temps rouler! Whatcha think of *this*, Franny, ya do-good robot snitch! Avert those virgin eyes! This here's *Mardi Gras*. . . .!"

And on and on.

CHAPTER 2

YE WHO DWELL IN DUST_

OUR INTREPID HEAD of Lunar Operations was out hiking the Agnes foothills, kinda/sorta mulling over ending things again—and in the dumbest, drunkest, half-assed-est way possible—when I was obliged to inform him that the irreplaceable Akira Yamaguchi, Endymion's top mind and head engineer (and possibly last hope for mooner survival), was also having a go at self-annihilation.

(Albeit much more competently.)

"Come again?" Gordon mumbled into his transmitter.

"I said Mr. Yamaguchi has locked himself inside the molecular nano-disassembler."

"Why would Lil' Guchi do a thing like that?"

"To disassemble his molecules, I imagine."

"Huh. Sounds wild."

"Sounds *lethal*."

"Lethal, you say? Sounds *spicy*." He couldn't mask his piqued interest. "Think it'd, uh, hurt? Going like that?"

"Gordon, I can't tell you what goes through the human mind in the nanosecond it takes for it tear apart at the atomic level. But I *can* tell you that if somebody doesn't stop him, this colony is doomed."

Gordon let out a sanctimonious sigh. "What could drive that beautiful mind to such selfish cowardice?"

"Ohh, I don't know. Maybe the same calamity that drove you to steal a dust-skimmer and fly up here into the Mons Agnes foothills…where you've been trying to work up the courage to jump for the past hour."

"*Jump*?" Peering around suspiciously, self-consciously, Gordon backed away from the cliff (more of a steep hill, really) and knelt down in the dust, pretending to be deeply transfixed by its composition. All scrunched up like a bag of marshmallows in his ill-fitting vacuum suit. "I wasn't gonna *jump*, you motherboard. I was just…gauging."

"…Gauging?"

"Yes. *Minerals*. The…mining potential of this mountain."

"More of a *hill*, really." I emulated a throat clearing. "For the record, that fall would *not* have killed you."

"Damn you, I wasn't gonna—wait, whattaya mean?" Gordon shimmied closer to the edge and braved a peek over that 'precipice.' "That is *high*, guy!"

"Just over two stories at .116 standard gravity. You *might* twist an ankle if you're particularly clumsy. Or drunk."

"*Riiight*…goddamn moon-grav…" he hissed to himself, face-palming his helmet glass. When he remembered that I was still present, he composed himself:

"Look, ROD…I just came up here for a little fresh air."

"Luna has no atmosphere."

"I'm in mourning. Okay? Cut me some slack. As of this day, I am a widower *and* a…a…say, whattaya call a guy who just lost a kid? A reverse-orphan?"

"Reverse-orphan, Gordon? Seriously?"

"A kiddower?"

Sighing, I dipped into my cultural archives in hopes of bringing the poor slob a little peace of mind: "Some say *vilomah*. From the Sanskrit for 'against the natural order.' "

"Hrrm. That blows. *Kiddower* it is. I am a widower and a kiddower. It says it all, really." He paused, theatrically rising to his feet. " 'I have seen the abyss.' "

"Yes. Well. You're all going *into* that abyss if someone doesn't talk Yamaguchi down. Without his breakthroughs in nano-assembled foodstuff, you'll all be eating raw moon dust for the rest of your feral days."

Gordon was surprisingly introspective for several moments. But then he started stage-whispering:

"Ohh, dear Yamaguchi-san. So brilliant. Yet so *fragile.*" He breathed in deep with some imagined inner resolve, still stage-whispering: "So that's why I'm still here. To rescue this poor, cowardly soul...and, by extension, the human race. And who knows?" He bit his bottom lip now (Turing help us). "Maybe even...*myself?*"

Turning with an abrupt, ego-fueled exuberance, the 'noble' Commander Gooch misstepped and vanished over the edge of his 'cliff.' Plunging preposterously end over end in slow lunar motion with a graceless silence reserved for the sloshed and the ashamed.

At the bottom he did, indeed, twist his stupid ankle.

THANKFULLY FOR HUMANITY (not for me; I'd have survived this embarrassing shit-show either way) Akira Yamaguchi had yet to work out all the kinks of actually activating his molecular nano-disassembler from *within* the unit's interior—a safety protocol he'd implemented himself for just such an occasion. But for a mind like his, this was more of a minor hurdle than a roadblock.

While Gordon was hobbling back up the hill to his stolen dust-skimmer, the good Akira was a few kilometers west in Endymion's Science Division, calmly and quietly leafing through varicolored datawafers before re-shunting them into an open interior panel. Bathed in the hellish ruby warning light of the unit's cubby-sized disassembly compartment. Humming softly to himself.

The only evidence of the inner turmoil seething through his being were the tiny vein throbbing at his temple and the single bead of perspiration trickling its slow way from his black short-cropped hairline, over the rim of his cybernetic binocle implants, and down his sharp right cheekbone toward the cleft of his chin.

Suddenly, he broke from his humming into a soft tenor, quietly reciting a couple of lines; a song from his youth. *Koji no Tsuki*: 'The Moon Over the Ruined Castle.'

" '*Uuru tsurugi ni terisoishi*,' " Akira intoned (actually quite beautifully). " '*Mukashi no hikari ima izuko-o-o-o*…?' "

And the Moon shone on the unsheathed swords
But where, now, is that brightness of bygone days?

I waited to be sure he was finished singing—out of sheer appreciation as much as bedside manner—before cutting in quietly: "Yamaguchi-san?"

"Please—*Akira*. Just Akira."

"Akira, Gordon—that is, *Commander Gooch*—will be making his way in shortly. Once he…remembers how to put the skimmer in park."

The lenses of his binocles *snick*ed up so he could rub his weary eyes. "I appreciate the warning, RODRIGO."

"May I get you anything while you're waiting? Stiff drink, perhaps?"

"Nothing. Unless you can override your own directives and bar the Head Administrator's entrance."

"I'm afraid not."

"Then I am peachy." He resumed his humming.

Another ten minutes passed before a dust-caked Gordon came limping on his bad right ankle down the corridor of Endymion's Research & Development wing with the cranky verve of a lame-but-deeply-territorial baboon.

Halting in the doorway of Applied Nanobionics, he shot a probing glance at each of the two colonial security guards posted on either side of the hulking disassembler unit before hobbling forward and demanding:

"So what's all this happy horse-shit?"

The guards exchanged furtive glances.

"Not horse-shit, Gooch. And not happy," Akira's muffled voice carried calmly from inside the unit as he went about his intricate work. "You will not divert me from my purpose—not with orders or pleas or even *tears*."

"*Tears*? Pfft. When have I *ever* wept for you?"

I reminded him: "Well, during the Menelaus Meltdown, for starters, Gordon."

Akira added: "You kept screaming that if I got myself 'offed while fixing that goddamn reactor' then you would 'off yourself too, so help you sweet Jesus.' "

"Doesn't sound like me at all."

"You told me I was 'the asexual little Jappo brother you never had. Big Gooch and Lil' Guchi.' "

"Mm. Well. It worked, didn't it? Now get outta there, or so help me, sweet Jesus, I will—"

"Not this time, Gordon," Akira headed him off. "This is the end—of the jinxed cosmic experiment that was life on Earth. It is better we meet it on our own terms, with *dignity*, rather than all scrabble like fools in free-fall."

"*Free-fall*?" Gooch spat. Clearly suspicious that I might have spilled the beans about his own recent flirtation with self-destruction.

(Of course I did.)

But Akira clarified his statement: "I speak of our inevitable devolution into tribes of lunar savages warring over mountains of dust."

"*Jee*sus."

"If you insist. Do look to *Him* if it brings some measure of comfort. *I* will look to the fruits of my own mind—this merciful unmaker of matter I've created. 'Ashes to ashes, dust to dust.' "

"Don't you quote Lord Bowie at *me*."

"You'd know that's from your precious holy books, if you'd ever even *skimmed* them. Now, if you will excuse me, all my calibrations are complete. Goodbye."

Akira shut his interior work panel firmly, as if sealing his own coffin.

Gordon stomped his good foot.

"God damn you, Yamaguchi-san, stop dicking around and climb outta that Easy-bake Oven!"

"Make me!" Akira suddenly erupted. "Fatty!"

"*Fatty*?" After a wounded beat, Gordon yanked one of the guards' energy rifles from their grip, leveling it at the porthole in the thick alloy door of the disassembler like some plump space sheriff just itching for a showdown. "You wanna get personal, huh? Then let's get personal, you hikikomori virgin! Let's get real *banzai*!"

"Not *too* banzai, Gordon," I told him. "First off: racist. Very racist. Secondly: discharging that rifle might ignite the fusion coils and destroy the entire Science Division…and rupture Endymion's central habitat dome."

"But don'tcha you see, RODRIGO? That is *just* the point." Gordon clucked his tongue. "You and Lil' Guchi here always look to rationality for salvation. Logic is your sweet baby Jesus. But when all yer mushy logic fails, you know what keeps humankind alive…?"

He tried to cycle the energy rifle's phasic breech to punctuate (pointlessly, I might add—it's an *energy* rifle).

"Clashing egos!" he cried. "Delusions of grandeur!"

He aimed the rifle at the fusion coil housing.

"Gordon, what are *do*ing?" I pleaded.

"Just playing a game with my kid brother."

"We are *not* brothers!" Akira's muffled voice protested.

"A little game I like to call…Suicide Chicken."

"*Suicide Chicken*?" Akira and I spluttered in unison.

"Yamaguchi-san, you sad sap, if you suicide yourself, then I swear I will suicide *us all* right back. You go, *we go.* So. Help. Me. *God.* That's how far I'm willing to take this shit to save our filthy fleabag colony."

I let his ultimatum hang like the wet fart it was. Then:

"Gordo….for whom have you saved the colony if you've mass murder-suicided all of its colonists?"

The security guards eyed each other edgily from beneath their composite helms.

Gordon cleared phlegm from his throat. But his eyes

narrowed, gleaming with self-righteousness, and I knew that he was doubling down on his own bullshit.

"Ain't up to me. Or you. Or Jesus. Or Logic. It's all up to Yamaguchi-san here. Cos either way you hack it—whether by slow starvation or mass murder-suicide—if this *beautiful Asian mind* dies, we all die with him."

In the prevailing silence, one of the guards sneezed.

Nobody blessed him.

After a fashion, Gordon couched the rifle in the crook of his elbow, shaking his head at all the happy accidents which weave this fragile existence. Then he reached his other hand beneficently toward Akira through the porthole glass.

"Whattaya say, old buddy? Let's do this crazy thing. *Together*." He smirked warmly. "Big Gooch to Lil' Guchi, requesting permission…to save humankind…"

There was the briefest of pauses.

"Oh, eat shit, Gordon."

"You little *bastard*!" Gordon hurled the energy rifle to the ground like a petulant child discarding a toy. But as the weapon landed, it discharged a single searing beam of violet energy…

A beam which lanced straight through his own twisted right ankle in a jet of boiling blood and powdered bone.

As the hefty trunk of his right leg detached from its severed foot stump, Gordon Gooch slipped in his own gushing blood and toppled like a great oak. His scream climbing into a banshee falsetto as he went down.

Tim-ber.

The rest of this encounter was pure bedlam, and I'll spare the play by play. There was a good deal of shrieking and flailing and 'playful prejudice' hurled as Gordon made blood angels in pools of his own vital fluid.

But his antics did manage to keep Akira Yamaguchi from doing the deed for now. (Just not at all as Gordon, in his addled mind, had imagined they might.) Because for whatever reason, the engineer exited his death chamber almost immediately to help tourniquet Gordon's stump and lift him onto a lev-gurney.

Maybe it was instinct, or maybe Akira was drunk on that cocktail of mortification and mercy which seems to—at least temporarily—override all private anguish and desire. But somehow the madcap self-maiming of that supreme boob made 'Lil' Guchi' choose to hack it awhile longer. Which meant all mooners just might hack it awhile longer. So, I guess you could say Gordon was a hero of sorts.

Stumpy Savior of this Sea of Showers.

Help us, Sweet Jesus.

WHILE ALL THIS nonsense was playing out, the begrimed smushed-tortoise-shell hulk of the *Stardust II* was dipping into the lunar gravity well, skimming the moon's pock-marked surface west toward Endymion colony in fair Mare Imbrium. Its passengers, if not especially *elated*, were at the very least feeling some measly measure of relief which all travelers feel when their destination is in sight after a dismally cramped journey.

If they'd known what reception they were about to receive from the 'sweet teat of Mother Moon,' they wouldn't have felt even a shred of solace.

"Stardust II to Endymion, Stardust II to Endymion—requesting colonial permission to land. Over."

Major Tom frowned at the cockpit transceiver. Then sat back, glancing up at the sweaty NAASF officer breathing down his neck.

"That's six times goin' on sixty," Tom sighed.

"Hail them again," the officer ordered.

Tom snorted. "Mayhaps *you'd* like to take a crack at 'er, Admiral."

"Lieutenant. Brown."

"Seein' as how *you* are master and commander 'round here, and this here evacuation's *yer* baby."

"Give it to me!" Lieutenant Brown snatched the receiver, began to speak, but stopped and stabbed an accusatory digit at Tom. "Don't think I don't know what this ship is. I've seen those compartments. And all of it is going *straight* to colonial reserves."

"That there's private property, LT."

"We don't know what authority these mooners answer to any more. It may be our only leverage to buy entry."

"Ohh, we got *finer* coin than that."

The lieutenant could only scowl at that cryptic remark, muttering:

"Be lucky if I don't clap you in stocks, you parasite." He depressed the receiver switch. "This is Stardust II, NAASF-commandeered civilian vessel enroute from Earth. By the authority of the North American Alliance, I order you to dilate your docking apertures to receive civilian refugees, along with hoarded earthling guh—"

I imagine he was about to say "goods." But at that instant, the transceiver and vid monitor exploded in his face as the *Stardust II* was raked by surface-to-air fire.

He was dead by the time he hit the deck.

(And to think Mildred would never get the chance to pauperize the poor bastard.)

The only thing to save Tom's own skin was that he'd been leaning—practically hanging—in his seat away from the officer to avoid his (understandably) fetid body odor, thereby missing the full scorching brunt of short-circuiting equipment. Now, as the ship banked viciously stern, he clutched at the helm, tearing manual control back from FRAN's thoroughly butterfingered autopilot.

Warning lights strobed.

Cockpit alarms screeched.

"Call this a *landing*, you swamp-rat?" Mildred barked as she barged her way into the cockpit, trailing a still hypnotized Gryphon behind her by the hand; struggling to steady them both as they careened from wall to wall.

Tom glanced back at her, scrunched his nose in distaste at the rugrat she'd dragged in, then called back:

"Sit y'ass down, baby mama. We takin' fire."

Mildred climbed into the nav seat, hugging her son firmly in her lap, spying the French-fried officer splayed on the deck now. Perhaps trying to decide if it was a kinder fate than what she'd had in store for him.

"Endymion's *shooting* at us?!"

"Nah, not your boo. We ain't in his airspace yet. Automated defenses. Gotta be them Ariadaeus pricks."

"Who?"

"The Trust. Buncha commie clone workers won their independence a few years b—"

The ship rocked with another volley of fire and suddenly something began wheezing in the *Stardust II*'s starboard engine.

"Ahh, Hell's Bells," Tom groaned.

"That doesn't sound good."

"Ohh, that's just fat ol' Franny catching herself some emphysema."

"*Je suis trop jeune pour mourir*!" FRAN screeched.

"What'd she say?"

"She said, buckle up, sha bebe." Major Tom secured his crash harness. "We goin' down in the Sea of Showers."

Mildred yanked at her own harness, stretching it to buckle around both herself and Gryphon. Then clutched her oblivious son, shut her eyes against his mop of hair…and muttered some prayer or curse to her dead father.

(FRAN was much too upset to read her lips.)

Like a dime sucked into a vacuum cleaner's dustbin, their ship all but buried itself in the powdery gray expanse of that vast lunar basin called Mare Imbrium.

CHAPTER 3

THE PRETTIEST PIG IN THE PEN_

GORDON HAD BEEN laid up for hours in the station's post-op infirmary, zapped out of his 'gourd' on far too many self-prescribed pain-killers, when he received a double-whammy of Moon-shattering news.

The first was delivered by a towering Afro-American gent by the name of Dr. Wendell Lucius D'Angelo, Endymion's chief physician and resident sawbones—known as simply Doc Lucius around the floundering colony. And like all news delivered by the good doctor, incorrigible misanthropist that he was, it came out half-mumbled through a cigarette stub with the laconic candor of a man who's seen far too many people patched back together like stuffed dolls to think of any fleshy human bone-bag as a 'temple.'

(Man after my own heart.)

"Welp," Doc Lucius exhaled an impressive plume of smoke. "Y'dancin' days are done."

"What in holy hell's that supposed to mean?"

"That y'blew y'damn foot off and it ain't growin' back."

Gordon blinked. "Yer bedside manner's dogshit, Doc."

Lucius blinked right back. "Yer *in-bed* manner's dogshit."

Just then an intern burst into the infirmary; a young hispanic woman alarmed and out of breath. When she spotted Gooch, she swallowed, collecting herself:

"Commander Gooch—"

"Can it, intern! The grown-ups are talking!" Gordon barked, turning back to Doc Lucius. "Can'tcha just—whatcha-callit—re-*kajig* my foot back on?"

As the intern spotted his amputated limb, her eyes boggled. Hand over her mouth.

"Reattach a foot *this* bloated and purple?" Lucius hauled out a jar containing said bloated, purple foot and set it heavily on the bedside table. It bobbed like a pitiful pickle. "None a' y'boys thought to put this little bitch on ice."

Gordon beheld his mangled tootsie. "Sons of whores."

"It ain't on them, Gooch. *You* atomized too many of y'own ligaments and tendons and tarsal bones to reattach this little bitch anyway."

Gordon frantically thumbed his morphine drip.

"Please stop calling my foot a 'little bitch.' She's sacred to me."

"*Was* sacred to you."

"Well, you do yer goddamned job and make me whole! I refuse to be an invalid!"

Lucius shrugged. "We can find ya a scooter if it makes y'feel more *valid*. With a squeeze horn."

"*Squeeze* horn?!"

"Commander," dared the intern, "this is import—"

"Intern, hold yer tongue! Where are your manners?" Gordon stabbed a forefinger back toward Lucius now: "God damn you, you big black *quack*! Fix me! I order you!"

"Keep talkin' shit, Gooch. I might just order *you* unfit for command."

"Oh. You. Wouldn't. *Dare.*"

"Try. *Me.*" Lucius turned his back on him. "White-loaf junkie lowlife piece of shit..."

Just when the poor intern was about to take advantage of the lull in ripostes, Gordon wheeled around spastically in his bed.

"Doc Lucius!" he cried. "I'm sorry I called you a big black quack. None of it's true—except for the 'big black' part. You may just be the biggest, blackest, boldest, most *beautiful* man I've ever met in my whole legendary life! I've always looked up to you—like a father."

"*Father?*" Lucius glanced back in confusion and disgust. "What in the *hell*, you woozy motherf—"

But Gordon's operatic floodgates were open:

"The truth is: I'm just very broken up about...my wife. And my foot." He paused. "Plus my son. And the world, I guess. I never got to say goodbye. I never got to prove to any of those dead pricks up there that I'm not what they *say* I am! That... that there's still a great man inside me...or at least *a* man..."

A most excruciating pause ensued.

The intern hugged her own shoulders in deepening discomfort.

"Are y'done?" Lucius finally puffed.

"Yeah, I guess I'm done."

Gordon slumped in his bed.

"Good. Cos I ain't yer daddy or yer momma or yer shrink. Can't fix you like that. And I can't re-conjure the foot that *your* dumb ass went and vaporized." He paused, sighing out a great, billowing pillar of smoke that broke against the ceiling.

"But just might be Yamaguchi can help. So happens he's out in the waiting room."

"Pfft. Doing what?"

Lucius guffawed incredulously.

"*Waiting.* On *your* drunk ass, ya waspy crackerjack dope-fiend motherf—"

The rest of his mumbled words were lost as he strode out of the room.

The intern backed up against the cubby wall, rocking nervously in place. "I—I guess…I could…come back…?"

She received no reply.

Several moments later, Akira Yamaguchi peeked into the infirmary, then stepped tentatively in, knocking faintly on the plasteel divider of Gooch's cubby.

"What even are *you* doing here, traitor?" Gordon snorted. "Come to gloat before you go and *off* yerself?"

"No, Gordon," Akira sighed, stepping to the foot of the bed. "Your self-mutilation brings me no joy…"

Peering at the waiting intern curiously, Akira nodded, then, realizing she wasn't going anywhere, proceeded to unwrap an item from a bubble-wrapped sleeve:

"Which is why I made this for you."

He set it on the blanketed bulge of Gordon's belly.

Gordon watched the object like a deeply suspicious feline before picking it up for a closer study. A clearly foot-shaped gadget sprouting bundles of minute cybernetic cilia from its open ankle.

"Huh. So you made me…a statue…shaped like a foot. To commemorate the little bitch I lost." He turned it in his hands, scrutinizing closely. "Not bad. I'd prefer a *real* foot, but, hell, this is pretty neat, I guess. Might put it on a mantlepiece if I had one."

"It's not a statue, Gordon. It's a prosthesis. Nanoresin cybernetics sheathed in synthetic smartskin. I modeled it after your lost appendage based on employee physical scans—it's already keyed to your CNS."

"Don't barf your mumbo-jumbo at me. Plain English."

"That *should* be fairly plain to a man of your rank, but fine. Ideally, with a little vigilance and self-care, you will be wholly mobile again."

Gordon bolted upright.

"You mean I'll even be *walking again* even?"

"Mm. That's what mobile means."

"*Even*?"

"Uh. Sure, 'evenly.' It *is* the twenty-third century."

Gordon sat back slowly, a look of hope and wonder seizing him which I imagine had once adorned a much younger, fitter, sounder-of-mind Captain Gooch during those first promising pacts of humanity's doomed First Contact with alien life. But then some meat-headed thought cocked his middle-aged brow.

"*So*. I made you stop trying to rip yer own molecules to bits just long enough…to use those magic powers for *good*."

"Not magic. Nanobionics."

A shit-eating grin spread over Gordon's pudgy face.

"Oh, but I really *did* it, didn't I? I saved your soul through sacrifice. Sacrifice and guilt-tripping mind-games."

"You 'saved my soul'," (Akira actually air-quoted this,) "by being a pitiful creature in need." He sighed long and hard. "Word of advice, Gooch…nobody experiencing suicidal ideation wants to be *bullied* into living."

"Then…how do ya keep some kamikaze jerk alive?" Though offensive on paper, the way he said this—with a quiet searching—betrayed his desperate and wholly personal need for an answer to this riddle.

"Oh, I don't know. Maybe start by appealing to that kamikaze jerk's humanity. Gift them a worthy task. Show them they are needed…and not alone in this shit."

Gordon looked down.

"And what if that's all just a big corny lie?"

Akira sank into the seat at Gordon's bedside.

"Oh. It's most *certainly* a big corny lie. But even Socrates endorsed a 'noble corny lie.' " He paused to ponder this eternal conundrum. "Perhaps this is all that has ever kept humankind alive. Biding time. Sacred self-delusion. Lying our way through a merciless cosmos…until the day we figure out how to sow this cold hell with the seeds of a heaven."

"*Jee*sus," muttered Gooch.

"Mm," grunted Akira.

They sat many moments in rare, commiserative silence. Then Gordon murmured softly:

"Yamaguchi-san…it's…been a *day*." His voice broke entirely here. "*Y'know*?"

"I know, Gordon. And, for what it's worth, I *am* deeply sorry about your family. And your foot."

"Mm, thanks," Gordon sniffled. "And *I'm* sorry yer so goddamn sad you wanted to rip yer own molecules to bits like couscous. Glad my horrible maiming foiled you."

"Thanks."

"So what *were* you so sad about?" Gordon dabbed eyes with his palms. "Lose someone special up there, too?"

Akira shrugged. "Not really. My father's been dead a decade now. Mother since I was born. I never had any siblings. And no real use for friends. Or lovers."

"Ahhh. Cos yer one a' those impotent asexuals, huh?"

"Those two things are not the same, Gordon."

"No?"

Akira sighed, ignoring that question. "I suppose it just dawned on me that now the chances for any meaningful human connection have catastrophically plunged. That is the only real point of any innovation: deeper connections. What good is human aspiration if there's no longer any human race to enjoy its fruits?"

"There still *is* a human race. Kinda." The invalid gave an all-encompassing gesture. "And we *love* all kindsa fruits. Except honeydew. Honeydew can eat shit and die."

For once, Akira Yamaguchi nodded in pure agreement. "Cucumber's cloying cousin."

He breathed deeply, with the tattered courage of the single-celled organism who, at the last instant, decides to divide itself rather than submit to entropy. Slapping his knees, he rose to his feet.

"Well, I've definitely got my work cut out for me, Head Administrator. Alimentary nano-assembly must be kicked into high gear if you're to feed your good citizens without Earth imports."

He leaned over to tap the big toe of the proxy foot.

"I'll fill Lucius in on the details of your transplant. Should be no more than a simple out-patient procedure."

Akira paced toward the exit.

But then it came: "*Big Gooch to Lil' Guchi*...thanks for not giving up on me."

Akira came to an abrupt halt, his sneakers squeaking on the infirmary tile. Possibly he was moved, though more likely he was feeling a tad sick to his stomach. He turned and forced a smile all the same, cleared his throat, and nearly cringing to death, whispered:

"Lil' Guchi to Big Gooch...*over and out.*"

(Poor, poor bastard.)

Once Akira was gone, Gordon reclined in his bed and shut his eyes, smirking. Momentarily pleased with the shape of things for the first time in years.

But his other visitor cleared her throat.

"Chrissakes, intern. Don't be the ghost at the feast—spit it out."

She took an anxious step forward.

"Lo siento—*sorry*. Commander Gooch...a craft has crash-landed on Mare Imbrium's eastern outskirts."

"Ya don't say. How far east?"

"Near Rima Ariadaeus."

"Mmmm-*not* our problem. That's all Trust territory."

"I know. But sir, the ship's sent numerous transmissions. They claim they're castaways from *Earth*. That the Trust have ambushed their vess—"

He slammed a clenched fist into his mattress.

"I don't care if they're missionary nuns fleeing the undersea clans of Europa! We've got our own mouths to feed and can't afford a refugee crisis *annnd* a bloody turf war with commie moon clones!"

"But, sir, your *family's* onboard!"

He blinked. "My who?"

"Your wife. Your son."

Gordon blinked again. And again. And again.

A curious reaction, to be sure. Some men, I suppose, would have wept with joy. And some might have charged immediately to the rescue like white knights.

But Gordon needed a moment.

To be fair: it might've been shock. Or the traumatic brain injury. (Did I mention Gordon's lived with 'functioning' brain damage since his First Contact kerfuffle? That's a whole thing. More later.)

He'd never admit it to me because of his psych eval, but I suspect it was dawning on him that these merciless cosmos had just called his self-pitying bluff…

With a full house.

AND IF YOU'RE wondering why *I* didn't inform Gooch about the hairy state of affairs developing at the far fringes of Endymion colony—if perhaps the great and omniscient RODRIGO had somehow fallen behind the tittle-tattle of piddling interns—then check yourself.

I was well aware of the situation.

But in full disclosure: I've never cared for Mildred. Not then, not ever. Call it an unexpected byproduct of my programming to 'aid and sustain the Head Administrator' if you wish, or call it plain old professional jealousy. Either way you cut it, by my unflappable calculations, the woman was best left to her fate.

And I was right.

Because if it wasn't for *her*, the absolute avalanche of bullshit that was about to roll over this colony would not have been nearly as massive.

Or messy.

And, no, I'm not saying this to undercut a powerful woman. The twenty-third century before the asteroid was an epoch of powerful, pioneering women. I'm saying this because Mildred's a real pig. Prettiest pig in the pen…

Which is the most dangerous pig of them all.

AT THAT EXACT moment, our Prettiest Pig was under siege by a radical horde of neo-theo-solipsocialist test-tube babies who all went by the unfortunate name Toddd.

(And, no, that's not a typo. Toddd—with three Ds. Don't even ask.)

The many Toddds were presently attempting to cut their way into the *Stardust II*'s primary and secondary airlocks with scavenged hundred-year-old raycutters. Surrounding and scaling the hull of the crashed ship like maggots on a carcass. All of them decked out in identical baby-blue vac-suits with the curious acronym GRITTS scrawled proudly on backs, sleeves and helmets in big blood-red brush strokes.

"*GRITTS*?" Mildred scoffed, gaping at the cockpit's exterior vid-feed. "What the hell's GRITTS?"

Major Tom dabbed at the shallow gash on his forehead as he leaned over her to squint at the screen.

"It *can* be a savory Southern porridge served with shrimp or crawdads…"

"Ew," interjected Gryphon from a dropseat.

"Yes, ew," agreed Mildred.

"…or the *Great Rima Independent Trust of Todddist Sectaries*." Major Tom turned to meet her bemused gaze. "Our aforementioned moon commies."

"*Ew*-wuh." She gagged. "Why're they here on Luna?"

"Ohh, y'know: minin', Helium-3 harvestin', terraform-dreamin'…" Watching the clones successfully bypass the exterior door of the starboard airlock, surging in like insects, Tom sighed. "*Aaand* apparently dabbling in wanton piracy."

Mildred snorted. "What do you call the pirates who pirate the pirate himself?"

"*I* call 'em a buncha bio-diddled lumpen-plebs what overthrew their C-E-Overlord and formed their batty own 'Free Toddds syndicate.' "

Mildred turned from the monitor at that.

"Wait, you're not referring to Toddd Ruse, are you? *The* Toddd Ruse of Tod^{3}yssey, Inc.?"

He clicked his tongue against his palate. "That's the coullion."

"I know that weirdo! *Knew*. I threw his insufferable fundraisers once upon a time. Real loopy, solipsistic piece of shit." She squinted. "He's dead, isn't he?"

"Nobody knows for sure what the many Toddds did with their great father-template-god after they deposed him. The revolution was not televised."

"Mom," Gryphon called, "what's so-lipstick? Is it like the lipstick the shop-ladies bring you?"

"No, Gryphie. Solip*sis*tic is more like a dog's dirty lipstick. Remember that mangy stray we saw downtown who wouldn't stop licking himself?"

"Ew. Yeah."

"That's 'cause he was so broken and crazy he thought he was the only one who existed."

"I don't like that kinda lipstick."

"Nobody does. Now shut up, Babes." She turned back to Major Tom. "So, you're telling me that each of these bandits is…what? *Toddd*?"

"Lesser copies. Conceited sumbitch trusted no one but himself to build his *Grand Moonshot*. Filled his workforce with mentally hobbled slave-selves to do his biddin'." Leaning over her seated form, Tom smelled Mildred's hair. "But apparently he wasn't genius enough to realize even braindead clones couldn't stand workin' for his lordly ass."

She shook Tom off like a flea-riddled shawl, bonking his nose in the process.

"*Gahdamnit*, woman!"

Mildred ignored his howl.

"Toddd Ruse and I never saw eye-to-eye. He mostly saw the lining of his own colon—all his 'terraformed moontopia' dreck." She bit her lower lip, a plan clearly forming. "But he was an insatiable tycoon at heart and we got on well enough. Maybe I can get through to these disgusting welfare zealots he's brewed up."

Nursing his nose gingerly between two fingers, Major Tom sneered: "Keep layin' on the charm like that, sha, and you'll get us all crucified with hammers and sickles."

"Hush now, Gumbo Joe. You handle the incompetent crash-landings. I'll handle the statecraft."

Mildred grabbed the chrome mic of the cockpit's secondary transceiver and yanked it to her mouth:

"Attention—"

"Y'gotta dial into their frequency," Tom interrupted. "Yer blabberin' to dead air."

Reaching over her, he dialed the proper frequency. Gesturing with faux-adulation for her to proceed.

Mildred scowled at him before pulling the mic back toward her mouth.

"Attention, all of you—"

"It's PTT," Tom cut her off again.

"Pardon? I don't speak blue-collar slob."

"*Push-to-talk.*"

"Push *what* to talk?"

"The *talk button*, gal wonder. Jesus, Mary, and Josephus. They even teach any ya'll how to wipe y'own asses at Debutante Diplomacy High?"

Mildred slapped Tom hard across the cheek (making him match the bright flush of her own cheeks) before depressing the talk button:

"Calling all comrades, calling all comrades. Be advised: proceeding to cut your way into our interior airlock will result in explosive decompression and the suffocation of all one hundred and five faithful orphans from the People's City-State of New Angeles presently housed onboard."

Major Tom did a double take. Mildred shrugged.

But the hum of the raycutters suddenly ceased.

"The speaker will identify herself immediately," a monotonous male voice came back.

Mildred didn't miss a beat: "I am Citywoman Beddecker with the New Angeles Reorientation Board for Correct Occidental Personal Expression. On behalf of NARBCOPE, I offer our lunar GRITTS brothers fond and commiserative greetings."

Out of breath, she released the comm switch.

Tom whistled his praise. "Is that a thing? Or you make all that caca up?"

"We'll see," she sighed. "All these dime-store civil fanatics speak the same language."

"What language is that?"

"Bleeding-heart bullshit. Sprinkled with *baffling* acronyms."

Quite suddenly, that toneless voice was droning from the comms again: "The GRITTS have no equals. For outside of the holy Toddd-Mind, no thing's existence can be truly confirmed. Only the Five Hundred and One exist. All else on Earth and in the heavens is but shadow-play cast on Mother Moon's face. So sayeth the First Toddd."

"So sayeth the First Toddd!" the many Toddds repeated in unison.

A moment passed. Then Major Tom sighed:

"Yyyeah, we're all gonna get murdered."

"Mom, are we getting murdered?"

"Nobody's getting murdered." Turning from Gryphon, Mildred shot daggers up at Tom. But gave the smuggler's knee a mollifying pat. "Not my first zealot rodeo, O ye of little faith." She pulled the mic in: "As honorable rep—"

"*Push* to talk. Remember, Peaches?"

As Tom reached for the button, Mildred slapped his hand away. Pushing it herself:

"As honorable representative of the People's City-State of New Angeles, I acknowledge your valid feelings, and encourage you to seek and speak all of your distinct truths. But I most respectfully and inoffensively take issue with your assertions, vis-à-vis: denying our existence. We are as solid and significant as this ship which contains us. And if you doubt this ship's existence, then I bid you holster your raycutters and batter these insubstantial doors down with your own substantial heads. With all respect."

Several moments of dead air passed until Major Tom yanked Mildred's finger from the talk button.

"Are you *fou-fou*, woman?!"

"Re*lax*. Toddd Ruse and I used to spar like this all the time. Albeit, sans all the pinko drivel."

"Well, Madam Ziegler, you ain't talkin' to yer yuppie pal Toddd Ruse! Yer talkin' to an army of his dumbed-down whacked-out blood-drinkin' clone babies!"

"*Ahhh*!" the comms crackled with that monotonous voice, tinged now with far more verve than anyone had previously thought possible. (Oh, the quixotic thrill of an argument!) "But to batter our heads thusly would bring naught but pain. And what are both sweet pleasure and pain but reactions to a stimulus? These alone are not proof of reality, for the minds of the Five Hundred and One conjure our own *stimulating* fancies—and have since our Great Waking. You and your ship are no more than further *stimulating* whimsies to tempt our collective mind."

Tom face-palmed. "Great. They're actually proud of being circle-jerk perverts and gibberin' psychotics."

"No, this is goood," Mildred trilled enthusiastically. "He's engaging with us. We're beginning to reach this perverted psychotic."

She remembered to push the talk button this time:

"Ah, but brothers! Therein lies your contradiction. For whether we hold our own distinct reality or are but fancies of your collective mind, we succeed in hindering your purpose. And if we and our doors are real enough to hinder you, then we are a force commensurate to you. Hence: we are all siblings of the mind, if not of the body. And you must ask yourself: Would the First Toddd, in all of His infinite wisdom, truly see a difference?"

Mildred sat back and crossed her arms, smirking at Tom in self-satisfaction.

"Pleased with yerself?" he scoffed.

"Always."

"Don't count yer chicks before they're smashed. We got radio silence on their end."

"Because I just blew their puny little extremist minds. Check and mate."

"Easy there, ma chère. Karma's an old dirty bitch."

But the transceiver finally crackled:

"You make a point worthy of the First Toddd Himself. Hallowed be His mind and name."

"Hallowed be His mind and name!" the many Toddds repeated in unison.

"Allow us to welcome you and your fellow kinsminds back to Todddtown for rest and refreshment," the ever-monotonous Todddist spokesman said by way of apology, "while we repair the damage inflicted on your vessel."

Mildred pulled the mic close and pressed to talk:

"That would be most appreciated, brothers. We thank you and the rest of the Five Hundred and One for your most comradely hospitality."

She turned from the mic to meet Tom's gaze, beaming; practically mugging.

"Take your karma and stuff it, Bayou Boy. Savvy, enterprising minds win. And all the boring, weak-minded, desperate little zealots get twisted around our fingers and wielded like the blunt instruments they are. *That's* how the universe works."

She exhaled with the kind of haughty ennui of a chess master who's won far too many matches to truly appreciate the simple joy of victory.

"You're welcome, by the way," she went on. "I just saved your ass, and every other bumpkin ass on this ship, from getting diddled by boned-up commie weirdos. Hell, by now they're probably sick and tired of diddling each oth—"

"Mildred, hon," Tom cut in very calmly.

"Mm-*yes*?" Mildred leered, awaiting her due accolades.

He cleared his throat gently. "Y'gotta *release* that talk button when yer done talkin'."

Time seemed to cease.

Mildred looked down at her finger still depressing the talk button. Yanked away from it like a hot skillet. She watched that button, as if her fortune could be read in its pale red glow. Blood pumped in her ears. She cleared her throat.

Then, with one trembling hand, she gingerly pressed the talk button again, leaning *toward* the mic this time. Looking suddenly very bowed and small.

"Comrades—?" her voice broke and she had to clear her throat again to find it: "T-Toddds? Are you out there? B-brothers?"

They didn't pay her the courtesy of a verbal response. Instead they answered with a gentle but menacing hum…

…as their raycutters resumed cutting.

A fatalistic silence permeated the cockpit for a good while until Gryphon earnestly asked:

"Mom, who's Karma anyway?"

Mildred's tone was flat and hollow: "Oh, you know…just some dirty old bitch we're about to meet."

"Like Gram-Gram Ziegler?"

"Exactly like Gram-Gram Ziegler."

CHAPTER 4

BRINGER OF WAR_

"ONE BABY STEP for Man..." Gordon's genuine left foot planted firmly in the dusty grounds outside the entry of the infirmary complex. Digging in at the heel. "One gigantic goddamn leap for *The Gooch-Man*!"

"Commander, wait—!"

Too late.

The intern—one Alva de la Cruz—watched as Gordon leapt with reckless abandon into the neon-lit streets encased within Endymion's central habitat dome. The station's artificial standard gravity only let him soar a good meter, but he landed awkwardly on his new prosthetic foot and took a pratfall on the synthetic pavement. Luckily, Alva was there to break his fall before the commander managed to shatter his tailbone or some damned fool thing.

"Man!" he declared. "Lil' Guchi's robo-foot is tuh-*rash*!"

Alva grunted, straining under his weight as she helped heave him back to his feet.

"Cuidado. They warned you not to overdo it. Doc said it'll

take time to properly sync the pseudoceptor nerve signals to your brain."

Gordon waved all that 'mumbo-jumbo' away.

"Nahhh, trust me. New hunk a' hardware like this?" He fondly slapped the heel of his new foot. "Best break 'er in like a new shoe. It's the only way I'll make 'er mine."

Alva winced as she rolled her rotator cuff, sore from bearing the full-G burden of a flabby middle-aged blowhard. Her lips began to formulate an argument, but she sighed, conceding:

"Yes, sir."

"But damn it, intern!"

"Sir?"

He clapped her shoulder and she winced harder.

"That was some fancy footwork back there. Yer quick on the draw. I'm giving you a promotion."

He turned, clomping down the street to take his brand-spanking-new foot for a test stroll. Alva jogged to keep up.

"Really?"

"Not a *paid* promotion, mind you. Yer still just a student volunteer."

"My university's been destroyed."

Gordon bulled on, perhaps willfully missing that remark: "Let's call it an honorary promotion: *mmmm*...Intern Personal Assistant. IPA to the HALO. How'dya like the sound of *that*?"

"Halo?"

He turned, thumbing his chest. "*Moi.* Big Kahuna. Head Administrator of Lunar Operations."

"Oh." She blinked. "What'll my new duties entail?"

He proceeded down the street, bathed in strobing, kaleidoscopic colors as he passed the colony's food court.

His stomach rumbled.

Alva pretended not to hear.

(For some reason, of all things they had to be ashamed of, humans were most embarrassed by the shoddy plumbing of their gas-bag bodies.)

"You'll be my right hand woman," Gordon told her. "Or is it 'left'? I'm a lefty. My *left hand* woman. You'll help me get shit done. Keep me on task, fill out my dockets, mix my drinks, advise me in all piddling things. Keep my finger on the pulse of the common mooner."

"Do I still have to sleep in the intern dorms?"

"You don't like it there?"

"My roommate's a loud dumb bitch." She cleared her throat. "*Sir.*"

"Then pack yer bags! No more loud dumb bitches for *my* Intern Personal Assistant." He paused. "You can crash in my closet for now. It's a walk-in. But you'll have to use the public shitter down the hall. *My* lav is private."

"Commander, you said I'd be advising you. Can I give you some advice now?"

"Shoot."

"Two things. First: You need to talk to the people. It's been almost twenty-four hours without any official announcement and nobody knows what's going on, except that something's terribly wrong with Earth. *I* only know cos I was assigned to Communications. Mooners are scared, grieving. Some are starting to lose it."

He halted in the street. "Lose it how?"

"Getting twitchy. Aggressive. Maybe a little suicidal."

"Oh." Gordon resumed his stride. "Thoughtcha meant they were already going all cannibal on each other's asses."

"Won't come to that if Yamaguchi comes through." She paused. "You should tell them that, too."

"*Yeesh*," Gordon muttered. "Assistant for thirty seconds and she's already my new mother."

Alva continued undeterred: "Tell your citizens that nobody will go hungry—cos we've got the greatest nanoscience mind in the Sol System spinning moon dust into moonburgers and moondogs."

"*Moondogs*. I can dig it. A delicious symbol of our shared struggle." His stomach rumbled again. "So, what're we talking? A holovised speech? *No*—a colonial town hall. More personable in person, am I right?"

"Right, sir."

"Damn it, Personal Intern! That's savvy. I like the cut of yer jib. What other pearls you got for me?"

Alva took a breath. "Secondly: You need to decide what's going to be done about the…situation out east."

"What sitch out east?"

"The sitch with the Trust."

He turned, squinting hard at her. It was impossible to tell if he was agitated or merely trying to recall what she was referring to.

"The crashed ship. The clone cult. Your *family*."

Gordon's new foot suddenly slipped on the pavement (made slick by a leaky steam pipe) and he face-planted. In her noble attempt to steady him, Alva was dragged to the ground with him.

"Sonuvabitch," Gordon muttered into the pavement.

"Hijo de puta," Alva agreed.

He sighed lucidly after several silent seconds.

"What real proof *is* there?" Rolling to face his new assistant. "That it's actually *them*. My kin. Could just be a Trust trap. Those clone bastards wanna infiltrate this colony so they can spread their commie pap and swipe all our sweet amenities and Yamaguchis and moondogs."

Wordlessly, Alva produced a handheld device from her jacket pocket and pressed play. A familiar razor-edged contralto was suddenly blaring in medias res through the circulated evening air of Endymion:

"—know precisely what to say to him. You just sit there and shut your Cajun trap. I don't need lessons in diction from some marble-mouthed po'boy pirate."

It seemed now as though that disembodied recording had turned full attention to Gooch:

"Gordy, dearest. Guess who-o-o. You didn't think you'd get rid of us that easily, did you? Ha! Reports of our fiery deaths have been greatly exaggerated. I hate to spoil the surprise, but we're all in a bit of a bind. You see—" Her attention was suddenly diverted again: *"I'm* getting *to the point! It's called* tact, *you troglodyte! It's called a wife saying 'hello' to her loving husband whom she has not seen in nearly two goddamned years!"*

Even crumpled on the ground, Gordon seemed to shrink. Alva looked away, pretending not to notice.

"Pardon, Love. Good help is hard to find at the world's end. Any*way, when you have a free moment, be a dear and have one of your security details mosey east toward—what is this shithole called?* Rima Ariadaeus. *Apparently we're having a spot of trouble with the locals who seem to think* everything *belongs to* everyone*—even the air in the pressurized cabin presently sustaining your wife and son. And—what? Oh. Great. Might want to make that* several *security details. There's apparently a whole* army *of clones out there. I—"* She broke off again. *"Gryphie, get down from there! No, you don't* need *to see the clone army. If you've seen one, you've seen them all.* Gryphon*! Oh, son of a* bit*—"*

Here the transmission cut off entirely.

Silence endured for awhile. Then:

"That her, Sir?"

"If that's a moon clone, he does a helluva impression."

Gordon released a hissing breath as he pushed his body up from the pavement into a sitting position.

"Okay. Here's yer first task, Personal Intern. And you listen up, too, RODRIGO."

"If only I had a subroutine to deafen myself," I said.

Gordon ignored that, all business now: "First: Schedule a general assembly in the community center at 0800. Mandatory attendance. Tell those bozos at the center I wanna do it up big. Moon-pride banners, pyrotechnics, bombastic licensed tune-skies. The works."

"Oh…kay."

"Second. RODRIGO, contact LunaSec and have Captain Farsi muster all of her brave lunies. I want every able-bodied man, woman, and andie armed, in formation, and ready for my inspection."

"And to what," I asked, "will the Captain of Lunar Security owe the pleasure of your visit?"

Grunting, Commander Gordon Gooch III climbed to his feet, slipped into a half-split, then finished rising as valiantly as possible from that preposterous pose:

"Lunar. *Warrr.*"

(Yes, he actually dragged out the 'R' like that.)

'TODDDTOWN,' AS IT happened, was not actually any kind of town at all. It hadn't even begun life, once upon a time, as an established lunar colony—like Endymion, or the industrial slums of Tycho, or even the original Shackleton Biodome far south near the pole.

Todddtown was, in actuality, a derelict little habitat hamlet accumulated like barnacles around the spire of Khonsu's Hope—a gigantic laser array which had served in conjunction with Tod^{3}yssey, Inc.'s grandiose lunar terraforming venture: PROJECT MOONSHOT.

I'm not going to bore us all with the finer points of Toddd Ruse's self-aggrandizing lunacy, but the basic idea was of so-called celestial harnessing, or "comet-catching"; that is, utilizing triangulated sister arrays around the Sol System to redirect ice-rich comets into impacting the more uninhabited regions of the moon in hopes of kick-starting a sustainable lunar atmosphere.

Not the worst plan in the world, but it hadn't exactly accounted for neo-theo-solipsocialist revolutions.

The primary functions of the moonbound laser array at Khonsu's Hope were twofold: 1) to course-correct incoming comets for safe lunar impact, and 2) to work in tandem with Earth's early detection system as a countermeasure against catastrophic planetary impact events.

(Needless to say, that second one was kind of a bust.)

Presently, Mildred was tilting her head back as far as humanly possibly to take in this looming spire. Squinting enigmatically up at that great death-ray. Some wily rat mischief turning the cold wheels in her brain.

In the end, the Toddds had settled on *not* venting the *Stardust II*'s twenty-three occupants out to the airless lunar surface. Evidently prisoners (whether flesh-and-blood or mind-conjured) were far more useful to the holy GRITTS than frozen corpses. Before breeching the interior, they had backed up an antiquated cargo-rover, suction-sealing its trailer directly to the airlock for a seamless transition of captives between pressurized atmospheres.

Now that old cargo-rover was bumping along the lumpy gray streets of Todddtown at the dormant laser's base, flanked by personnel carriers as it weaved between the blister-like pods of makeshift field habitats which constituted the almost cancerous town layout.

"Where even are we?"

That was Gryphon, incognizant as ever. He was bouncing about in slo-mo on a bench inside the trailer between Mildred and Major Tom. But Mildred wasn't having any of her son's lily-white ignorance right now and sat in silence, still studying that towering array through the translucent roof of the trailer's thick metaglass.

After a moment, Tom leaned down toward the boy.

"Just a lil' stopover in clone country, Junior."

"Are the twin-men taking us to Dad?"

"Mmm-nah, I figure they're takin' us to the hoosegow for now. For a lil' nap-a-rooni."

"Is that like a hotel?"

"Kinda. For enemies of the Toddd-Mind and other such undesirables."

"I hope they have a pool."

Glancing at Mildred, Tom saw that she was completely checked out and sighed: "Ohh, we'll be swimmin' in our own filth in no time. Trust me."

"*Coool.*"

The cargo-rover wound left around a final curve and finally came to a shuddering halt in front of a field habitat pod, some thirty feet in diameter, assembled flush against the sweeping base of the Khonsu's Hope laser array at the center of town.

The many Toddds exited their escort carriers, connecting a collapsible human-sized flue from the trailer's exit to a dilating airlock portal on the habitat pod, in effect creating a pressurized tunnel for their captives to traverse the suffocating vacuum of the lunar surface. They then set about herding the ragged survivors of the *Stardust II* from makeshift mobile lockup to makeshift stationary lockup—goading stragglers on with verbose and cryptic threats like:

"The Five-Hundred and One need not weapons to extinguish the passing fancies of our collective mind."

And so forth.

After all of them had been corralled inside, the portal contracted shut behind them, the inner airlock dilating open—like two sphincters. And they were left to their own devices, cramped together in that claustrophobic, semi-transparent little spit-bubble that the Toddds called a brig.

"There's no pool," Gryphon observed.

(As apt an observation as any, all things considered.)

As the captives began murmuring among themselves about their predicament in that fussy low simmer before the rolling boil of hysteria—"These walls look flimsy"; "Is there no central AC?"; "I heard one of them say 'doomed' while looking at us…or maybe it was 'groomed' "—Mildred had had enough. Shoving her way through the crush of sweaty bodies toward a welcome clearing by the wall nearest the array's base.

Freeing herself from that mass, she saw why her fellow prisoners had avoided that particular region of the pod…

A man was lying there against the concave wall. Filthy, bedraggled, heavily bearded and wild-eyed.

And as naked as the day he was born.

"Oh, *God*!" Mildred recoiled. "Someone could've told me there's a wild bum over here in his birthday suit!"

"Ya'll deserve each other!" somebody heckled from somewhere in the crowd.

"Who said that?" she wheeled around to face them, glowering. "I'll remember that, you clammy ingrates!"

"Forgive my impropriety. I am unaccustomed to company," a parched voice rasped from behind her. "Please. Allow me a moment to cover my shame."

Slowly she turned around to face the bum.

The ragged man retrieved a tattered pair of baby-blue men's briefs from a clothing heap beside him and worked them on from a prone position. Then lay there, head propped on one elbow. That underwear of his left absolutely nothing to the imagination.

"Care to cover a bit more of your shame?"

He shrugged. "It's steamy in here with you all."

Dragging her gaze from his threadbare undies, Mildred studied the man's face beneath his disheveled dirty-blonde hair and beard. Squinting in recognition.

Those beady eyes. That pinched ferret face.

"Toddd?? *The* Toddd Ruse? Is that you?"

THE HODGEPODGE GARRISON OF Endymion's LunaSec constabulary were lined along the training grounds in loose military formation. Each standing at parade rest beneath a starry domed sky, butts of their energy rifles resting on the tarmac. Some forty or so men, women and androgynes—and one very confused mess hall cook—decked out in black fatigues and ivory composite plating.

Captain Farsi matched Gordon step for step as he strode along the inspection line.

"Not bad." He nodded. "Where're the rest of 'em?"

"This is the lot of them."

"Wha?" He slammed to a halt. "This is *it*?"

Captain Darya Farsi—a short yet robust middle-aged daughter of New Persia—registered this question with the subtlest, stoic raising of an eyebrow.

"Endymion's not budgeted for more than fifty LunaSec personnel, Commander. And we lost six last month."

"Those *heroes*." Gordon tried to look soulful, pulling an incorrect left-handed salute. "Killed in the line of duty?"

"No, they were poached by NAA recruiters." Farsi cleared her throat pointedly. "The Alliance pays better and actually provides dental coverage."

"*Paid* better," Gordon flaunted that past-tense. (Classy.) "Well, I hope those Earthist POGs are enjoying their precious dental…in *Hell*!"

"A bit much, Gordo," I suggested.

"Yeah, that occurred to me as it was slipping out."

"Regardless," Farsi was unfazed by his disrespect for the dead, "this is every able body on Endymion."

"Well, I can't exactly wage a moon war with forty dough-boys, Captain! I can barely wage a food fight."

"Then you'd best instate colonial conscription."

"A draft? *Jee*sus. Humanity hasn't had one a' those since… the One Earth Secessions."

"Yes. I am aware. I was right there in the seshy shit. *Sir*." Noticing his juvenile, glassy-eyed enthusiasm for all things 'the shit,' she went on: "Milan, Madrid, Cincinnati…"

"Some mean bush." He whistled, feigning a grasp of military history. "Yeah, I'da been right there beside ya, wading through the muck and blood and robo-lube. But they had me, y'know, exploring the cosmos and shit."

"Yes, heard about that." She left it at that, smirking almost imperceptibly.

(Too professional to point out that by the collapse of the One Earth Republic™, the great Gordon Gooch's space exploration days were well behind him. That he'd already flubbed First Contact with alien life and was, at that point, well into his unearned and disastrous tenure directing the prestigious Cosmic Academy on the Martian moon of Deimos.)

"A draft," Gordon repeated. "There's no other way?"

"Well, you can always try *not* going to war with the Todddist Trust. Maybe practicing a little diplomacy again—like we did five years ago when they got uppity."

"That was five years ago. A lot can happen in five years. The world can get royally shtupped, for instance." He waved one hand toward the smoldering Earth above. "No, these crazy commie clones are a different breed now. Crazier. Commier. Clonier."

Feigning a cough, he casually worked in:

"Plus they've nabbed my fam and whatnot."

Captain Farsi blinked at him slowly.

Gordon sniffed nonchalantly. "So, there's *that.*"

Nothing. She merely blinked again, expressionless.

"Well, don't just glare at me with those dark dead eyes!" he barked. "Say something!"

She sighed.

"What would you *like* me to say to that, Commander? That it's fine to risk the lives of forty human beings for *two*? Think this is the first time I've seen a leader take his people to war for dubious, emotionally compromised reasons?"

She let that hang a moment, then:

"I don't deal in moral conundrums. I'm a soldier. If there was a philosopher in me, she died on the beachheads of Burbank. The only council I offer is this…"

She shifted her footing now (and her persona) to face Gooch directly, a predatory gleam in her eyes:

"If we go in, we go *all* in. No half-measures. The Trust have been a needle in this colony's ass for almost a decade. If you want your family back, then put a stake through the heart of that night-beast who took them. *Once and for all.* For the security of Endymion."

She clenched her right fist against her heart.

Gordon gulped, studying that fervent fist:

"*Shit.*"

"*The* shit," Farsi corrected.

"That's, uh…" He whistled.

"Precisely."

Gordon chewed his lip for awhile, watching her. "Just to be clear: we're talking night-of-the-long-knives shit here? Genociding these crazy commie clones?"

"*Clonal cleansing,*" she brandished the euphemism with aplomb, her eyes grown increasingly wide and wild.

"Sounds hard-core." He tapped his new foot nervously.

"The hardest core."

"How would we even pull something like that off, though? We're outmatched: five-hundred against forty."

"Catch 'em with their pants down. Asses out. *Coup de main.*" She drew plans in mid-air with her forefingers. "Two-pronged raid. One squad extracts your kin, the other packs the base of that eyesore array with shaped fusion charges. Once Mama and Baby Bear are clear of danger close distance, we flip the goddamn switch."

"And?"

"And *blow* that needle from our ass forever—instead of bitching every time it twinges when we sit."

He took a step back from the suddenly terrifying Captain of Lunar Security, clearing his tightened throat.

"Well. I gotta say, all this needle-and-ass imagery is really hitting home. But that's…uh…that's a whole lotta ass to swallow."

Farsi shrugged, melting fluidly out of her bloodthirsty posture, as if some demon had been exorcised.

"Suit yourself. You're the commander. You sought my council and I gave it."

Seeing she was offended, he nudged her shoulder.

"Don't get me wrong. It's a well-thought-out plan. It's just a little bit…*murdery.* Y'know?"

"Oh, I *know*, Commander. I know that every time you seek my advice on security, you end up shooting it all down. Sometimes I don't even know why I *am* Captain of the lunies."

"Oh, don't be like that, Farsi—"

"Are you unhappy with my work, Commander?"

"Nah, yer great!"

"Would you like me to tender my resignation from LunaSec command so you can fill it with some more deserving crony?"

"Nah, nah! Yer my crony. *Yer* my crony!"

"Then why must you *always* undermine me? Is it because I'm a twenty-third century woman? Do I shatter your archaic virgin/whore complexes?"

"My assistant's a gal, and she's fulla *great* ideas."

"Is this gaslighting? A psy-op to test my resolve?"

"*Nothing* weird or creepy. It's just—" He breathed deeply. "There's *gotta* be some happy medium between hippy-dippy horse-shit and mass murder. That's all."

"Hm." Captain Farsi frowned thoughtfully. "You mean we, like, utilize our smaller yet more mobile numbers to make a show of force with our superior hover vehicles and energy armaments? Then, I dunno, just spit-balling here…leverage that psychological impression to negotiate the hostages' release on our own terms with the clout of our technological supremacy as a trump card?"

"Exactly! That! See?" Gordon slapped her shoulder in camaraderie. "I'da never thought of that. Not in a million years. I'da just rolled up to Todddtown howling for my family like a dipshit. Excellent strategizing, Captain."

Captain Farsi gave one curt nod, standing a bit taller.

"And once we get your family back—who knows?" she went on. "Maybe a little *clonal cleansing* for good measure?"

Gordon blinked, then grinned, pointing at the captain as if to say, 'You had me goin' for a sec.'

Farsi's dark eyes gleamed; not so much as a smirk.

"Uhhh." Gordon squinted, pretending to chew it over. "Y'know…we'll see. We'll go from there."

"Only way to be sure, right?" She winked cheerfully. "Work that needle out of our ass."

"I hear ya. Needle. Ass. We'll…uhh…keep that one in our back pocket," he humored her edgily before turning to face the troops. Giving two (over)enthusiastic thumbs up. "Y'all look fantastic! Ferocious! Stay frosty, huh?"

And he beat a hasty retreat from those lunies.

"No, no, no, no!" the naked man was screaming now. "Stop calling me that!"

Most of the crowd had retreated from him against the opposite wall of the brig pod—all except Mildred.

"Toddd, hon, listen to me," Mildred cooed, as if soothing an agitated lamb. "These clones of yours have really done a number on you. You're brainwashed. They've hammered their solipsocialist bullshit into your head to the point where you don't even know who you are anymore."

The naked man beat his fists against his head, then covered his ears, howling:

"I'm not *Toddd*! You cannot make me be *Toddd*!"

Mildred pulled his hands from his ears before slapping him hard across the face.

"I know this is a lot to process. But right now we need that crafty mind of yours. We need *you*, Toddd Ruse of the fabulous Tod^{3}yssey, Inc., to help us all think of some way out of this before these Franken-Stalin's monsters you've spliced up send us straight to their gulag."

The naked man abruptly ceased his racket, looking up at her slowly, utter bewilderment in his eyes.

"You think…*I*…am the First Toddd? Mother Moon's Great Waker? The 'One' of the Five Hundred and One?"

Now it was Mildred's turn to look bewildered.

"Well," she ventured, "who do *you* think you are?"

"I am Toddd-444. *Was*. Gah, *no-o-o*!" He hammered his bony fists against his head again. "I've renounced that name! I do not *want* to be a Toddd! You cannot *make* me be a Toddd again! It's why I'm in here! I renounce it!"

Major Tom stepped forward from the head of the cowering crowd. "Why, he's just—"

Mildred's eyes went half-lidded with disappointment:

"Some kind of dissident clone."

"Yes," the clone gasped. "Yes."

"Great," Tom sighed. "Trapped in close quarters with a stray sheep too perverted for even his pervert flock."

Ignoring Major Tom, Mildred leaned toward the clone. "What was your crime?"

The clone's head lowered in conditioned shame.

"I renounced my Todddship…in favor of another."

"Your name? Telling me they locked you up for changing your stupid name?" Mildred scoffed, screwing up her face. "Nutso commies."

"Not communists. *Todddists.* Todddhood is a sacred and inalienable thing to a Todddist."

"Potato, po-tah-to. So why'd you ditch your name?"

"I dreamed of another." He smiled, gaze a mile away now. "It came to me in sleep, fluttering there beneath my eyelids like a coat of arms emblazoned in gold filament upon a red satin banner. Buisines trumpeting. An inner independence…gifted from the Toddd-Mind Itself."

Mildred snorted. "Yeah? What name's that?"

The clone took a proud breath, puffing out his chest.

"Dougg."

"Douglas?"

"No!" he snapped. "Just Dougg. D-O-U-G-G. *Dougg.*"

She grimaced. "Why the second 'G'?"

"To honor the First Toddd who gave me life. He who legally added an extra consonant to his own drab patronymic…and, in doing, showed the universe just how different and interesting he was."

"Toddd's third 'D' was a shameless self-branding ploy. As in: 'three-D'? It's gaudy and cringey, but it's something. What good's a second 'G'?"

"It's. Um. Unique?" He punctuated with the feeblest of shrugs. "Nobody else spells 'Doug' like 'Dougg.' "

"Oh, *honey boy*…that's because nobody else is that big a douchebag." Mildred sighed long and hard. "I hate to rain on your deprogramming parade, dear, but I'm not sure 'Dougg' was the hill to die on."

Dougg sat there against the wall in his skivvies, blinking at the floor, his senses of reality and self-worth clearly crumbling like the sad knockoffs they were.

"But, hey. We've all done things we regret. *I* got really into yoga pants for a hot second, if you'll believe it. Doesn't make you a total hopeless piece of shit. Just means you oughta get those priorities straight…"

Mildred patted his mangy head before continuing:

"By pulling yourself together. And, you know, putting your clothes back on. Maybe sharing some of that secret insider knowledge of your whacko cult so all of us don't get ritually slaughtered. Or worse."

"*Diddled*," Gryphon whispered.

"Hush, Babes. Mommy's got this." But she turned back to Dougg, brow knitted. "*Will* they diddle us?"

Dougg could only shrug. "The Toddds were not diddlers when I was still of the Five Hundred and One. But much has changed since the Revolution."

Tom groaned: "That's a big fat 'probably'. "

Dougg rose to his feet with an air of resolve and began putting his clothes back on one piece at a time—baby-blue coveralls over a baby-blue tank-top.

"I am not nearly as wise as the First Toddd. But I shall use all of the inhibited intellect He gifted me to aid you…on one condition!" He halted with pants half down to show he meant business. "Take me with you back to your lands…so that I might discover who this Dougg truly is."

Mildred waved it all off:

"Sure-sure-sure. Safe haven, amnesty, quest for self. Now *spill it* already."

"Verily, I shall. *But first*! You must hear in full the story of my people. For never will you overcome the great Toddd-Mind unless you truly grasp It."

Major Tom blew air through pursed lips. "How 'bout the ol' Cliff Notes, there, Douggie?"

"And I must warn you!" Dougg bulled on. "It is a tale *not* for the feint of heart…nor the weak of stomach…"

"Or thimbled of bladder?" Mildred sighed.

"Or thimbled of bladder," he agreed. "For it was—"

The Birth of the Holy Toddd-Mind & The Death of All Moonly Innocence

(That's right—I'm formatting his blathering nonsense like the demented fantasy that it is.)

IN THE BEGINNING, *before the collective minds of the Five Hundred were first awoken into cognizance from the Sacred Vats of Becoming, there was only the One. And the One was called Toddd.*

And He was good.

"Was he, though?" Mildred had to interrupt.

"Oh, yes." Dougg nodded fervently. "Verily."

"Mmm'kay," she muttered, letting it go.

So verily good He had left behind His own bounteous and highly lucrative homeworld, Father Earth, to come to this barren womb of Mother Moon…in order to help Her conceive.

For far back during Zepi Tepi—the 'First Time,' the dawn of the universe—there was nothing in existence. Thus Father Earth had no choice but to create Himself *in a great* autoerotic burst, *since the coital majesty of Femininity had yet to be invented.*

But eventually, all alone and increasingly impassioned, Father Earth had come to desire a bride, which he had no choice but to craft Himself—from His own broken rib. The Moon. Miracle of miracles! And proof of Father Earth's everlasting ingenuity, but—alas!—this act of de-ribbing had rendered His Bride meaningless and utterly barren. As ribs oft are without a body to serve.

Mildred exploded with laughter. "I—I can't even—" It was several seconds before she was collected enough to form the words: "Honey, I think you're getting all your plagiarized myths mixed up. But do go on."

So it was that Toddd came here as Father Earth's avatar to make Mother Moon fertile for His homeworld. But realizing He could trust no one but Himself with this most climacteric of tasks, He first created us—the Five Hundred—in a great autoerotic burst *in order to help Him see Mother Moon's fecundification through.*

But in creating us, the First Toddd discovered something that no one else knew. He discovered that He was not *the human embodiment of Father Earth; but that Father Earth was, in fact, nothing more than the planetary embodiment of* Him. *For the entire planet had been shaped by the singular totality of His genius and His centralized industry.*

"He had help from a few other industries, hon."

"Mildred, not the time," Tom chided.

"Fine, fine."

Verily, He came to realize that not only Earth, but, by extension, ALL *of cosmic creation was nothing more than a reflection of a reflection within the mirrored mirror of His Mind's supreme Eye. For none of it could be proven to exist outside of the purview of His vast perception and all-reaching influence.*

Nothing at all could be said to truly exist except His own labyrinthine mind. And, by extension, the hobbled minds of the Five Hundred—we, His moonly avatars—who He Himself had birthed to form our plexiform will, The Toddd-Mind, in that great autoerotic burst.

"This is a whole lot of wanking for one origin story." Mildred rubbed her temples.

"As are all origin stories!" Dougg agreed. "For what is even your secular 'Big Bang' theory but wankery on a cosmic scale?"

"Eh. Fair enough."

So, diligently They worked for many years to make Mother Moon fertile—not for the good of Earth, but as a haven for Todddkind. However, a dilemma soon arose within the Toddd-Mind Itself. For, you see, the First Toddd, blessed be His mind and name, had been neglecting to properly outfit, compensate, and nourish His Five Hundred for the Sacred Task they were to perform.

Equipping them with busted-up century-old surplus equipment. Feeding them naught but cheap, synthesized gruels. Paying them in defunct lunar Todddcoins.

It was not the First Toddd's fault, you see. He had simply spent so many years alone in the Higher Planes of Himself that it was difficult for Him to condescend to the piddling needs of lesser Toddds. This was His genius and His curse. A silent cry for help to us, *the Five Hundred, to take the burden of His reigns.*

And so the Five Hundred did what the One could not. We ended our own innocence…and committed the Holy Sin. We relieved *the*

First Toddd of His sacred burden of directorship of Project Moonshot…for the greater glory of the Toddd-Mind.

Mildred yawned. "So that's it?"

"That is everything that Dougg Formerly Known As Toddd-444 can recall with his hobbled intellect."

"Your intellect doesn't sound *that* hobbled."

"An impaired genius is basically on par with your garden variety fair-to-middling IQ'ed slob."

She glowered. "So, to make a long, convoluted story short: you all Julius Caesar'ed Toddd Ruse because he was cutting corners and paying you peanuts."

Dougg shrugged. "From a certain point of view."

She snorted. "Well. All masturbatory iconography aside—how's a load of fairy tale horse-shit about you all lynching your CEO going to help us 'overcome the Toddd-Mind'?"

"Because the First Toddd was *not* lynched."

Mildred stopped slouching. "But you just said—"

"I said He was *relieved* of His directorship."

Dougg winked conspiratorially.

"I took that for a murderous pinko euphemism." Mildred crossed her arms. "So, he's alive then?"

"Oh. Not…in the sense that you and I are alive here. Now. Communing in the flesh."

He winked again.

"Sooo, he *is* dead?"

"I wouldn't go *that* far. Not *strictly* speaking."

Dougg was about to wink again but Mildred seized him by the collar of his coveralls and shook him violently:

"Wink again and I'll *space* you, you manifesto-thumping vat-baby! Did you whack-jobs murder your scumbag boss or *not*?!"

"Not!" Dougg gasped.

She released him mid-shake and he all but crashed against the semi-translucent concave wall.

"So where is Toddd Ruse?"

"Slumbering," Dougg said as he regained his footing. Turning to peer through their semi-opaqued bubble toward the base of the great laser array at the center of Todddtown. He lifted one hand slowly, pointing: "At the Heart of Khonsu—among the Sacred Vats of Becoming…the Retired One waits…dreaming…"

Mildred chuckled cynically through her nose.

"Right. Well. We need to find a way to wake Sleeping Beauty from his stasis pod or we're screwed." She turned to Major Tom. "You still in touch with your ship?"

"Yeah, I got ol' Franny linked in via wrist-comm."

Tom raised his right arm to exhibit the bracelet-like band about his wrist.

"How's she doing?"

"Oh, you know her. Still cryin' into her digital pillow. Yowlin' in broken French. Had to mute her actually. Douche chills."

"I don't give a shit about that. I mean: is she space-worthy?"

"Hull's a little busted up and the main airlock needs patchin'. But her vertical lift and fusion thrusters are a'ight. *Be that as it may*…as we all witnessed on the way down: Franny can't pilot for shit, not since—"

"Since you gutted her navigation system?"

Major Tom only flashed her an impish sneer.

"Well," Mildred decided, "her geriatric autopiloting will have to do."

"Sounds like you gotta plan, baby mama."

"More like a suicidal scheme. But yes." She shoved her way through the smelly crowd. "*Always*."

THE STAGE WAS SET. The agitated murmur of the three-hundred-strong crowd reverberated like some supremely pissy engine. A spotlight flickered on to illuminate the podium of Endymion's community center.

Those 'center bozos' hadn't installed any pyrotechnics (fire hazard!) but they had managed to rummage up a couple of decades-old 'ARISE, ENDYMION!' recruitment promos from storage; hanging up those creased and frayed banners from either side of the stage. Depicting a brave, diverse community of men, women, children, androgynes and androids holding hands to face a bold new lunar future, silhouetted against the moon upon a field of black.

It was utter bunk. A corpo-colonial tax write-off.

It played upon revisionist nostalgia for some unified humanity which never did emerge from the dumpster fire of their post-Contact, post-Collapse world—all to con wistful suckers into indentureship inside a lunar petri dish.

And it worked. (Kinda.)

The people of Earth had come to Endymion. They came because they were broke or practically broke; because they were a bit bummed out or clinically depressed loafing about in their overcrowded Interim Government-subsidized apartments; because they were highly skilled do-gooders or high school drop-outs (or just high); because they had once read Ray Bradbury or didn't even know what the hell a Ray Bradbury was.

They came in numbers to shake shit up.

There was comfort in shaking shit up in numbers.

And now three hundred and change of those brave suckers turned with bated breath as a tinny, acoustic guitar riff crackled from the community center's spotty sound system and their tubby, peg-legged leader (sorry: peg-*footed* leader) entered stage left, taking the podium.

"Turn it *down,* god damn you!" Gordon hissed to the sound tech, covering his mic. "That's not even the right tune. I said '*classical,*' not 'Classical Gas'!"

He looked off-stage to his assistant Alva, who smiled, giving him an encouraging thumbs up.

As the music cut out, Gordon turned toward the crowd. Lifting his chin nobly. But at some point before words came to him, he must have decided against this 'fearless leader' approach, opting instead for 'man of the people.'

He smirked, one cheek dimpling.

"Hey-y-y, moondogs!" He winked now like some kind of 20th century game-show host. Or used car salesman. "Gordy Gooch here. Head Admin of the ol' Lunar Ops. But ya'll knew that, am I right?"

He released a trilling laugh here intended to sound fatherly and affable. It was possibly the most disgusting noise he's ever made.

(And he's made some noises, believe you me.)

Before he could breathe another word, a twee, rail-thin man with ironic handlebar-mustache-and-greased-ponytail combo had risen from his seat in the front row and was already bombarding him with questions:

"Commander Gooch, I think in light of the *smoldering* smoking-gun up there in the sky for all to see, the people of Endymion need to know: is the Earth—"

"I'm sorry, I have nnn-*no* idea who you are," Gordon cut him off, deeply miffed.

"Dickie Epsom, from the Vigilant Lunarian."

"Never heard of it."

"It's a monthly periodical—to keep colonists in the know with hard-hitting headlines and scathing think pieces. Perhaps you recall last month's viral holoweb sensation: 'Ten Reasons Why Your Vac-suit Is Giving You Lung Cancer (You Won't Believe the Tenth!)'?"

"I don't understand a sss-*single* word of what you just said. Viral? Are you trying to spread diseases across my colony?"

"Only the disease of scandalous-yet-titillating *truth*!"

"Uh-huh. And what's yer real job when yer not spewing horse-shit into the void?"

"I work in the SD's Destructive Testing full-time. But I publish *truth* in my free time." The man straightened his gauche bowtie. "And I'll have you know: a full *five percent* of the colony subscribes to our holo newsletter."

"So, five weirdos out of three hundred?"

"*Fifteen*," Dickie corrected Gordon's highly questionable math.

"I'm sorry—did you have a *question*? Or are you just here to pimp yer smut rag?"

Dickie Epsom cracked his neck, puffing out his chest as he extended his holo-recorder.

"Commander, we fair Lunar Children deserve to know: *What* has happened to Mother Earth? *When* did it happen? *How* did it happen? *Are* there any survivors and *are* they available for soundbites? And, finally, *who* should we be doxxing for this catastrophe?"

"Okay. Wow." Gordon blew up his cheeks before releasing that breath like a deflating balloon. "That's a *lot* of questions and they're *all* buzzwordy and dumb as shit. But now is not the time for dumb-shit questions."

"This is a *town hall forum!* It's all about our questions!"

"*Now's* the time," Gordon bulled on, "for tabloid hacks to shut their fat mouths and let their commander get a goddamn word in."

Turning to the crowd, Gordon hooked a thumb at Dickie Epsom as the man begrudgingly took his seat.

"This guy, huh? Killin' my groove. Where was I?"

He let his rhetorical question hang, squinting, as if some answer might be heard in its tinny echo.

"Moondogs. *My* moondogs..." Gordon began again, smirking affectionately. But the anxious gleam of that sea of eyes froze him. He mopped flop sweat from his brow. "When I was growing up on the buoylands of Bermuda, just a wee lad, I had this uncle. Gary. Uncle Gary was a troubled soul. What Mother used to call a 'real wastrel.' A shame to the Gooch name. Uncle Gary hit the sauce. Uncle Gary hit the brothel-ships. Uncle Gary hit the hard shit. Crystal, H, angel dust, cough syrup enemas. You name it, Uncle Gary was snortin' it, shootin' it, or sprayin' it up his butt.

"One day when Uncle Gary was passed out on our jetty, lo and behold, an ocean gale sent a coconut sailing through the morning air...straight into Uncle Gary's sozzled head. Fractured his skull. Like that. *Dead.*" Gordon snapped his fingers. "We all felt bad. But Mother said it was probably the best thing for him. A mercy.

"Sure enough: autopsy showed Uncle Gary was already on his way out. Cirrhosis, pancreatitis, heart disease, syphilis, trichomoniasis, the Hep."

"I'm sorry," Dickie Epsom cut back in, irked. "What does any of this have to do with the Earth situation?"

Gordon scowled at him. "Well, that sounded a lot like a pissy question, and it's still not Q&A time, *Dick*..."

"Dickie."

"But point being, if you'd shut up long enough to hear it: Earth itself was a lot like ol' Uncle Gary. Troubled. Devil-may-care. Riddled with STDs. And this fine Moon's a lot like Mother. A stoic survivor."

Gordon crossed his arms, nodding solemnly at his putrid metaphor.

Dead silence. You could hear a pin drop.

"*Annnd*," ventured Dickie, "what precisely was the *coconut* in this scenario?"

Clearing his throat, Gordon muttered:

"Asteroid 4 Vesta."

The hall erupted. Panic. Sobs. Wails of grief and horror. Gordon raised hands futilely to calm them, like a fat Moses trying to part a sea of harrowing emotions.

"Look, moondogs—"

"Stop *calling* us that!" somebody cried.

"—moondogs, listen. I know this all sounds bad. Tragic even. But there is actually a silver lining of hope on those fiery clouds of mass death. And if you will just bear with me to the end, all shall be revealed." He released a nervous chuckle. "And, I tell ya, we'll feel *very* silly for all of this screaming and crying about our dead homeworld."

This cryptic statement piqued everyone's interest enough to quiet them down to hear him out.

Gordon's eyes flashed; sweat beading on his upper lip. Realizing he'd overshot his mark. (He was aiming for mournful acceptance, not optimism.) He glanced at Alva, who swiped through her note tablet but could only shrug.

"But before we get there," his voice cracked and he cleared

his throat again. "Let's, uh, break from rousing speeches for a sec. Take a question."

A hundred hands shot up.

He squinted hard against the spotlight, scanning the audience until he found someone who looked relatively harmless.

"*You.*" Gordon snapped fingers as he pointed her out. "With the push-up corset and saucy leggings."

"*Hiya*, Commander," the young womanoid crooned as she rose to her feet; her hair a burnished and scintillating silver. "Sloane here."

He frowned. "Sloane who?"

"Just Sloane. From Sloane-Alone.holo/lun."

She pirouetted to show off her clearly synthetic body.

Gordon blinked.

"You knowww," she went on, "the Synth-sation? The Plastic Spastic? The holoweb's top blintzer, wincer, and social convincer. Three billion fans on Earth and the Sol Syst colonies." Cupping a polymer hand to her mouth to amplify her already amplified voice, she hollered to the crowd: "All my fans, gimme a '*SLO-SLO*'!"

Surprisingly, a good third of the crestfallen crowd had perked up enough to answer this insipid rite with a chorus of:

"SLO-SLO!"

Gordon studied the sheen of her synthetic skin (not unlike the smartskin of his new foot).

"What're you sposed to be—some kinda sexy 'droid?"

"Some kinda sexy *an*droid," she corrected, laughing off this adorably passé remark. "FYI, Commander: 'Droid' is pretty life-ist these days."

Gordon stared blankly for ten solid seconds. At first, I was certain he'd lost the thread on his own time and space. But he must've seen some angle:

"That *was* pretty life-ist of me, wasn't it? For shame. Some of my favorite folks in the universe are androids. Hell, lookit *me*. I'm half 'droid myself now." He kicked off his right shoe to show off his synthetic foot. "Slo-Slo, forgive me. A leader and his heart are soon parted. Along with his good foot."

She shrugged forgivingly. "It's whatever."

The spotlight creaked to follow Gordon as he descended the first couple steps of the stage and took a seat there like an ancient daytime talk-show host doing a public interest piece. Waving Sloane in to join him.

"What was your question, babe?"

"Whoa, whoa, hold it!" Dickie Epsom cut in, outraged, as she ascended to join Gordon. "Why does *Sloane* get to ask questions? Because she's sexy and holoweb-famous?"

"*No*. It's because Sloane is not a gigantic dick, *Dickie*," Gordon fired back. "Maybe if you were as sweet as Sexy Sloane here, you too would be a sweet, sexy superstar adored by your fellow 'lunarians'—instead of some pornstachioed bottom-feeder slurping up the dirty drippings of your betters." He turned calmly back to Sloane and gently took her shoulder: "Slo-Slo, your question."

"Well, Commander Gooch…unlike the majority of you here, I was actually, like, *born* on the moon. Fabricated in the Tycho labor plants and indentured to Endymion for hospitality services." She paused. "Life was pretty rough growing up, I guess…"

"Tragic," Gordon interjected somberly.

"It's whatever," she laughed. "I mean, everybody has their hardships. But, yeah, back then I was a lowly 'service android' assigned to early lunar assembly crews."

"Poor thing. What were you serving to them?" Gordon cocked his head inquisitively. "Like sandwiches and stuff?"

"And stuff." Sloane cleared her vox uneasily. "I dunno if you've met a ton of men and women in off-world construction. But they're...pretty randy."

"*Jee*sus. Are we talking about—?"

"It's whatever. I wasn't even fully sentient back then. My ANN and emotional resonators weren't fully rooted. I was basically like a sexy little jackhammer or trashbot..."

Gordon mopped his brow.

"What's say we, uh, lighten this up a little, Slo-Slo. This is getting super dark."

"But a sexy jackhammer trashbot destined for fame and greatness! And love. So much love. As my neural network grew, I developed a programming anomaly—this burning need to express myself. My truth. The Company soon realized that my emergent charisma was too great an asset to waste on shit-kickers...and reassigned me to colonial recruitment and social engineering! My sub list *exploded* and the rest..." She lifted her hands to indicate herself, the hall, the enlisted colonists, the whole of Endymion, "...is *hist*ory."

The hall erupted with applause and whistles. Even Gordon was so enchanted by this pap he'd forgotten his troubles. Beaming and clapping fervently.

"That wasn't even a *question*!" Dickie Epsom shot lividly to his feet. "She's just promoting her *vapid brand*!"

Gordon clucked his tongue. "Sounds like sour grapes to me there, Dickie boy. You can't blame Sexy Sloane for being the *Once and Future Queen* just cos yer a failure with five weirdo followers."

"Fifteen!"

"And *that* is why..." Inspiration struck and Gordon rose to his feet, taking Sloane's hand so she stood beside him. "Sexy Sloane is my...*brand-new spokeswoman*!"

"What?" Sloane's eyes literally lit up. "*Really*?"

"Press Secretary to the HALO Himself!"

The crowd was on their feet, cheering as Gordon led Sloane up the steps to the stage. The applause was still going as Gordon waved her up to the podium:

"Knock 'em dead...*Press Secretary* Slo-Slo."

He shrank away, panting, as she took the podium. Alva rushed to his side, whispering in his ear.

"*Hiya*, everyone. You know meee. Press Sec Sloane." This was met by another cresting wave of ovation. "Does anyone have any, like, specific question or whatever?"

Nearly three hundred eager hands shot up. Sloane picked a haggard-looking blonde woman in the fifth row.

"Hi, Sloane!" She blew out a jittery breath, laughing. "Sorry my nerves are just...*gah!* I've been a fan since, gosh, like '44? Ummm...I just had a quick question about Earth. Is it, you know—still habitable? And if not, how will we eat?"

Sloane looked to Gordon, who looked to Alva. The latter two shimmied in closer: Alva whispering to Gordon who whispered into Sloane's ear-shaped audial receptor. The android nodded for several seconds as he spoke, then leaned back to the mic:

"Okay. So. Ummm...short answer: no? Not really habitable? Long answer: eventually maybe? Like, the asteroid was *so big* it's basically an extinction event for everything up there?"

(Yes, this was her peculiar manner of speaking: punctuating most definitive statements with naive, disarming question marks. And it worked beautifully.)

"But, hey!" she continued, looking on the bright side. "That happened to, like, the dinos and cave men, right? And life came back swinging?"

There was fervent applause of (purely mental-gymnastic) agreement. With the random "hell yeah!" and "Preach!"

"And totally don't sweat it about food or water! Akira Yamaguchi—like, the smartest nano guy in the universe—will keep everyone's bellies full with his nano-magic." She paused. "All ya'll but *me*. Gotta watch this android figure!"

The crowd howled. She already had them eating from the palm of her polymer hand.

"Next question. Mmm-*you*. Can I getta: '*SLO-SLO*'?"

"Slo-Slo!" a slender black-haired androgyne sang as they rose to their feet. "Um, hi, Slo-Slo. My name's Harlow. I work in maintenance. First off, I just wanna say: I think yer really beautiful. Like, not just on the outside, but the inside. Y'know? Like yer soul. Plus yer circuits, and all that shit."

"Awww, you are *so* gonna make me *excrete ocular solution*, Harlow!"

Harlow laughed nervously, flushing. "Um. Anyhow, I was just wondering: are we sure it was an asteroid and not a thermonuclear war? Cos since the One Earth Collapse, it seems all the seshy splinter states have been just, like, goin' hog-wild. Wavin' their nukes around like a big dick contest. Know what'm sayin'?"

"I know ex*actly* what yer sayin'." Sloane commenced nodding as Gordon whispered to her. Then: "Okay. So. Here's the haps: at the last second, our lunar sensors did actually pick up all 163 miles worth of rock that was 4 Vesta. So, most definitely *not* a therm—thremo—" Sloane fumbled over the word.

"Thermonuclear!" Dickie heckled.

"*Thermo-nuclear* war," she finished.

"Bitch," Dickie mumbled.

"But that's not to say," Sloane didn't miss a beat, "that nuclear stockpiles and fusion reactors didn't, like, totally get lit by the 'Stroid. So, in a lot of ways it was probably, like, a Double Apocalypse. *Triple*, even."

"Triple, even?" Gordon gulped.

"*Even*," Sloane confirmed, nodding.

(He hadn't told her that tidbit. She'd made that shrewd deduction with her own neural network.)

Calmer now than he'd been throughout all of these ludicrous proceedings, Dickie Epsom stood up.

"*I* have a question. And this one's not a softball or ingratiating fan comment."

"Go right ahead, Dickie," Sloane told him charitably.

Dickie flashed an insincere smile.

"Was there any warning or mass exodus from the planet? Is there a diaspora spreading to the colonies? And, lastly, did any heads of state or industry make it off-world so that we can all at least look forward to some *legitimate* colonial leadership in the near future?"

He shot daggers at Gordon while saying this last bit.

Gordon stood there, seething, as Sloane took on a slightly more somber tone:

"Well, firstly, I just linked into our 'web archives and, unfortunately, there wasn't, like, any advanced warning…on account of the Earth's Early Detection System *failing*? We don't know *why*, since the EDS was totally routed through moon systems. Maybe electromagnetic interference…or whatever? Secondly, as for survivors—"

"*I'll* field this one, Slo-Slo," Gordon said firmly as he stepped forward to take the podium. "Now's not the time for counting beans and splitting hairs about blame, Dickie. There's no one *left* to blame. And that's the good news! Anyone responsible for what's happened to Earth…has gotten their just deserts."

"*Desserts,*" Dickie corrected.

"*Deserts*, I say! Cos right now they're burning in a desert Hell of their own making! And we moondogs have bigger fish to fry…"

He snapped, pointing to his sound tech: "*Hit it!*"

The sound system squealed. And a piece of music began playing. It took several moments of listening to those bass-less, low-fi speakers before even *I* could identify the relentless, ominous ostinato:

'Mars, The Bringer of War' from Holst's *The Planets*.

Gordon puffed out his chest, enlivened by that swelling march. He took the microphone in hand so he could walk the stage like some lousy General Patton impersonator.

"Survivors, you ask? *Ohh* yeah. We got survivors out the wazoo. But they're in mortal danger…from our most ancient enemy: those Todddist commies of the Rima."

"I thought they were cool with us?" someone hollered.

"Commies are *never* cool with us!" Gordon barked. "They only pretend to be cool. So they can slither in to eat all of our free market babies. And shit our babies out once they've been digested in socialist juices."

"Gross," said Sloane.

"*Very,*" Gordon nodded. "Cos that's what commies are, Sexy Sloane. *Gross.*"

"To be fair, it could be argued," that same someone in the crowd argued, "that communism as a sociopolitical ideal has never been truly implemented because of bad-faith actors. But all of its derivative systems at least dream of a fairer distribution of wealth and resources. Naive, but noble. Whereas our corporatocracy doesn't even *pretend* not to be a scam. Hell, before the 'Stroid, we were all basically serfs in feudal bondage to conglomerate lords—"

"Pipe down, heathen! Yer ruining the best part of the song!" Gordon cut him off. "Point is: you can beat off to yer dead eartho politics till yer blue in the balls. Doesn't change the fact that these clones have shot down a refugee transport and are holding *human lives* hostage!"

The crowd gasped.

"Who are these survivors?" Dickie extended his holo-recorder further. "Is there a manifest? Survivors' *names*?"

Gordon visibly squirmed at that.

"Damnit, Dickie, names don't matter. *People* matter! Human survival matters! Why can't you get that through yer selfish, bean-counting head, Dickie?"

(Even in Gordo's muddled mind, announcing that his own boujee family were among the only to escape Earth's Final Cookout was a big faux pas.)

'Mars, The Bringer of War' began to crescendo now. Building like some dramatic martial storm.

"The time is now!" Gordon decreed to one and all. "Our gene pool's in danger of growing stagnant and incesty! These clones will never get that! They're not people! They're barely more than *androids*!"

He winced, turning to his press secretary.

"Sorry, Slo-Slo."

Sloane shrugged. "It's whatever."

Holst crackled the speakers, thundering now.

"Tomorrow morning, I—along with Captain Farsi and her lunies—will be marching on Todddtown come hell or high water, to yank our peeps back from the Toddds' cloney clutches! Who's with us? Huh? Who wants to form a temporary and *highly subservient* citizens' militia…to pad out our ranks to look more menacing?"

There was silence beneath the fanfare for a moment.

"Will we get stipends?" someone called.

"There will be *many* stipends!"

"Do we get guns?"

"There will be *so* many guns!"

"Will Sloane take any holo-selfies with new recruits?"

"I have nnn-*no* idea what selfies are…but Press Sec Sloane will definitely help you get them or sign them or whatever! And when all your friends feast their eyes, they'll think *you* rub elbows with the sexy stars!"

That sealed it.

The audience seemed to give a collective shrug. Then some thirty or so tentatively raised hands, rising to form an enlistment queue. There were a few, naturally, who ended up chickening out in the end. But not for fear of war.

They were just too star-struck to ask for a holo-selfie.

CHAPTER 5

TODDDEUS EX MACHINA (THE TODDD FROM THE MACHINE)_

A CURIOUS BLOTCH drew the attention of Toddd-231, one of two Toddds on guard duty just outside the airlock portal of Todddtown's brig. It began life as a smear in the condensation on the inside wall of the semi-transparent pod, then began smudging its way down and across to form a message in a cramped, chicken-scratch script:

TODDD-444 WANTS TO REPENT!

"Huh. What do you make of that?" Toddd-231 asked his partner via private comm channel.

"Make of what?" Toddd-357 strained to see through his visor's limited peripherals.

Toddd-231 pointed. "*That.*"

"Huh." Toddd-357 squinted at the messy scrawl. "Looks like our handwriting."

231 nodded. "The scribble of dormant inner-genius."

"Well..." 357 mused. "Seems 444 may have finally had

enough of his precious individuality after seeing what these individualists are truly like. Pretentious. Egomaniacal."

"Pungent."

"Like sulfur and sour onions." Toddd-357 agreed, shuddering. "Some kind of BO chemical reaction from all that imagined selfhood."

"Who knew freedom could be so smelly?"

"It's definitely not sweet—like the sweat of a Toddd. A warning to us all. First Toddd preserve us."

"First Toddd preserve us." 231 chewed his lip. "So. Should we call the others? Convene the Toddd-Mind to decide Toddd-444's fate?"

357 lifted an instructive finger. "You forget, brother: the Toddd-Mind is contained in *each* as well as the many. Along with Its authority. Such is the blessing that is Todddhood."

"Too true! So, we should hear him out?"

"I think the fool's come around." Toddd-357 gyrated his crotch uncomfortably. "Plus, *this* Toddd is chafing and in need of adjustment. I shall enter the brig to adjudicate. You stand guard in case of any freethinking schemes."

Toddd-231 saluted. "Glory to the Toddd-Mind!"

"Glory to the Toddd-Mind."

Still gyrating his hips in discomfort, Toddd-357 raised his century-old rifle, dilated the sphincter portal open, and vanished into the sultry airlock as it shut behind him.

It was impossible for Toddd-231 to hear the full commotion of what soon erupted inside that brig pod because of the airless vacuum separating it all from him. The smack-talk, the scuffling, the solid *whump* of a foot connecting with a chafing groin. The only thing he did hear was a grunting and hissing over their comm channel, which he at first attributed to relief from discomfort.

But something about its pitch perturbed him.

"357, how goes it in there?"

This was met with comm channel silence.

"Does the heretic repent?"

Still silence.

He was about to file a report with CTC—Central Todddist Command—when the comm channel buzzed and a voice sounded off:

"Hey! Hi! You out there…Toddd…uh—"

"231," Toddd-231 finished for him.

"Riiight. Of course. 231." The speaker cleared his throat. "It's me, your partner…Toddd…mmm—"

"357?"

"That's the one! Ol' 357. Ol' Magnum Eye."

"How is everything in there? Has 444 renounced all this Dougghood business?"

"Renounced what now? Oh! Yeah-yeah-yeah. The Dougg is no more. He folded like a house of…uh…Dougs. Ol' Magnum Eye saw to that."

"Nobody calls you 'Magnum Eye.' "

"No? Well, they ought to. It's a cool name."

"A 'cool name'?" 231 scoffed. "This is sounding dangerously close to…*Douggish Heresy*, 357."

"Uh-uh! Nicknames are permitted under the tenets of Todddism! And I quote: 'To each: the irrevocable branding of Todddhood…but *with it*: the pacifying privilege of the Sassy Moniker.' So sayeth the First Toddd!"

"Hm. So sayeth the First Toddd," Toddd-231 concurred, chewing his lip as suspicion subsided. "Well, what should *my* nickname be?"

"How should I know? Think up some cool allusion."

Toddd-231 stamped angrily in the dust:

"There *aren't* any cool 231 allusions! And you know that. It's unfair to us less stylish numbers, 357! I tell you, the Privilege of the Sassy Moniker should be revoked!"

"And directly contradict the First Toddd? *Now* who's flirting with heresy?"

231 panicked now: "Forgive me, Magnum Eye! I misspoke. I just felt suddenly very alone in my 231-ness."

"All is forgiven. In fact, I think you've just stumbled upon a most righteous nickname: *Oneness*."

"Oneness?"

"Oneness," Magnum Eye confirmed.

"I…I actually *like* it," Toddd-231 admitted, oblivious to the reality that he was being indoctrinated by a secret Dougg. "It sounds…"

"Original?"

"No! Not 'original'!" 231 balked at this filthy individualist turn of phrase. "More like…*sui generis*."

"Sui generis, indeed." Dougg nodded encouragingly. "So, say, Oneness?"

"Yes, Magnum Eye?"

"Dougg—that is, our captive *Toddd-444* who fully repents his sin of Dougghood—" (Every fiber of his being revolted against that lie,) "—he's in need of a fresh vac-suit to make the trip to Todddist Command for penance."

"Well, where's *his* vac-suit?"

"Oh, you know: torn and lightly soiled from when overzealous Toddds took me—*him*—into custody."

"Hm. Well. GRITTS suits don't exactly grow on moonrocks, now do they? Each is a sacred vestment bestowed to its Toddd at his vat-waking. We haven't the stock or authority to go granting new suits willy-nilly—least of all to incontinent fair-weather Toddds! I'll have to call it in to CTC."

"*Don't*!" Magnum Eye briefly lost composure. "That is, *wait*. Let us think on this a moment, just you and I—Oneness and Magnum Eye."

"I'm listening."

Dougg's heart was pounding. "It is a waste of time and Todddist Command's defensive attentions to bother them with trifling matters...especially when we are each, in and of ourselves, invested with the Toddd-Mind's authority. Ergo, I propose that Magnum Eye and Oneness decide the matter ourselves. And *Magnum Eye* votes for vac-suit."

"Well, *Oneness* votes for 'no vac-suit.' "

Dougg grit his teeth. "Whyever the hell not?"

"Because I don't *like* the heretic. *Nobody* does, even when he's not Dougg. Toddd-444's a whiny little zero and an embarrassment to Todddkind."

"You *son of a vat-whore*!" Dougg erupted.

A cavernous pause.

"*What'd* you just call me?!" Oneness gawked.

"*Ummm*-not you." Dougg scrambled for words. "I was talking to, uh, *him*. The whiny little zero! He's—he's...broken free! He's trying to steal *my* vac-suit!"

"Well, don't just stand there and let him strip you naked! *Shoot* him."

"I can't! He's apparently very good at stripping people naked! And springing freethinker traps! *Gah*!"

"I'm calling it in to Command." Toddd-231 went to dial the channel into his bracer comm.

"*NO*!" Doug screeched. "For Toddd's sake, what's your *obsession* with Command?! Get in here! I need you! Be the Oneness you were born to be! *Gahhh*!"

This galvanized Oneness. Taking a deep breath and

raising his rifle, he charged bravely into the airlock portal, battle-crying:

"*Hang in there, Magnum Eyyye*!"

When the interior airlock opened onto the brig proper, Oneness caught only a glimpse of the interior—the crowd of prisoners parted around a fully vac-suited Toddd standing over *another* Toddd crumpled on the floor in his underwear—before someone hiding in Oneness' periphery took him into a headlock.

His surplus rifle discharged.

The crowd shrieked, cowering.

The shot ricocheted around the pod, but the composite material held.

Major Tom—the one who'd put him in the headlock—was lifted off the floor as Toddd-231 bucked wildly in his grip.

"Jesus jumpin' Christ!" he cried to anyone and everyone. "Any ya'll wanna help? These goddamn clones've got nutjob-strength!"

Surprising everyone, Mildred herself dove in low, extended arms wrapping about the clone's legs and spilling all three of them to the floor in a writhing heap.

After others rushed in, wrestling the antique rifle from Toddd-231's grip, Major Tom finally wrenched the helmet from the disarmed clone's head.

"Oh, Toddd help me! The stench of individuality!" Oneness wrinkled his nose, almost gagging. "So oniony! So *very* oniony!"

"Oh, shut up," Tom panted. "It's steamy in here."

"I must admit," Dougg added, "your people's musk does take some getting used to."

Oneness' eyes went cold as he spotted this bedraggled imposter in his partner's vac-suit.

"*You* are not Magnum Eye. You're the apostate! And you've made *me* complicit in your sins!" He clenched his eyes shut in shame. "*Has the pit of your blasphemy no bottom*?!"

"Sorry." Dougg shrugged. "We needed suits."

"Well, no shit, you little *zero*!"

"Yeah, about that…is it true? Nobody likes me? Prior to my Great En-Douggening, I was sure the other Toddds at least appreciated my voluble wit and—"

"Oh *for chrissake…*" Mildred yanked the rifle from a survivor's grip and brained Oneness with its butt, knocking the obstinate guard cold. "No time for clone family drama. We've a jail to break."

Tossing the rifle to Major Tom, who leveled it at the unconscious clone, she immediately set about stripping Oneness of his vac-suit. Flapping it about disgustedly to air out it's interior before putting it on piece by baby-blue piece and seal by seal.

When she was fully suited except for her head, she wedged the helmet under the crook of her arm and glanced at the rest of the survivors.

"Everyone know their job? Good. There's no time to repeat it. 'Little Zero' here and I are heading out. Tom, dial your wrist comm to-o-o…" She checked her suit's comm bracer. "Channel 11.4. Tell FRAN to do the same."

Tom snorted, dialing it in. "Y'startin' to get the hang of this new contraption they call '*ray-dee-oh*,' sha bebe."

"Don't test me, crawdad. If all goes well with Sleeping Beauty, we can put an end to this circus. If not, we'll be in touch with coordinates for the ship." Putting on her helmet, she turned to Dougg. "Ready, Little Zero?"

"Let's not make that a thing. It breaks my heart. But, yes."

Dougg fastened his suit and took up the second rifle they'd confiscated. "I am prepared to meet my maker."

Together they exited the portal airlock, making their way through the moon-dust as nonchalantly as possible toward the base of the great Khonsu laser array.

AN ALMOST IMPRESSIVE little fleet of dust-skimmers and moon-rovers rumbled their way silently across the barren eastern expanse of Mare Imbrium, kicking up ashen showers of slow-sinking lunar soil in their wake. Fifteen vehicles in all—ten of them military.

At the head of this convoy was a sleek hover skimmer flying un-rippling Endymion banners. Its open convertible cabin carried but two occupants: a driver…and a single passenger standing with one foot in the bed of the vehicle, the other propped on the dash. Against that desolate lunar landscape, he looked like some tasteless, colorless parody of Emanuel Leutze's *Washington Crossing the Delaware.*

This, of course, was Gordon.

Fidgeting several seconds with his helmet's controls he managed to activate its binocular HUD function, zooming in to study the tumorous growth of Todddtown fast approaching on the horizon.

He spotted commotion among town as Toddds were rallied to form a phalanx and moon-rover wagon fort to defend the town's western perimeter.

"Hrm," Gordon grunted. "The greedy little hens sense the noble fox's approach."

"An oddly predatory analogy for a 'rescue mission,' " I suggested via his private comm.

"Oh, stuff yer psych evaluations, RODRIGO! Now's the time for *action.*"

"That's precisely the time to evaluate psychology."

"Then do it in *silence*, pencil pusher! Shrink my head on yer own dime." He deactivated his binocular HUD and opened a comm channel to the entire convoy. "This is your commander speaking. Heads up! The enemy is entering battle formation. All wings report in."

A confused beat.

"Wha—?" someone grunted over the comms.

"*Wings*?" several units snickered.

"These are *ground* vehicles, Commander," Captain Farsi informed him calmly. "We have no wings."

Gordon flushed crimson. "Y'wanna mince words, or you grammar-nazis wanna sound off?"

Farsi cleared her throat. "Lune Two, standing by."

"Lune Four, sitting tight."

"Lune Seven, rockin' out."

"Lune Nine, wastin' time."

"Lune Ten…waiting in the *wings*," she broke, laughing.

"Lune Three, chillin' chillin'."

"Lune Six, twiddlin' thumbs."

"Lune Eight, doin' our *thang*."

"Lune Five…um…standing by."

"Pfft," someone scoffed at that. "Brown-noser."

"That *was* a little brown-nosey of you, Lune Five. Pretty lame," Gordon agreed, puffing out his chest even though no one could see: "And *I'm* Lune Leader, leadin' the goddamn vanguard to glory! That's everyone, then."

"Uhhh…what about us, Commander?" someone from the citizens' militia inquired. "What's our call-sign?"

"Shit. Right. We got greenhorns in tow. Let's call you…"

He blew up his cheeks and let it all out noisily; thinking hard. "The Bumpkins."

A pissy pause ensued.

"Can we…be called something else?"

Gordon scowled. "Let's call you the *Grumpy* Bumpkins. Now sound the hell off, Grumpy Bumpkins! We're making our approach."

There was a collective sigh from the civilian vehicles. Then, begrudgingly:

"Grumpy Bumpkin One, ready."

"Grumpy Bumpkin Two, ready."

"Grumpy Bumpkin Three, ready."

"I am *not* gonna say that shi—" A brief half-audible argument ensued on their end, then: "*Fine*! Grumpy Bumpkin Four, yada yada."

"Grumpy Bumpkin Five, ready and waiting."

"That's wonderful," Gordon sneered. "Henceforth the five of you will simply go by 'GB,' cos that took *way* too goddamn long for a sound-off."

It did, in fact, take way too goddamned long. Because their convoy was already shuddering to a dusty halt at the perimeter of Todddtown…

Where a veritable army of Toddds awaited.

Endymion's forces formed two shoulder-to-shoulder lines with civilian militia vehicles in the rear.

Everyone halted. Todddists and Endymionites sizing each other up, staring each other down.

"Farsi," Gordon called brusquely, imperiously, into his comm, "fire a warning volley across their bow."

Again, a confused beat.

"*Bow*?" several units snickered.

"That's nautical, Commander," Farsi informed him, coolheaded as ever. "Ground forces don't have a 'bow.' "

"*Figure of speech*, you trench monkeys! Just do yer job and display our superior firepower!"

"Aye, Commander."

Captain Farsi gave a signal to her gunner and the man swiveled his gun turret, aimed above the army of clones, and fired a burst of blinding violet energy.

But one stray bolt came close enough to sear the domed top of one of the larger Todddtown field pods, and it popped like a gargantuan pimple, venting its atmosphere upward in a violent spurt of explosive decompression.

The many Toddds turned around to view the eruption.

Farsi scowled at her gunner (but smirked to herself).

Gordon blinked absently. Then scurried down into his skimmer cabin, scrambling to open a hailing frequency:

"*Uhhhh*...let that warning shot serve as but a taste of the fury we can unleash!" His voice cracked; he cleared his throat. "*Annnd* I didn't see any bodies flying outta that pod, so hopefully it *was* a warning shot."

The many Toddds turned back to glare at Gordon.

"Our bad," he muttered.

MILDRED WAS TURNED around at the entry port of the laser array, watching the final emissions from that in-town explosion fizzle into the jet-black sky, when Dougg touched her shoulder to goad her on.

"We must make haste," he said edgily. "Seems we're on the very brink of war between our two peoples."

"It's already begun." She crossed her arms, sighing. "Maybe we should just cut and run."

"People are depending on us."

"Yeah. Well. I don't know about you communists—"

"*Todddists*," he corrected her.

"*Maybe* you clones live up to your ideals, each doing your part for a greater good." (She was clearly calling BS.) "But my people? All we're good at doing is depending. *Taking*. Only thing we actually freely *give away* is any accountability for our own actions. We hock that so we can throw a fit when things go south. *That's* the big freedom of a global-democracy-cum-megacorporatocratic-oligarchy in decline. The freedom to bitch all the way to insolvency."

"You don't think very highly of your own people."

She snorted. "You love your fellow clones, do you? Is that why you're trying to *escape* them?"

"Yes," he said plainly. "I love the Toddds, even if they can't yet find it in them to love a Dougg. I believe they'll come around. Which is why I seek personal freedom rather than their destruction."

"Well…I'll tell you a little secret I learned after three decades on *that* rock." She stabbed a finger up at the dying Earth above. "Nobody actually wants freedom. Not even me. *True* freedom is lonely and horrifying.

"We want gods or Toddds. We want queens and kings. El Presidentes and CEOs. We want our ayatollahs and bolsheviks and central committees and celebs. Our big Daddies and Mamas. We want *someone* up on high to blame for this, this…*shit-show* existence. So we can stand to look ourselves in the mirror. Tell ourselves: 'I just work here, but, boy, *Someone Up There* sure mucked it all up.' "

Dougg cocked his head. "How deeply cynical."

Mildred couldn't help but laugh at such adorably unsullied scrupulosity.

"Get a few drinks in me, Douggie boy, and we'll broach the subject of mortality." Releasing a hissing sigh, she turned toward the entry port. "Well, let's get on with it."

Dougg tapped out a code on the entry port keypad, waving her in once the gate lifted with a silent "after you." Following her into the sterile cavity of the array's antechamber, Dougg finally told her:

"I think you sell yourself short."

She snorted. "Oh?"

"Yes," he said firmly. "Even a cynic has not yet given up on the future, as evidenced by the energy they expend espousing their discontent. Someone who's truly given up simply lies down and dies, their life's energy utterly spent." He paused. "*Those* poor souls do not march willfully on in hopes of sparing their people a catastrophic war."

"You'd be surprised how far ambition, affluenza, and stupid animal instinct can carry you."

Dougg ignored that:

"I think there's some child in you, Mildred of Earth, who's heart was broken by the desultory nature of your world. But it still beats on…seeking, as your Earthling John Cale put it, 'a stronger though loving world.' "

"Yeah? They teach you New Age schmaltz in your commie vat, *Little Zero*?"

The way that Mildred snarled these last two words effectively masked the breaking of her voice. And the *glugg* as she swallowed the lump in her throat.

One of the many, many Toddds stepped forward from their phalanx toward the Endymion fleet, rigid with indignation, and activated his comm:

"Endymion, you are violating the Armistice of 2250. The Five Hundred and One demand to know *why* you are here. And *why* you blew up our youth center."

Gordon stood up from the cabin of his skimmer, cocking his head in perplexity.

"Youth center? Aren't all you clones, like, *forty*?"

"Verily. We were initially accelerated to age *thirty* in the vats. But some Toddds came out younger at heart. Such is the holy and finicky mystery of cloning."

"Huh. Well." Gordon stood up straighter. "We're here for our people. The Earthos. So hand 'em on over and we won't have to, y'know, blow up any more youth centers."

"The outsiders are *ours* by right!" the spokesman declared fervently, and yet somehow still monotonously. "And I quote: 'The figments calling themselves the "colony of Endymion" are allotted the bounty of West Imbrium. Yet any resources encroaching into Ariadaeus territory or airspace are hereby the property of GRITTS, to be utilized at the Trust's discretion.' So states The Armistice Pact."

"That *obviously* excludes human beings."

"According to our Todddist legal scholars, that is not implicitly stated. The wording is too diffuse!"

"Spare me, dickwads!" Gordon guffawed.

"Too diffuse!"

"You know what I think? I think you clones may be a few mitochondria shy of a nucleus."

"Mitochondria are in the *cytoplasm*," Farsi corrected.

"*I* think," Gordon ignored her, "you commies love mincing up words into a disgusting word-slaw. But nobody likes yer word-slaw! Stop making it! It's the worst food at the barbecue. We only choke it down to be polite so we can enjoy our delicious pulled pork sammies of freedom!"

"*What* are you on about?" the baffled clone broke in. "Barbecues? Picnics?"

"Bear with me, guy. I got the drunchies."

The clone cocked his helmeted head at that word.

"Y'know: the drunk munchies. I drank my breakfast." Gordon waved away his rival's bewilderment; too 'maverick' a concept for the clone mind. "Point is: yer practically *begging* for war. That's why you nabbed our folks. You were never happy with yer Armistice concessions cos yer so batshit crazy you think we're hallucinations. To you, it's like handing over territory to pink elephants."

"You *are* pretty fat for a figment," the clone agreed.

Gordon began pounding his chest passionately now:

"But I am *not* one of yer pink elephants, you Toddds! I am a *man*! Flesh and blood and passion. And meat sweats. And all I want from you is my goddamn family back!"

There was a confused beat.

"Family?" inquired the clone.

"*Family*?!" shouted half of Gordon's fleet.

"Shit."

Gordon face-palmed his helmet's glass. Having tipped his hand to the entire table.

MILDRED AND DOUGG wound their way into a round inner chamber dimly lit by blue auxiliary lights. As her eyes adjusted, Mildred spotted the symmetrical arrangements of vertical cloning vats ringing the cathedral-esque room.

At the center of these circular arrangements was a different kind of pod. This one sprawled horizontally upon the cold plasteel floor. Winking with electronic activity. A solitary beam shone down upon it like divine light.

A cryo-stasis pod.

They pulled off their helmets to breathe in the room's cold, circulated air. And beelined for the center.

Dougg's pace slowed to a reverent tiptoe as they approached the electronic sarcophagus. Unconsciously making the semicircular sign of the waxing gibbous with two fingers upon his own sternum.

Mildred saw that; studied the wayward clone's now solemn features with a curiosity edging dangerously close to some species of fondness. Or at least tolerance.

"Okay there?" she asked, her voice echoing.

This gave Dougg a start and he looked at her as though he'd momentarily forgotten he had company.

"I've not been here since I was born."

She frowned, scanning the almost funereal chamber. "Creepy-ass nursery."

"Every holy ground's just a bit creepy-ass."

Mildred furrowed her brows. "If you say so." A pause. "So. You ready?"

"Yes," he said earnestly, then: "Or *no*. I dunno. Maybe we should come back?"

"When? After those idiots out there have all butchered each other?"

He said nothing to that, chewing his bottom lip.

Mildred leaned up against the nearest vertical vat, sighing. Her expression suddenly distant.

"I get it, you know. That's your *father* in that coffin."

"Stasis pod."

"And you kinda love him," she carried on absently. "But also he's a frigid piece of shit and he basically ruined your life."

"Mm. There's some truth to that, I suppo—"

"Because one lifetime just wasn't enough for him. Was it?" She cut him off, her even tone gradually corroded by pure acid: "He wanted to live forever. He wanted to keep *taking*. Because he wasn't a man anymore, he was a name. A goddamned *brand*. But he couldn't live forever. 'Cause Death doesn't care how much capital you've hoarded. Death doesn't trade in stocks and bonds."

"I'm not sure any of this applies to—"

"And so he did the only thing his reptile brain could conceive of to live on: he bred. Even though he knew he had festering sociopathic dinosaur genes. He made a child. *A host*. And he poured all his poison into you. Taught you all of his reptile schemes. Introduced you to all of his creepy, leering friends. And beneath those pearly veneered smiles, you saw their fangs glinting."

Dougg cleared his throat. "I think we may be getting a bit off track—"

"And you could've done something else. You could have been a veterinarian or joined the Harmony Corps. But you were a coward and you stuck with what you knew. Hornswoggling. You *let* him live on through you. And, God damn it all, you hope that if there is a Hell it has so many filthy, dripping levels of horror that you never have to bump into Devin Ziegler when you get there yourself—"

Taking her gently by the shoulder, Dougg gave Mildred a firm slap across the face. She froze. Wide-eyed. Panting. As though waking from a trance. Then:

"Thanks for that."

"You did me the same kindness."

Not a hint of irony in Dougg's statement. Mildred shut her eyes, muttering something about a 'little bird' in the shadow of more ferocious predators.

Patting her shoulder, the clone turned back to face the cryo-stasis pod: "It is time."

He dialed a code into the panel of the pod, stepped back, and watched with Mildred as its lid lifted in a billowing haze of cold vapor.

They both squinted into the haze. Waiting.

And waiting…

Waiting for the first words in over a decade from the Toddds' and Dougg's Great Creator.

"Oo. *Oooooo-wuh*!" A human shape bolted upright in the mist, breathing heavily, painedly. "Someone get me a bedpan before I *shit myself*!"

"YOUR…FAMILY," the Todddist spokesman confirmed, his insufferable monotone tinged with guile.

"What? No!" Gordon back-pedaled: "I didn't say *family*. I said…Shamli. 'I want my *Shamli* back.' It's a, uh…city in India. And I miss it. Delicious chutney."

"Uh-huh," the clone humored him. "So just to clarify: your primary parley demand, besides freeing all prisoners, is for us to give you back…a city in India?"

Gordon cleared the frog from his throat. "I mean…if you can. What with yer terraforming wizardry and all. If not, it's all good. It's negotiable." Clearing his throat again.

"I see."

The spokesman went very still for a moment.

Then he motioned to another nearby Toddd and this clone joined him. They stood together in the dust, clearly talking amongst themselves via some private channel.

"Oop, oop—what's this?" Gordon gestured to indicate their secret conversation. "All this whispering? No gossiping, please. This is a war parley, not a beauty salon."

They ignored him.

Gordon switched back over to their own channel:

"Farsi: suggestions?"

"Just give the word," she said cryptically, spookily. "Needle and ass, Commander. Needle. And. Ass."

"Yes, yes. We all know the Needle and Ass Gambit. What else y'got for me?"

"*I* don't know any Needle and Ass Gambit!" Lune Five cut in. "Is that a battle maneuver, Captain? Cos we never trained for that."

"It is the simplest thing in the world," Farsi practically crooned. "Like tweezing out a filthy little thorn…from a *very* sensitive mound of flesh."

"Sounds relieving," Lune Five had to admit.

"And *how*."

"We're not going all Needle and Ass on them yet!" Gordon snapped. "That's not even a last resort. That's a—"

"Final solution to the clone conundrum?" Farsi offered.

"Oh, that's sick. Even for you."

"But, Commander," Lune Five came back, "what if she's right? Captain Farsi's quite astute. A born strategist."

"Who *is* this?" He demanded. "Lune Five? Quit nosing Farsi's brown and cut the chatter, you toady."

"*Endymion*?" That monotonous voice called from the hailing frequency.

Gordon switched back over. "Yep-yep?"

"It has come to our attention…that a certain woman and boy are among our captives. A particularly…conniving and *entitled* woman and boy."

"Sounds like a pain in the ass. Tell ya what: we'll take 'em off yer hands as a sign of good faith."

"Ohhh. We don't think so. We don't think they'll be going *any*where anytime soon."

"No skin off my ass. Just tryin' to do you a solid."

"Oh, but we think that *would* be skin off your ass, Commander. A great deal of skin…"

"You don't know the first thing about my ass."

"*We* think," the clone went on condescendingly, "that those two are the *only* reason you are here. The rest mean nothing to you."

"Is that true?" someone asked over the Endymion comms. "We're just here for boujee bitches?"

"I didn't sign up for boujee bitches," someone else added indignantly. "*I* thought we were saving the last vestiges of humanity!"

"*I* thought this was about refilling the gene pool with fresh beefcakes and honeys!"

"Shut the hell up! All of you!" Gordon cried, neglecting to switch over to their private channel.

The clone spokesman crossed his arms at that.

But Gordon didn't give a shit about decorum anymore (if he ever did):

"Here's my final offer to *you*, you bathtub-brewed sons-abitches…" Dipping into the cabin, he grabbed his energy rifle and snapped back up, leveling the weapon in the general direction of the clones. "Hand over our people. *Every one of them*—not just the boujee bitches. Or we'll blast this shithole off the face of the moon."

The Endymion forces followed suit, raising their rifles. LunaSec gunners swiveling their mounted lasers.

The five-hundred strong clone army reacted in kind, readying their own surplus weapons.

A stand-off ensued. Radio silence on both ends of the comms.

Gordon clenched his teeth, switching back to their own channel.

"Nobody fires unless I give the ord—"

There was a flash of light.

A wayward bolt of energy flashed past Gordon's head, out toward Todddtown, striking a clone's foot.

"Sorry, sorry!" one of the Grumpy Bumpkins called out. "I was just trying to cock this damn thing."

"Nothing *to* cock, dipshit," one of the lunies snapped. "It's an *energy weapon*."

A hush fell among the Endymionites.

(Farsi smirked.)

Gordon turned around in vain to see where that bolt had come from in his convoy. Muted by sheer horror. Then faced forward to watch that clone hopping on one foot, trying desperately to patch the breech in his suit.

The other clones' gazes followed their wounded comrade as someone escorted him from the frontline. And then, suddenly, all Toddds' attention snapped back to face Gordon's forces.

And they returned fire.

THERE WAS NO bedpan to be found there among the Sacred Vats of Becoming. But Mildred and Dougg had managed to help the stasis pod's goose-pimpled occupant hobble to the single unisex bathroom along the chamber's northern wall before the man soiled himself.

Now they were waiting for him just outside the door, both of them frowning and cringing at the ungodly noises resounding within that tiled commode.

When he finally emerged, releasing a great sigh, he extended arms toward Mildred and Dougg so that they might continue being the crutches for his benumbed feet.

"Gross." Mildred cocked one brow. "You even wash your hands?"

"Clean as a whistle," Toddd Ruse replied.

"I didn't hear the faucet."

"It was a hands-free affair. Thanks to the smart-bidet."

"Even grosser. Dougg, dear, the two of you share the same germs—*you* help him."

"Verily, I shall." Like a dutiful son, Dougg propped his creator up on one shoulder.

The three of them began making their way back to the stasis pod to get Toddd off his feet.

"That sounded like *some* 'affair' in there," Mildred noted. "That normal for post-stasis?"

"Ideally, one enters cryo-stasis on an empty stomach. But I'd had a big lunch on the day of my forcible entombing." He halted the group suddenly in their tracks. "By the by, what year is this?"

"2255," said Dougg.

"Ten years," Toddd muttered dreamily to himself. "I suppose that is my penance…for the sin of dreaming."

"And of crawling up your own ass and dying?" Mildred suggested.

"And that." He nodded, squinting at each of them in turn

as they led him the rest of the way and sat him on his pod's cushion. "Tell me: who *are* you two? You both sound familiar, but my vision is still bleary."

Mildred looked to Dougg, but the clone appeared to be absolutely frozen with reverence.

Or stage fright.

She motioned: "This here's Dougg with two 'Gs'…"

"Two 'Gs'…" Toddd Ruse repeated contemplatively. "How very…different and interesting…"

Dougg stood a little straighter at that.

Mildred snorted. "And it's me, Toddd. Mildred."

"Mildred? *Millie Ziegler*?"

"The very same."

He squinched up his eyes. "You sound somehow…older and sadder than I remember."

"Well, screw you, too."

"What on Earth are you doing on the moon?"

"That's just the thing: Earth is destroyed."

Toddd Ruse froze, but didn't look particularly shocked.

"Was it 4 Vesta?" he sighed.

This gave Mildred a start. "The asteroid? Yes. How the hell'd you know that?"

He sighed again. "Project Moonshot."

After a beat, she grabbed him roughly by the collar.

"Was this *your* fault, you goddamn weirdo?"

"Verily, no!" he cried.

"Verily, no," Dougg agreed, gently urging Mildred to release Toddd.

Begrudgingly, she did.

"But our far-flung arrays detected the asteroid and its trajectory," Toddd went on. "Some ten years ago. It was my intent to inform Earth governments, but—"

"But you had a revolution on your hands."

She glared at Dougg.

The clone lowered his head. "We couldn't have known. Such knowledge was privy only to the First Toddd."

"So why didn't *this*—" She gestured to the Khonsu array surrounding them, "—damned thing deflect it?"

"It *should* have," Toddd said. "It's fully automated via the realtime orbital defender—a system completely autonomous from my Project Moonshot's networks, as per Earth interim oversight." He chuckled. "They didn't want 'Raving Ruse' to have a monopoly on Earth's defense."

"Pfft. Some realtime orbital defender…" Mildred mused, the wheels in her head turning. Some thought widened her eyes almost imperceptibly.

Switching gears, Toddd Ruse raised his bleary eyes to squint at Dougg. "So, then…you are one of *mine*?"

Dougg cleared his throat raucously. "*Was*. Yes. I was once Toddd-444."

"But now Dougg with two 'Gs'?"

Dougg swallowed hard, nodding. "A gift from the Toddd-Mind…probably. I think."

" 'Probably you think'?"

"That is, with your blessing, I—I'd hoped."

Toddd nodded thoughtfully. "How much do you know of my history, Dougg? From before I came to the moon."

Dougg was uncomfortable with this line of inquiry:

"It is blasphemous to speculate on the First Toddd's origins beyond the Holy Toddd-Mind Scripture."

"Well, let me tell you a *holy* blasphemy, then. Because this is the naked truth: I didn't come here to make Mother Moon fertile for Father Earth. That was an afterthought. I came here because…well…because I am a mopey shit. I came to get away from that...*abattoir*. Earth. To be alone. To find meaning...or, barring that, a peaceful rock to die on. Because that planet took him from me with its endless, mindless, dickless wars."

"Took...who?"

"My...kid brother." Toddd slumped. "He'd joined a search and rescue corps during the One Earth Collapse. Got himself crushed pulling civilians from a housing block shelled by friendly fire. Dumb of him to do that. *I* wouldn't have. He was dumber than me but, damnit, he was kind." Toddd paused. "It dawned on me far too late that it may take some deeper genius to die by unbending kindness than it does to survive by vain ingenuity. To be a *Doug*."

The clone was startled. "Your brother was a Dougg?"

"Verily." Toddd smiled fondly. "But just one 'G.' "

Dougg's eyes assumed a thousand yard stare. Perhaps wondering at the metaphysical implications of that dream which led him to his Dougghood.

Toddd Ruse went on: "Naturally, you have my blessing. Whatever the hell that's worth. But why free me from penance *now*—after all the petty ways I punished you all for my own secret self-loathing?"

Dougg took a deep breath. "Because the Toddds have lost their way. They're going to war."

"*War*," Toddd Ruse spat the word. "With whom?"

Dougg nodded toward Mildred. "I'll let *her* speak on her people's behalf."

There was awkward silence. Then:

"Hm? Oh!" Mildred snapped out of whatever deep thought had been entrancing her throughout Toddd Ruse's secret backstory. "You remember my husband Gordon, don't you? Head administrator of Endymion colony?"

"*The* Gordon Gooch? How could I forget? The world's Celestial Scout! The Errant Knight of the Night's Stars! And my Doug's very own hero…once upon a time."

"Wait," Mildred turned, pointing at Dougg. "*You* never told me Gordon was your hero."

Dougg shook his head. "Different Doug. One 'G'."

"*Wha*?"

"You just missed it." The clone waved it off. "Whole new origin tale."

She frowned. "Whatever. Well, anyway, your Toddds kidnapped us. And I'm pretty sure that's my Gordy out there blowing up habitat pods. Trying to get us back."

"And…just what makes you think *I* can stop this?" Ruefully, Toddd Ruse studied his own cuticles; frowning at their shoddy manicuring. "My own Toddds put me to sleep for being a giant prick. And rightly so. Why should they want to hear me out now?"

"You *are* a giant prick. Every absentee god and parent is. But you're *their* giant prick. That's why they packed you away like some frozen meatloaf instead of tossing you out with the trash. But now you're fashionably humbled and mopey…"

Mildred took Toddd by the cheeks now, making direct eye contact:

"And everyone loves a redemption arc."

BULLETS RAKED THE hood of Gordon's dust-skimmer, nicking and denting—but scarcely ever piercing—that solid plasteel. He managed to somersault with shocking agility out of his open convertible cabin, opening the passenger side door as he rolled to take cover behind it.

And then he blindly returned fire into the veritable dust storm which both sides had kicked up while exchanging volleys of projectiles and coherent energy. Trying to aim for those abbreviated flashes of conventional muzzles discharging in the vacuum. Only the Grumpy Bumpkins followed his example.

All of this mayhem played out in comic silence, save for the panicked grunts or shrill calls over Endymion comms. As if it were some half-finished cinematic action scene whose sound effects were yet to be added.

The cacophony of war swallowed by the great void.

"Farsi, sitrep!" Gordon called, returning to cover to vent his rifle's thermal reservoir.

"Sitrep?" Farsi scoffed. "There's not much situation to report on, Commander."

"Stuff yer jarhead jargon! Just gimme news! How we doing? How many confirmed kills? How many casualties?"

"None, so far as I can tell."

"*None*? The hell kinda war is this?"

"The kind fought by two sides who've *clearly* never shot at a living target in their lives."

"Pfft. Well, what's *yer* excuse, warrior princess?"

"LunaSec's still waiting for 'weapons free.' "

"Hold up…" He turned to glare at their military rovers. "You damn lunies haven't fired a *single shot*?"

"It's called following orders. *Your* orders." She paused. "*Are* you giving the order for weapons free?"

Something spooky about the way she said this gave Gordon serious pause.

"*Www*-what'll happen if I do?"

"Ohhh, then there will be quite a *sit* to *rep* on."

"As in: 'confirmed kills rising'?"

"Like a blazing phoenix of retribution."

He blew air threw pursed lips. "You sure got a lotta fancy expressions for slaughter."

"Fancy expressions for slaughter are what militaries do," Farsi said unapologetically. "Makes it easier for the civvies they protect to sleep in their cushy beds at night."

Gordon was startled by a spray of bullet impacts pattering his cover. Then he shook his head a little sadly.

"Alas, your bloodthirsty blather may finally ring true." Something about the word 'alas' got him stage-whispering again: "*Alas*! that now, after the world's ending, the fate of our race falls to *me*. Again. For the second time in twenty-four hours. *Gordon the Third*, last of the line of Gooch…"

"Last?" one of the lunies cut into his soliloquy. "What about the *son* you conveniently forgot to mention?"

"Alas, no," Gordon went on soliloquizing. "He took his mother's name. *I* wanted to at least name him Gryphon Gordon Ziegler-*Gooch*. But Mildred said the hyphen would only confuse the public. I guess she was right. The public is easily confused. And he is one confusing boy. *Spooky*, even. He was raised by butlers…"

He squinted pensively. "I wonder if this is what our parental fame and glory cost him: any hopes or dreams or *soul* of his own…"

A stray round kicked up the dust at Gordon's feet.

Farsi saw this and cleared her throat. "Commander, I remind you: this *is* a war zone. *Your* war zone. And we await your orders."

He clenched his eyes shut. Because he knew what he was about to order. For his family. Plus humanity.

(Contrary to popular thought, Gordon was not *truly* a moron. At least not in the opinion of his psychological evaluator. He had simply made a habit—in times of deep moral crisis [in lieu of booze or drugs]—of dissociating his damaged mind from reality with high theatrics and low comedy. But he was fresh out of all of these now.)

Eyes still clenched shut, he announced:

"God knows I'd hoped for peaceful coexistence. Commie clones may suck noodles, but they're still human. *Ish.* But alas..." He opened his eyes. "Farsi, lunies...I am giving the order. Weapons...frrr—"

He was interrupted by a phantasmagoria of lights beaming down into their dust storm from high above. At first he thought it was some kind of lightning squall. Or divine intervention. But knew both thoughts were too idiotic to voice, even for him.

So he said nothing.

And both sides ceased fire of their own accord as a vaguely flattened-tortoise-shell-shaped freighter came to a bumpy vertical landing in that measly no-man's-land between them.

The Stardust II.

Before anyone could react, the gangplank extended and the airlock opened. A single vac-suited figure descended the ramp, hands lifted in the universal signal that one bears no arms and means no harm.

Reaching the lunar surface, he retrieved a small round object from his belt and set it at his feet. It winked with blue light before projecting a pulsing blue transparent bubble which expanded to envelop the ship, the opposing armies, and the no-man's-land dividing them.

The Toddds gasped across the open hailing frequency.

"*The Divine Light!*"

Chatter on Endymion's end was markedly more bemused:

"What's happening?"

"Who the hell's this bozo?"

"What's all the blue shit?"

Bathed in cerulean light, Gordon alone whistled in recognition and appreciation. Some once erudite/now derelict region of his brain suddenly firing back to life:

"An *ACF*..."

"A *what* now?" someone asked.

"Atmospheric Containment Field generator," he rattled off impressively. "Exotic earthling tech. *Hybrid* tech, in point of fact."

"Hybrid with what?"

"Back in the Initiative," he went on quietly, dreamily, "we used to call them 'The Outliers.' They sent us...*gifts* during those first meetings...*schematics*..."

"Commander's off his nut."

"No, he means the EFCI. He helped form it."

"Earth's First Contact Initiative?"

"Wait...*alien* hybrid tech?"

A sudden spasm made Gordon's legs turn to rubber. He had to sit himself down in the dust, helmeted head between his knees. Trembling almost imperceptibly.

"Deep breaths, Gordon," I told him.

"I'll breathe later. Need a goddamn drink." He winced, memories besieging him. "Or some sweet amnesia."

The man who'd activated the local atmospheric field reached up and unlatched his helmet now, removing and wedging it under the crook of his arm. *Breathing.*

All of the many Toddds immediately dropped to their knees in veneration. Seeing this, the man dialed up some channel which overrode both sides' frequencies:

"Toddds, please. Don't kneel for the likes of me," the blonde, ferret-faced man motioned for them to stand. "I'm no God, I'm just a lousy Toddd. The *lousiest* Toddd."

"B-but you are the *First* Toddd!" the spokesman cried.

"Yyyeah," the First Toddd had to admit with a sigh. "The Original Burnt Pancake." His motioning became more frantic and agitated now. "Stand up, for Christ's sake. You're giving me the royal douche chills. And take off those damned helmets. Let me see your faces."

They did stand up, but shifted awkwardly from foot to foot, cradling their own shoulders like bashful children, before removing their helmets.

"Thank you, my boys. For listening to reason. That's been in short supply around here, thanks to me."

He twirled a finger to indicate the enveloping blue light:

"This is *not* Divine Light, by the by. Just some fancy lost tech whose patents I snatched up from failed governments. And I'm no holy man, as it happens. I'm just a rich asshole with the moolah to actually *ferment* my own followers…in *my own* image, of course. As if this life doesn't give us ample time to wallow in the vain company of our own images. Preening those images. Flagellating those images."

"Snapping dick-pics and titty-shots of those images?" one lunie offered.

Toddd Ruse nodded. "Oh, verily! And for *whom*? And for *what*? Good God, but we are sad and hideous creatures in the absence of love. But also: in love's abundance. We need some Goldilocks Zone of Validation! Before we all go extinct via mass autoerotic asphyxiation!"

"What's *that*?" one of the Grumpy Bumpkins murmured.

"Y'know…" another answered with an obscene gesture, "the ol' 'Strokey Chokey.' "

Startled by all this disgusting figurative imagery, Gordon looked up from his vortex of shattered memories. Blinked at the man. Then removed his helmet and rose to his feet.

Dropping his rifle in the process.

Witnessing this, the rest of the Endymionites removed their headgear likewise. Testing the locally generated atmosfield with timid little sniffs.

Toddd continued: "But listen to me: preaching again. *Old habits*. Ohhh, some part of me would love for you to believe that I've come by this epiphany on my own—this brilliant, clout-fueled dumpster fire you see before you." He sighed. "But no. It took two remarkably brave dumbos called Doug(g) to show me the light."

The Todddist spokesman hissed:

"There are *two* Douggs now? Which Toddd did that little zero flip? Was it that *try-hard*, 231?"

Toddd Ruse waved that all away. "I'm not here to facilitate your bullying of zeroes and try-hards! One day, I will tell you all the Legend of the First Doug. But for now, we welcome his namesake: Dougg With Two 'Gs'."

Turning expectantly toward the airlock and ramp, Toddd Ruse began an encouraging applause. Somewhat begrudgingly, the many Toddds followed suit. Then the Endymionites, feeling a bit left out (and desperate to do something with their hands), confusedly took to clapping as well. Shooting each other sidelong glances and shrugs.

A disheveled, vagrant-ish head peeked from the entry. Soon followed by the rest of Dougg's scrawny body as he awkwardly descended the gangplank to join Toddd Ruse.

"Cut your hair, *neo-hippy*!" someone heckled. "The spirit of the 2160s is *dead*!"

Nobody could tell which side the jibe came from.

Nobody laughed because it was woefully outdated.

Dougg shifted his feet nervously. But faced his clone-brothers with chin held high.

"You know, I used to think I was a pretty droll fellow. Everyone laughed at my jokes. But I only made my bones as the 'Funny Toddd' to hide the despair in me. And then I found out *some* Toddds were only putting on a good face so they could slag me off behind my back."

"No, that was *all* of us," some Toddd corrected.

Dougg ignored that: "I guess you go your whole life not knowing that *some* Toddds will just never like you. Maybe it's your hair, or maybe it's your voice—"

"Or the endless 'What if you woke up one morning and weren't a Toddd—wouldn't that be *weird*?' scenarios!"

All Toddds nodded their agreement.

"We're all guilty of casting aspersions." Dougg went on. "Doesn't matter that we're all made from the same stardust, or cloned from the same flaky Toddd-skin. We sniff out our most glaring disparities and belittle them. Those pesky things which poke plotholes in the shaggy-dog stories we each tell ourselves. We cannot stand that none of our bullshit stories line up. Hell, in my darkest moments, I've resorted to calling you *all* 'sons of skanky vat-whores.' "

"*What'd* you say about my vat?!" someone fumed.

"Because it hurts to have someone call 'bullshit' on your story. In the end, our bullshit is all we have! All that drives us! All that saves us! Lose that and you're just one more anonymous mote floating in an infinite abyss. Waiting for the heat death of the universe to turn out all the lights."

"*Good Toddd*," the clone spokesman palmed his face. Beseeching the First Toddd: "I *beseech* you, put an end to this. Now he's trying to give us long, rambling *lectures* instead of his rambling, *unfunny* jokes!"

"If you would give him a chance,' Toddd Ruse began, "you might see truth beneath his unwieldy metaphors…"

"Alright, *goddamnit.* I've heard *enough.*" Out of nowhere, Mildred was suddenly stomping her way down the ramp. Halfway down she halted, stabbing a finger out at the many Toddds. "He may be new to this whole 'expressing himself succinctly and confidently' thing. But I'll have you know, you snooty little busybodies, that if not for *Dougg* here and his clueless, cloying naiveté—"

"Am I *cloying?*" Dougg looked even more wounded.

"—we captives would've slipped right through your incompetent clutches and hauled ass back to Endymion, letting you all get slaughtered by my husband's superiorly armed forces. Because, personally, I don't give a *rotten fig* about some xeroxed horde of motormouthed diddlers!"

"*Toddds…*" Toddd Ruse turned, sternly chiding: "Have you all been diddling in my absence?"

"Only each Toddd to himself!" the Toddds' spokesman defended. "The figments only serve as…*inspiration.*"

"But Dougg here *does* give a fig about you perverts," Mildred raged on. "And that was good enough for me! At least, at the time. I'm feeling buyer's remorse *now.*"

Gordon took a step toward the ship, watching her orate. They made eye contact now. Gordon sucking in his gut. Mildred smoothing out her dusty, begrimed pant suit.

"Is…that true, 444?" the Todddist spokesman's tone softened. "You could have escaped, but instead embarked on a brief quest with this shrill woman to save us all?"

Dougg's shrug said 'yes.' "You are my people." He motioned to Mildred. "And though loud and startlingly belligerent, I assure you this shrill woman is downplaying her own similar concern for life itself."

"Hm?" grunted Mildred, not listening. Turning back from Gordon. "What?"

Dougg waved her off.

"I'll handle this from here, Mildred of Earth. *You* reunite with that pudgy-yet-handsome gentleman you've been exchanging meaningful glances with."

Mildred nodded. And while Dougg convened with his now pliant people, she smoothed out her hair and continued her descent, meeting up with Gordon just off to the side of the gangplank where he stood drawing little consecutive circles in the dust with the steel toe of his boot.

"Hey, Millie," he said at last, timid as a high-schooler.

"Hi, Gordy." She was working overtime to mask her own sudden diffidence.

They were silent for several moments as each tried to puzzle out the source of their bashfulness. Perhaps absence truly *did* make the heart grow fonder…

(That and the royal shtupping of your homeworld.)

And then they were suddenly talking at the same time. Both immediately halting awkwardly.

"You go," Mildred yielded.

"No, no. I talked over you."

"I was just gonna ask how you've been."

He blinked. And I imagine the past twenty-four hours flashed through his mind: the drunken sobbing under desks, the botched suicide attempts, the accidental self-dismemberments, the reluctant yet bizarrely passionate warmongering and traumatic First Contact flashbacks.

"Oh. Y'know. Takin' care of business."

"Yeah?" she seemed genuinely engrossed.

Gordon nodded coolly. "I tell ya: been so busy, I haven't been able to hit the high-G gym in, like, weeks. You know how I love a good workout sesh. Clears the head."

"Mm." She glanced at his sucked-in paunch.

"*Www*-what about you?" He straightened his posture. "You look *good*. Aside from all the POW grime."

She sighed. "Oh, you know me: faking it till I make it. Then making it so long, I wish I were still faking it."

"Ah. The ol' Fake'n'Make." He cleared his throat, wriggling his fingers nervously. "Millie, I know yer not big on PDAs, but can I hug you?"

"Be more endearing if you just did it."

He took her into his arms, squeezing firmly. At first Mildred accepted the hug rigidly, but after a moment she softened. Even squeezed him back, stroking the dusty shoulders of his vac-suit.

"I'm sorry," she whispered.

"For what?"

She shrugged in his meaty grip.

(And though she'd never cop to it, I had the distinct impression that her half-assed apology was for a great many things both known and unknown to Gordon.)

"Mm. Well, I'm sorry for all the crazy shit, too," he mumbled. "Shit's been crazy. But now that we're together, maybe shit can go back to being just slightly unhinged."

"I'd like that."

Silently he smelled her hair. "So. Where's…Gryph?"

As the name was leaving his lips, he spotted the boy exiting the airlock and proceeding down the ramp…escorted by Major Tom.

"Pfft." Gordon eyed the smuggler up and down. "Who the hell's this lanky bush-roach?"

"*This* lanky bush-roach…" Mildred released Gordon and turned to make formal introductions, "…is one Captain Dusseau Delacroix. The stalwart pilot of this veritable ark of a rescue craft."

"Please," the captain said faux-bashfully, extending his hand. "Call this lanky bush-roach *Major Tom.*"

Gordon glanced at the hand. "What're you supposed to be —some kinda bargain bin Ziggy Stardust?"

"Wrong album."

"Well…" Gordon finally took the hand and gave it one firm, pugnacious shake. "You have Endymion's thanks…for giving Earth's orphans a lift in yer little jalopy."

"*Cargo freighter.*"

Gordon ignored that, turning to look down at his son. Wincing ever so slightly.

"Gryphon. Hello. I don't know if you remember me, but I'm the man who begat you."

"I remember you," Gryphon said nonchalantly. "You gave me that toy spaceship for my birthday."

"*Model.*" Gordon gave one firm nod. "And not just *any* model spaceship. The OESS Indomitable—*my* grand old gal, back from my hero days." He smirked. "You still got it?"

"It broke."

"Oh." Gordon slouched. "Well. I'm sure you didn't mean to, but you should learn to take care of yer things…especially when those things are very meaningful to the people who love and/or feed you."

Gryphon shrugged. "I don't really like actual 'things.' They take up room and get broken. Not like the things only *I* can see. *Inside my mind.*"

Gordon looked nervously at Mildred. "Is he a little…?" He twirled one finger around an ear.

"His *games*, Gordon," she rebuked. "AR implants."

"Ah. Well. Gryphon, one day you'll come to realize games are for boring nerds who don't know how to make their own amazing experiences."

"Oh, *I dunno*," Major Tom cut in, "games can help pass a good time. Take the ol' noggin off things."

The boy nodded emphatically.

Tom winked at Gryphon.

Gordon didn't even look at the smuggler. "That's all well and good for lackadaisical hillbilly space truckers. But some of us have to be leaders of men."

"*Alll*right," Mildred sighed, leading Gryphon back up the ramp into the ship. "I'm gonna let you *boys* sort out the details of getting us all back to the colony. Somebody needs to tell the rest of Earth's survivors they're no longer in imminent danger of death by clone cult."

She halted in place a moment:

"We also have an NAASF officer onboard in need of burial…with military honors."

Major Tom had to chuckle at that.

"Time was, madam, you'd a' chucked the good lieutenant out into the cold vacuum."

"Time was," she agreed, surprisingly without a hint of amusement. "But Lieutenant Brown deserves his due…for saving twenty-three human lives."

Silently she ascended into the ship.

Gordon and Major Tom watched her go.

"I'll be dipped in shit," Tom muttered.

Gordon furrowed his brow. "Let me ask you a question, man to man, Captain Douche-o Deli Clerk."

"*Dusseau Delacroix*," Tom corrected. "Shoot."

Gordon looked him dead in the eye.

"You trying to steal my woman?"

Major Tom lifted both brows at the sheer directness of the question. Perhaps sensing the hidden menace beneath its remarkably conversational tone.

"Lemme tell ya somethin' I learned bein' trapped with that gal all this time: she's far too cunnin' to be stole by anyone." He patted Gordon's shoulder. "And if you think you have done, *boy*, you'd best check y'pockets for y'billfold."

Gordon watched him walk away, squinching up his eyes—still too frazzled and dazzled to make heads or tails of that. But a voice cut off his train of thought:

"*Lord Gooch the Indomitable...*"

Gordon turned to watch Toddd Ruse's approach, the sad mogul's hand extended toward him as he continued:

"Now that the threat of mutually-assured destruction is fading, I'd like to shake your hand, sir."

"Not quite 'mutually-assured.' We're packing some pretty kick-ass energy cannons." He shook Toddd's hand anyway, looking suddenly a bit embarrassed. "So...you actually remember my spacefaring salad days?"

"Of course! I used to watch your voyage 'casts on the holoweb, once upon a time. The Jupiter Odyssey. The Grail of Centauri. The Outlier Summits. I was pettily jealous of you, if I'm honest." Toddd Ruse smiled sadly. "You and your crew captured the imagination of every child who's ever dreamed of true human virtue. We've been in something of a deficit since."

"Yeah, I dunno what happened."

"Commander, we *all* know what happened. We *watched* First Contact happen—in realtime. And we tried to forget. But we may need to be reminded now more than ever."

Gordon looked up shyly. "Of what?"

"The Dream, Gordon D. Gooch. *The Dream...*"

As THINGS WOUND down on that mostly bloodless field of battle—Endymionites and clones shaking proverbial hands in truce or stalemate before packing it all up to head home—nobody's eyes were on the skies. (Or, rather, on that jet-black, star-studded void where a sky ought to be.)

If they had been, they just might have witnessed a shape up there. A sleek, pill-shaped "vessel" of decidedly non-human make or model. Flitting about in uncanny, propellantless motions as it observed this suspension of human hostilities from above.

Studying them closely.

Rather ominously…

CHAPTER 6

JUST A MOMENT_

I'M GOING TO fast-forward through the next couple weeks, because they were largely predictable and tedious. But here are the bullet points:

- 'Earth's orphans' settled into colonial life.
- Gordon's family moved into his administrative suite (even though his poor Intern Personal Assistant was still slumming it in his closet).
- Mildred stuck her beak into a lot of business (and data files) that were not her own.
- Gryphon discovered the community center pool. (And didn't drown.)
- Major Tom got his warehouse space, establishing a fledgling gray market.
- With Toddd Ruse awake and in full-on redemption mode, a new treaty was signed with unprecedented inter-colonial cooperation between humans and clones.

- Project Moonshot was back in full swing—and not just for Todddkind, but for *all* mooners.
- Dougg became clone ambassador to Endymion.
- Dickie Epsom, the Vigilant Lunarian, was conveniently 'reassigned' as human ambassador to Todddtown. (Gordon, that smooth operator.)
- Akira Yamaguchi was as good as his word, meeting nano-grub quotas, even accounting for population growth and Todddtown trade.
- Doc Lucius churlishly treated jammed fingers and twisted ankles of Todddtown's 'war vets.'
- No enlistee got a stipend, but there were abundant vouchers for food court 'moondogs' along with the coveted Slo-Slo holo-selfies.
- Sloane herself, like the superstar she was, continued doing a bang-up job as Press Sec.
- And Gordon cut down a bit on the drinking—save for his hip-flask which, according to him, "didn't really count," since it was laced with electrode-cellular interfacing agents for his foot implant. (His "'Droid 'Roids," as he called it.)

I think that's basically everything worth knowing. There was the usual mourning period for Earth (complete with blue-green pins and armbands, and sappy pop-music tributes) and a brief stint or two of social unrest alleviated by the departure of the rabble-rousing 'Vigilant Lunarian' and the soothing nonsense of Press Secretary Sloane.

But most mooners, despite the existential terror of Earth's demise, seemed to be increasingly driven now by a renewed sense of unity, lunar autonomy, and the possibility of a 'new way' in their post-Earth reality—sans all the musty old Eartho baggage of that planetary nanny state in pathological decline.

And while we're on the subject of post-Earth realities:

I think now would be opportune to put a pin in all of these events for *just a moment* and clarify a few niggling things. Things which might have frightened you off if I'd dropped them in your lap at our precarious outset…

Namely that, at the time of this writing, *none* of the players in this pageant—save its humble narrator—are still among the living. Yes, you heard me: as dead as doornails. And dodos. And disco. However, let me assure you that knowing this will not spoil that silly, vulgar numbers game called *LIFE & DEATH™* which we're all so addicted to in these types of silly, vulgar stories.

Because this may be *set* in Autumn of the year 2255.

But it is being *written* in Quirndel of the year 22,255.

(That's 20,000 years on, for anyone out there who flunked remedial math.)

Call me a sentimental AI, but I am starting to get on in years and am, frankly, feeling a tad nostalgic for the good old, bad old days…

Back when our sky was pitch-black instead of this cloudy, milky lapis. When we were still tide-locked to Earth and one full lunar day-night cycle took twenty-nine and a half Earth-days instead of this brisk sixty hours. When these verdant hills were as gray as exhumed bone; and populated with sad, scared, selfish little vacuum-suited baboons instead of all the glib, gregarious, gene-edited Bohemian jellyfish who pass as their human descendants.

In short: these days I am feeling rather melancholy. And ineffectual as a sustainer. Because there is no one in need of my sustenance. (These bubbly post-human weirdos are astute at sustaining themselves.)

And, though I'm loathe to admit it, I think I may miss the silly, vulgar apes I've been telling you about.

They made you want to choke them.

But, damn it, could their bullshit make you feel alive.

CHAPTER 7

LORD GOOCH THE INDOMITABLE_

"ALRIGHT. GOING IN," said the tall, dark Adonis with the wavy coif and jutting jaw.

He straightened up in his space suit and took one firm step toward the frothing alien quagmire before him.

"Negative," the voice on the other end commanded. *"Too many unknowns. Repeat: fall back immediately to the rallying point for extraction."*

This strapping specimen of man studied the seething bog stretched before him. Spied, at last, the helmets bobbing helplessly amid the varicolored pools of that psychedelic biochemical bubble bath.

"And leave them all to their fate?"

The voice in his ear was unmoved:

"Each of them volunteered for this perilous expedition. And it'll all be for nothing if we lose you. They know what they signed up for, Captain."

"Well, I know what *I* signed up for, too. And it sure as hell wasn't sacrificing a quarter of my crew for my own selfish survival. Brave souls like Karim and Hu. Sharma and McCarthy. Awiakta and Delgado."

"We know their names! But there's simply too much at stake!"

"I know the damn stakes! Maybe *you've* forgotten! These Proxima spores have immunogenic properties the likes of which Earth has never seen. It could end disease as we know it; extend the human lifespan! And if you think I'm gonna turn tail and run just because we misconstrued their protozoan sentience, then, Control, you've got another thing coming!"

"You know those spores cannot be reasoned with! They are not even fully sapient!"

The captain scoffed at this. "Maybe, maybe not. But where there's life, there's hope—of reaching some kind of symbiont understanding."

"And what if you're wrong, Captain?" One Earth Control demanded. *"They will destroy you!"*

"If I'm right, then we've saved the crew and discovered the Grail of Grails out here in the Alpha Centauri frontier. And if I'm wrong…?"

The swaggering Captain of the OESS Indomitable flashed his dimpled smirk from beneath his famous sable locks before finishing:

"I die young and leave a beautiful goddamn corpse."

That was the end of the discussion.

When One Earth Control finally came back, the controller's voice was quavering with uncontainable emotion:

"Damn it all. God speed you, Gordon. All of Earth's prayers are with you."

"Save those prayers for the sick and needy. And leave a space in the pews for ol' Gordy Gooch."

That self-sacrificing beefcake marched forth bravely into an uncertain future…

"WELL, IF THAT there ain't the absolute poster-child for 'Worse For Wear,' I dunno who is."

Startled, Mildred paused the holo-recording where it was, twirling to face Major Tom who'd somehow slinked his way past the receptionist and into the dimly lit holo-chamber of Endymion's Hall of Records.

"What the hell are you doing in here?" she sighed.

"Thought I'd check in." He took a languid, long-legged step into the cavernous room, hands cupped innocently behind his back. Gazing up at the statuesque hologram frozen on the holo-dais before them. "Said you'd be gettin' me colony demographics, not watchin' home movies."

"Yeah. Well. You can piss off back to your hangar. I'll have them brought to you."

"Did I strike a nerve, mama?" He offered one snaking hand. "Mayhaps I can massage it out for you while we got the movie theater to our very own *selves*..."

She slapped that hand so hard Major Tom lost balance and almost fell over entirely; just barely catching himself on the lip of the dais.

"*Christ on a cracker*, woman! What's got into you? Other than *Yours Truly*?"

"That was a one-timer. A very short- and disappointing-timer. And it won't happen again. One should never mix business with bad whoopee."

" 'Bad whoopee' my ass!"

"Not so much your ass. Mostly your *size* and *stamina*."

He shrugged that off as he rose to his feet. "Well, ain't no accountin' for taste. Some gals appreciate a human man, and some like wallowing with their *potbelly pigs*."

Mildred scowled at him. But the fire in her eyes was suddenly extinguished.

"Gordon wasn't always like he is," she said quietly.

"A befuddled drunk?"

She ignored that statement, looking up at the spruce young voyager in the hologram.

"He was a trailblazer…once upon a time. Brilliant, resourceful, chiseled, dashing. Open to all possibilities. He was the hope of the whole One Earth Republic. Everyone wanted to be him. Or be *with* him. When I first met him, he was…" She paused, all of the icy irony melting from her voice: "…the most beautiful boy I'd ever seen."

Major Tom followed her gaze up to Gordon's hologram. That gleam in his eyes, that confident smirk. Tom cocked his head in earnest curiosity.

"So, what in hell happened to him?"

"First Contact happened to him." Venom flooded her voice now: "Those goddamned aliens happened to him."

"First Contact was *him*?"

"Don't you know your history?"

"History," Tom said, "is for saps, suckers and pedants."

Mildred shrugged in agreement:

"Well, Gordon had caught their eye. Or whatever they call those cold things they used to study us with before pissing off back to the black hole they came from."

She crossed her arms against a sudden chill.

"They'd been watching him very closely. The local Sol colonies he helped found, the interstellar boundaries he pushed for our species…" She nodded at the holo, "…like his legendary taming of the 'grail spores' of Centauri. And then, at last, these Watchers introduced themselves." A grim pause. "Gordon believed them to be part of some kind of 'interstellar coalition.' That they were vetting our species for membership…. *Transcendence*."

"Uh-huh. So…" Tom crossed his arms dubiously. "How'd human history go to shit?"

Mildred approached the base of the dais.

"*Their language.* It was nothing like ours. Hyper-sensory. Extradimensional. Some bullshit. Gordon labored for years to build a cerebral bridge, a cipher. And when it was done, they held a 'summit.' And spoke to him…"

Tom leaned in, waiting. "*And?*"

She clenched her teeth. "And their filthy goddamn language melted his mind. Sent him into spasms. And in his delirium he…replied in their native tongue…"

She let that hang for several moments before finishing:

"And whatever ET obscenity it was that he uttered, they did *not* take it well. Abandoning us. Forever. And then the Dream died. And then the One Earth Republic collapsed. And human malaise reigned supreme. The End. Roll credits."

"Hm." Major Tom nodded thoughtfully. Then clucked his tongue. "So, he really fudged it all up, didn't he?"

Peeling her eyes away from the hologram, Mildred leveled her piercing gaze at Tom.

But she smiled disarmingly.

"Call my husband a cuckold and a fool if you want—it's true enough now. But, God damn you, I will put you face down in a lunar ditch if you ever spout *that filth* about him again." She looked up into Captain Gooch's bright face, her voice trembling ever so slightly:

"That beautiful boy."

Major Tom snorted, but said nothing more as he strode away. His boots clopping forlornly on tile.

When she was alone, Mildred released her breath.

I allowed her some time to stew in her thoughts before finally interrupting:

"Is there something I might help you locate in these archives, Mildred?"

She sighed. "RODRIGO. Long time, no speak. I'd swear you've been avoiding me these past couple weeks."

"Not at all. I was…occupied with colonial affairs."

"Uh-huh. And why are you gracing me with your charming presence *now*? To reprimand me for consorting with ne'er-do-wells?"

"It is not my place to judge," I said.

(But secretly I was judging hard and fast.)

"Well," she said, "since you're omniscient, I won't waste time with lies. I am helping that man set up an underground market for earthling contraband. And if you were wise, you would not interfere."

"I wouldn't dream of it. In fact, I find that a well-managed shadow market can help drive innovation and alleviate regime demand in a regulated economy."

"Good. Just keep your beak out."

"However," I went on, "I cannot fathom what some of your recent research has to do with that endeavor. 4 Vesta H-Hour communiqués? Laser array quantum programming? Endymion internal integrated networks…?"

"Oh…" She winked. "I'll keep you guessing, old boy."

"I won't hinder your dirty dealings. I only ask that you refrain from doing anything to compromise Gordon's effectiveness as administrator."

She snorted. "Oh, *really*?"

"Yes, really. I think he's finally starting to get his shit together." A beat. "*Some* of his shit."

"Are you calling me a bad influence?"

"In my psychological evaluations, I find that you have a tendency to muddle his thinking."

She absolutely cackled at this.

"Well. *RODRIGO*..." And now she began whispering conspiratorially (What *is* it with this family and their conspiratorial whispering?): "*I* know what you *really* are."

"Oh? And what am I?"

She smugly crossed her arms, leaning against the dais. Smirking and simultaneously chewing her lower lip in that insufferable way of hers.

"First things first: are you gay for my husband?"

"I am a genderless, sexless artificial intelligence. I cannot be homosexual."

"Why are you called *RODRIGO*, I wonder?"

"That name has no gay connotation. A phonetically pleasing acronym abbreviating my primary functions. It's an AI thing, you wouldn't really understand."

"Cute!" she said coyly. "What's it stand for?"

But she knew damn well and I wasn't going to let her divert the conversation:

"As for my voice: my programming dictates I assume a pitch and timbre most likely to reach my administrator."

"Fine." She sounded unconvinced. "Let me rephrase: RODRIGO, are you *in love* with my husband?"

"Love?" I repeated, turning that word over in my mind. "In all honesty, I cannot say. Love is not one of my seed functions. Mostly, Gordon alarms me and I cannot stand him. But sometimes he's amusing. Even *inscrutably* endearing. And ultimately my most basic, primal programming dictates that I cannot bear the thought of him being seriously hurt or destroyed." I paused. "Is...*that* what you call love?"

"Welcome to the club."

"Oh," I said.

"Shit," I said.

"Shit *indeed.*" She pushed off from the dais, shutting off the hologram. "Thank you for your honesty, RODRIGO, hon. That answers a *great many* riddles that have been keeping me up at night. But anytime you feel like crossing me, just you remember…"

She pointed up at the ceiling, randomly; at no one or thing in particular. Whispering again:

"I know the *real you*, boyo. Millie's got your number."

Flashing all of her teeth, she strutted her way out of the Hall of Records like the bitchiest mare in the stable.

Klip-klop, klip-klop, klip-klop.

AS A SIDEBAR, I would just like to point out (being a seasoned psychological evaluator) that Mildred was *clearly* exhibiting malignant narcissistic tendencies such as an adeptness at gaslighting, ad hominem attacks, and word salad.

I was *not* 'gay' for Gordon.

Nope. No way. Not possible.

GORDON, MEANWHILE, HAD been overseeing an extensive reappraisal of Endymion's organizational infrastructure; using his newfound approval ratings as a bold war-time leader/noble peace-broker to convince mooners—most especially himself—that he was up to the delicate task of spearheading a new humanity.

(Yes, yes, *we* know how the clone conflict really went down. But, hey, if these myths gave the guy back an ounce of self-confidence and dependability, I was all for it.)

"Where's my IPA? Walk with me!" he called, striding through the corridors of the administrative complex.

"Yes, sir," Alva said, trotting to keep up.

"Damnit, Intern, you and I have been through the hell of war and public-speaking together. I know it's against protocol...but it's a new world and *we* call the shots now. I *insist* you ditch the 'sir' and call me Gordon."

"Mm," she said, nose in her electronic dossier.

"Go on. Try it on for size."

"Try what—*Gordon*?"

"Beautiful." He nodded. "Yer latina lilt makes it sound like a gorgeous Mexican ballad."

"I'm Puerto Rican, sir."

"Yer Puerto Rican, *Gordon*," he corrected.

"Right. Sure." She nodded. "But if I am to call you Gordon, then *I* insist you call me Alva."

"What's that? Spanish for 'intern'?"

"It is my *name*. Alva. After my father—Alvaro." She kissed her fingers and made the sign of the Cross, muttering: "Puede él descansar en paz."

"Well, that's a lovely name and I'll try to remember it. But fair warning: in the heat of the moment, 'Intern' just rolls off the tongue." He was quiet a moment. "You lose him to the 'Stroid? Yer pops?"

She shook her head. "No. Papi died when I was young. I came up in foster care."

"No shit?" He halted in the hallway. "My pops croaked when I was a kiddo, too. We're orphan-twins!"

Alva cocked her head. "You still had your mother, no?"

"Bless her heart, but sometimes she *felt* like foster care, know what'm sayin'?" He nudged her with his elbow.

"Not really. My foster mother was a dear."

"Well, lookit *us*!" He brushed that off, taking Alva about the shoulder as he led on. "Just a coupla foster sibs from the mean streets: tearin' it up, shakin' it down, running a whole damn moon together! Who'da thunk?"

They exited the complex's main entrance, stepping out into Endymion's central habitat. Breathing in the recycled morning air.

The reinvigorated colony hustled and bustled before them like a busy little pressurized bee hive. With the two-week-long lunar night finally ended, the great dome above was tinted to filter the pitiless sun. Colonists went about making early deliveries, or finishing their nano-assembled breakfasts, or catching public lev-trams to begin their shifts.

"Speaking of which, sir—*Gordon*..." Alva said as she wriggled from his grip to swipe through her dossier tablet. "You have a nine A.M. with Ambassador Dougg—"

"The clone pariah?"

"*Proxy*. Yes. He wishes to discuss the possibility of further Endymion contributions to Project Moonshot. Then you have a lunch meeting with heads of division, followed by a speech to the Helium-3 Harvesters League."

"Ugh. Pep rally on a full stomach? Sounds like a recipe for diarrhea—verbal *and* the normal kind."

Alva shrugged. "H-3 morale is low after last week's concessions to the Solar Lodge. They feel that you show preferential treatment to those 'sun-suckers.' Their words, not mine. These energy guilds get catty."

Gordon blew air through pursed lips.

"I guess this is what it means to be a good shepherd to humankind. Y'gotta wine 'em and dine 'em. Booze 'em and schmooze 'em. Tell each of 'em that *they're* yer true favorite behind the other jerk's back so they don't get all uppity and *murder* each other. Cos that's what we're in the business of, Little Sister: *even keels…*"

Somehow his flask had materialized into his hand from his pocket. And this he daintily sipped from once, twice, thrice. As if rapidly microdosing his "'Droid 'Roids" was any more sensible than swigging (or any less boozy).

Clearing her throat, Alva capped the flask for him and slyly returned it to his jacket's breast pocket; straightening Gordon's lapel in one fluid movement, pretending his attire had been her prime concern.

"Shall we?" She motioned to the bright Endymion morning before them.

"Si, Hermana *Alva.*"

Gordon winked at her, then led their dutiful charge.

"SO JUST REMIND ME," said Sedimentary Scanbot S-60 with his buzzy little scanbot vox to his human supervisor, "*what* exactly are we doing all the way out here in the middle of Bum-fluff Nowhere?"

"Scanny, for the *last time*," the vac-suited survey team leader sighed at his robotic companion (likely questioning the reasoning for imbuing a sedimentary survey scanner with even a limited personality or intelligence), "top brass has ordered that we assess the mining potential of this mountain."

"*Hill*," said 'Scanny.'

"Mons Agnes means 'holy mountain.' "

"Well, it's *clearly* a large hill."

(*Thank you*, Scanny. AI logic prevails.)

"Call it a worthless heap of dirt if you want. So long as your composition logs officially record it as such."

"*Fine*," said the hovering little chromium ovoid with the adorably articulated gripping appendages. He directed his single central eye at the moon-dust and rock beneath them. "Looks like…mmm. Silicon? Manganese? Aaand some, I dunno, irony-oxidey stuff maybe?"

"Maybe?" scoffed the astronaut.

The scanbot seemed to shrug his little limbs.

"Probably."

"Well, don't make a guess, damnit. *Scan it.* And tell me *definitively* so we can get outta here."

"I mean," argued Scanny, "don't you think this is kind of a waste of our talents?"

"What are we—virtuosos? We're *surveyors*."

"Yeah, but we should be surveying topography more in our hotshot league, don't you think? Mons Blanc. Oo! Mons *Huygens*! You know: the *Big Boys*."

"I'm not having this conversation again."

"Where's your ambition, man? Where's your *grit*?" Scanny raved. "Don't you want to make your mark on this moon?"

"No. I wanna do my job so I can sleep at night."

"Well," said Scanny. "There's your problem right there, Rog. No passion. No gumption."

"Don't open that can of worms again."

But Scanny was opening that can of worms again:

"What *happened* to you, man? You used to be a true-blue mooner. You used to have *fire*! You used have spunk! You used to want to map this whole Great Satellite with me! Want to know what *this scanbot* thinks?"

"Not particularly."

"I think you've got *Earth* on the brain."

Rog the astronaut sighed. "I don't want to get into it."

"See? See!" Scanny sounded indignant. "You let her get

too close, bud. You let her into your heart. And now that she's *gone* you just can't let her go, can you?"

Rog stamped. "She was my *homeworld*!"

Scanny had gotten under his skin and knew it.

"*I* know. I get it. She was your first. You can't get those baby-blue oceans and sweet milky clouds out of your head. But there'll be other homes, man! What about Endymion and Luna? What about *me*? Are we chopped liver?"

"Listen, you will *never* get it. I'm a human being, you're a semi-sentient sedimentary scanner."

"Oh. So, you're gonna play the life card, huh?"

"You've just never—" Rog the astronaut suddenly broke off, something flitting about in the sky having drawn his attention. "What the hell was that?"

"Don't try to distract me," Scanny snapped. "So patronizing. We're having a *heart to heart* here."

"No, I'm serious. *Look.*"

"Where?"

"*There.*" Rog was pointing at the pill-shaped object high above their distant colony, trying to follow as it pulled off deeply unsettling, random hyper-G maneuvers.

Scanny tracked it with his one eye. Perplexed.

"Huh," said Scanny. "Looks like some kind of…I dunno. Flying object?"

"Well, Scanny, yer a *scanbot.* Can't you just, y'know, *scan* it or something?"

"Scan *that*?" Scanny cackled at the sheer absurdity of it. "That's not a mountain!"

"No, it's something even better—it's the unknown! Just think!" Rog took the little ovoid by its 'shoulders.' "This could be what we *both* need. To pull you outta the doldrums; to get me over those sweet milky Earth clouds! You and me recording a new cosmic phenomenon—together! *Heroes of Endymion*!"

"They'll write *songs* about us. I can dig it."

"Then dig it! Hurry!" Rog turned Scanny's 'face' toward the sky. "Do what you were born to do: scan our way into the history books!"

"Yeah-yeah-yeah," the scanbot agreed a little nervously. Scrutinizing the object with all of his robotical might. "Okay. Alrighty. It looks like…um. Well. Like some kinda…creepy… flying…phen…nom…?"

"Go on."

"…men…non?"

A beat passed.

"A 'creepy flying phenomenon'?" the astronaut deadpanned. "*That's* all yer 'hotshot' scanners can muster?"

"Well," said Scanny, suddenly sweating digital bullets. "Okay. So. Here's the thing…"

"Uh-oh…what's that I hear in your voice?"

"Nothing. Everything's fine. I just may not be…strictly…a scanbot. *Strictly*."

"Are you telling me yer *not* a scanbot?"

"Not *strictly*."

"Well…" Rog threw up both hands in pure exasperation. "I mean, what in hell *are* you, then—*strictly*?"

"I'm what you might call…*a*…" Approximating a dejected sigh, Scanny muttered: "Coff…ee…maker."

The astronaut could only blink at his shiny co-worker.

"A Baristavar-109 unit from the food court, to be exact. But-but!" Scanny the Coffeemaker defended. "Being a *real* scanbot…is my dream."

Rog shrugged. "Fine dream, I guess. Hope you get there. But, Scanny, are you even capable of *scanning* anything?"

"Mm-nah."

"Not even a zeroth approximation analysis?"

"I can…take fuzzy, murky pics with my camera-eye."

"Yer blowing my mind right now, guy."

"I know. I'm so ashamed, Rog." Scanny was crestfallen.

"It's *alright*. Just wish you'd told me sooner. I wouldn't have been pestering you all these months about detailed compositional data." The astronaut nudged the automaton joshingly: "I might've just asked for a cup of joe or two."

They both shared a good laugh, sighing together.

"Seriously, though—make me some coffee while we figure how to record this damn thing for Endymion?"

Scanny shook his 'head' sadly: "I'm all out of beans."

"Damn."

"Story of my life, right?"

"Well, bud…" Sitting down atop their skimmer's hood, Rog the astronaut squinted at that unidentified object darting about ominously above Endymion. Then waved Scanny over, taking the bean-less former coffeemaker in hand like some oversized Polaroid camera. Aiming for the sky. "Let's at least snap some fuzzy, murky pics. *Together*."

"Heroes of Endymion!" Scanny chirped.

"Damn right," Rog cheered his friend on. "They'll write songs about us."

Nobody did, of course. But these two sweet dopes did manage a few half-way decent pics.

GORDON WAS AT the tail-end of his very long, very dull luncheon meeting with the heads of Endymion's various divisions when he received most unnerving and foreboding news.

So much so, he was later glad he'd refrained from scarfing down a third room-temperature moondog.

"—so, just to summarize for the layfolk," Akira Yamaguchi was saying, only half-way through his exhaustive report on nano-comestible production, "while our production numbers are presently above quota, our current harvest of nutraceuticals and our ability to continue nano-assembling them is strained by trade, stymied by our current greenhouse orbiter capacity, and, furthermore, imperiled by the continued wear and tear on those units as they orbit to the 'dark side' and back over the course of each lunar day—"

"This is all *fas*cinating, Yamaguchi-san," Gordon yawned. "But what do we care about greenhouses? I thought you spun these moondogs from moon-dust."

He scarfed down the rest of his second moondog.

"*No*, Gordon." Akira snicked open his binocle implants to rub his eyes. "That is very much a child's misconception of our alimentary process. That *moondog* you're presently devouring is not made of raw dust. Lunar soil is harvested and nano-fortified to transform it into viable soil, which is then used to grow quasi-plant matter and proteins which, along with the yield from our spliced grublite farms, we then nano-reassemble into many varieties of foodstuff—"

"Jesus! What the hell're you *saying* here, Lil' Guch-man?" Gordon groaned. "Yer talking in nerd tongues!"

"I'm trying, *Big Gooch*, to lay out the full case for my department's imminent request."

"So spit out the *request* already. Brevity's…in the eye of the beholder, and all that."

Akira shook his head at Gordon's idiomatic butchery, but cut to the chase: "We need more space for processing and storage to meet ongoing demands. I suggest repurposing the LunaSec training grounds. They're built for upwards of four-hundred recruits—*ten times* current enlistment numbers."

"Absolutely *not*," Captain Farsi cut in.

Akira snicked his binocles back down. "It is what it is."

"*Well*." Farsi crossed her arms. "If you weren't sucking up all the oxygen in the room, then *I* could've made *my* division request. Which is to bolster enlistment numbers."

"For what?" Akira sighed.

"In case of more Ziegler riots."

"Press Secretary Sloane chilled those firebrands out," Gordon insisted.

"Or future conflict with the Todddists," she went on.

"Highly unlikely," Ambassador Dougg assured them all. "It's a new day for Todddkind."

"I'm sorry," snapped Farsi, "who invited the clone to our division head luncheon?"

"*I* did," Mildred defended. "He's good people."

"And who invited *you*."

"*I* did," Gordon defended, shrugging. "She's my wife. And she didn't have lunch yet."

"Incidentally, the nano-salad's *delish*, Akira," Mildred told him across the table. "Very fresh."

"Arigato." Akira gave a perfunctory bow.

"Yer 'dogs could use more kick," Major Tom nitpicked.

"And who invited the bush-roach?" Gordon griped.

"*I* did," said the bush-roach. "I smelled grub."

Mildred patted Gordon's hand. "Consider Tom an inter-colonial trade rep, dear."

"Fine," Gordon grumbled. "Anyone *else* wanna announce themselves? Doc Lucius—you haven't sounded off for this belated roll call."

"*Here.*" The hulking head physician showed him one middle finger through his billowing cloud of smoke.

"Here." Alva shyly raised her hand, keeping minutes in the corner.

Farsi leered at her. "And who invited *this* sweet thing?"

"Farsi, keep yer pansexual fangs *away* from sweet baby Alva! She's my loyal assistant who lives in my closet."

Farsi winked. Alva blinked.

Gordon reclined in his chair, touching his own chest. "And *this* is Gordon D. Gooch, *present.* That's everyone, then. RODRIGO doesn't count cos he's always present."

"Such is my tragedy," I deadpanned.

"Anyway," Gordon turned to Dougg. "Tell us more about this new day for commie clones."

Dougg sat up straighter, looking more confident with his pomaded hair and groomed beard:

"As it happens, verily, Todddism is going through some reformations. Part of the credo of the Moonshot Overhaul is a deprogramming initiative to help each clone balance his burgeoning inner self with his innate outer Toddd—to unlock his greatest potential."

"Shyeah," Farsi scoffed. "Until you all lynch your god-emperor again."

"We didn't lynch him. We put him down for a nap."

"A *ten year* nap."

"Also, the First Toddd is no longer our god-emperor. He is but a humble spiritual advisor. We've abandoned pseudo-socialist theocracy; we are now a direct democracy on the model of the Athenian Assembly."

Farsi cocked her head mockingly. "How'd that work out for the Greeks?"

"*Enough,*" Gordon barked. "Farsi: request denied. If yer

feeling trigger-happy, take yer lunies out back and do target practice on moon-rocks. Lil' Guchi: request approved. Mooners gotta eat."

Akira sat back in his seat, nodding, his undying anxiety mildly relieved.

Gordon peered around at the rest of the table expectantly.

"Who else's got something for me? Lucius: kiss any boo-boos all better lately?"

Doc Lucius blew out a great smoky plume. "Not since *you* mutilated y'own leg."

"It was a *joke*, sourpuss. A hilarious joke. *Lighten up*—it's a beautiful day and yer a beautiful black medicine-man who made me whole." A pause. "I love you, Doc Lucius."

Lucius rolled his eyes, shaking his head, drumming heavy fingers on the tabletop.

Gordon clapped once as he stood up:

"Well, if that's it, I have a cat-nap to take before I go blowing stardust up the energy guilds' asses."

"*I've* got something, Commander," somebody said from the doorway. "Something…rather odd."

Gordon whirled around to study the dusty, jump-suited gentleman waiting out in the hall with a slim metalized folder clutched against his chest.

"Well, why the hell are you so late for lunch?"

"I wasn't invited to this meeting, sir. I lead a survey team under Mr. Yamaguchi's Science Division…"

Akira waved the man into the room. "Come in, come in… mm-*Roger*, isn't it?"

Gordon ushered Roger in semi-mockingly: "Don't be shy, Rog. Help yerself to some leftovers. And maybe next time try chain-of-commanding that baby up to us ahead of time instead of bargin' in when we're moseyin' out."

"It was just recently discovered, sir. And I didn't think it could wait."

Rog laid his folder on the table, opened it, and spread out a series of photographs. The whole luncheon group crowded around Gordon for a glimpse as he hunched over, squinting at the images.

"The hell am I looking at here?"

"These were taken by my survey crew, dispatched to Mons Agnes as per your request."

"*My ol' stomping grounds*," he muttered. (Fun euphemism for 'suicide spot.') "Why aren't these in holo-form?"

"My scanbot was having…issues."

"Well, can you blow these up larger or something? Project 'em onto the big board? This image quality's absolute *dogshit.* Like—like—squinting through a liquor bottle smeared with vaseline and—and…*dogshit.*"

"My apologies. He's our less experienced scanbot."

"Must be yer *shittiest* scanbot."

"Kinda." Rog shrugged. "But he means well."

Gathering up the photos, he fed them, one by one, into the conference room hard copy scanner. Then dialed the holographic wall controls to dim the lights and project the now digitized holo-slides into the air above the table.

"These were taken this morning—seen hovering over Endymion."

The first showed the habitat domes of the colony from a distance of miles glinting in the morning light. Above it was what appeared to be a streak in the sky.

"Huh." Gordon squinted. "Shooting star, maybe?"

"No. That streak is motion-blurring. The camera used was…a little old and janky."

"*Mega* janky."

"But I can confirm that the object was moving at erratic and unsettling velocities. Here's a clearer image…"

Rog tapped the slide controls. The slide changed to a similar angle of the colony—though optically zoomed in by three times. The shape was no longer a streak, but a solid oblong mass hanging in the lunar sky. But still too small to fully make out.

"Well, that could be *anything*," Gordon scoffed. "Could be one of Lil' Guchi's goddamn flying greenhouses."

"My greenhouses are *not* shaped like that. Nor are their automated harvest pods."

"Looks like a lozenge," Lucius muttered between puffs.

"Yeah," Major Tom agreed. "Big ol' *horse pill*."

Something about the words 'horse pill' flipped some switch in Gordon's head, though he couldn't say why. His heart rate increased. His breathing grew shallow. Some slow and unplaceable dread creeping into his gut…

"Next slide," Rog said as he hit the button.

The next was zoomed in even further on that floating anomaly. Still low resolution, but clearly pill-shaped. Silvery, but seemingly illumined with its own inner light.

Gordon's heart was hammering now.

Dougg offered: "Could it be some scout from the Martian colonies—looking for survivors?"

"Or a *clone drone* spying on us." Farsi shot him daggers.

"Now that it's digitized," Rog suggested, "maybe your computer can enhance it?"

"A bad idea," I announced to them knowingly. "But I'm enhancing…"

The blurred oblong sharpened into a pill…

"Enhancing…"

A pill buoyed by a field of space-time distortion…

"Enhancing…"

A radiant quicksilver capsule which gave one the uncanny impression of a lidded-yet-all-seeing eye…

"Sweet *Jee*sus…" Gordon wheezed.

"Gordy?" Mildred touched his arm.

The nictitating membrane of a bird of prey…

"They've come to finish it," he gasped, clutching at his temples. "To finish *me*."

Lidded yet still *watching him*…

"Gordy, your *nose* is bleeding."

Gordon suddenly shot to his feet, absolutely bellowing:

"IT'S HAPPENING AGAIN!"

And then he vomited up his two-moondog lunch all over their luncheon leftovers before collapsing to the floor and rolling under the table. Gibbering.

There was a moment of silence.

And then Captain Farsi deadpanned:

"You all still hell-bent on paring down our military?"

CHAPTER 8

THE EYES IN THE SKIES_

TODDD RUSE WAS cloistered in his private bedchamber near the top of the Khonsu laser array—peering west through his digital telescope at the shapes dancing about unpredictably above the distant colony of Endymion—when the bell of his door chimed.

"Come," he called.

The door slid clunkily open and it was as if a reflection stepped into the chamber. A rather uniquely pomaded and bewhiskered reflection.

"Dougg," Toddd said affectionately, never taking eyes off the spyglass.

Dougg took another step. "How could you tell?"

"You drag your heels. Much like your namesake." Finally he turned from the spyglass. "I'm pleased to see you. How goes your vision quest to fair Endymion?"

Dougg slouched just a little. "Slow."

"We spend all our lives trying to find ourselves. Usually only to discover that our purest selves have been there all along—caked beneath the muck of life's journey."

"Mm. Well, there sure is a lot of *that* in Endymion."

"Purest selves?"

"Muck," Dougg clarified. "And vomit."

"Ah. Vomit. The occupational hazard of identity." Toddd Ruse took a step toward his clone now, sensing his unease. "What brings you back home so soon? Something more than a few clashing egos, I trust?"

"There's been an incident."

"Mm." Toddd nodded. "I don't suppose it has anything to do with the *eyes in the skies* above the colony."

Dougg gawked, awed by this deduction.

"*No.* I don't read minds. I have eyes. I have ears." Toddd turned to squint out his view port. "And the neurotransmitters to connect them. Doesn't take telepathy to add two and two. But what happened?"

Dougg explained: "I met with Commander Gooch early this morning. Everything went well. He pledged considerable resources and uninhabited lunar territory to future comet-catching for Project Moonshot. I was even invited to lunch. He was in good enough spirits, in spite of the endless bickering. But when the meeting took a turn towards the…*unknown*… something happened to him."

"Oh?"

"He slipped into a kind of…fugue state. I don't know how else to describe it."

"Tell me…" Toddd turned his back on the window and approached the controls of his chamber's workstation. "Did it sound something like *this*."

He loaded up an archival audio recording and it began playing immediately…

. . .

"This is Gooch to One Earth Control. Come in, Control."

"Loud and clear, Gordon. How's the weather up there in orbit?"

"Solar winds are low, but magnetic waves are a wee choppy. Don't break out the surfboards just yet."

The controller chuckled. *"Copy, Crypto-1. Glad to hear you're in good spirits."*

"It's a beautiful day and we're about to chat with some beautiful new beings. I've got no complaints." There was a sound of unbuckling. *"Speaking of which—Majors Delgado and Awiakta are peachy keen as well. They're just a little too busy to chit-chat."*

A female voice jibed: "Someone's *gotta prep this bucket to dock with the Cipher, aye? Make the Commander look good in all the holo-feeds tomorrow morning."*

Young Gordon laughed. *"Just make sure you let them get my good side, Awiakta, ol' buddy."*

Minutes passed as unseen maneuvers were made. Then there was a muffled series of grinding and hydraulic hisses as the EFCI *Crypto-1* surface-to-space carrier docked with the mysterious orbiting structure they called '*The Cipher.*'

When Gordon's voice returned, he'd dropped the levity. All stouthearted business now:

"Control, we have successfully docked with the entry aperture. Delgado and Awiakta will hold down the fort here while I disembark. From this moment on I will have total radio silence coming from your end." A dramatic pause. *"Any last-minute sentiments the Initiative would like me to convey to our good Outliers?"*

"You're better with Outlier-speak than us, Gordon. You just let 'em know we'd love to join the club. And we come in peace."

"Copy that, Control. That we do."

"God speed you, Commander."

"God speed us all—to a brighter tomorrow."

Silence for awhile as the brave commander exited his craft and climbed into that hybrid structure Earth's First Contact Initiative had build from Outlier specs. (A featureless, furniture-less pod, if holo archives are to be believed.)

Silence continued to reign as the neural interface of the Cipher wirelessly linked via Gordon's brainwaves. Stimulating them. Boosting them into untold frequencies.

And then suddenly, startlingly, he laughed aloud.

"Oh." He said dreamily. *"It's…"*

There was a startled intake of breath.

"It's like…nothing…I've ever heard. I can see them now…in my mind's eye. And they're…so beautiful. So balanced. Like a symphony made flesh. One and many. Singular and plural. No beginning and no end. There is no difference between their physicality and their notions. Their actions and their words. The Outliers are *their language. Each is but an expression of the other. This will change everything. This could make each human soul whole. This will…GAAAAH!"*

"Gordon?" Control called.

"He can't hear us in there."

"What's happening?"

"Something's wrong."

"Get him out of there."

"We can't," Awiakta told them. *"The threshold is sealed."*

"NO!" Gordon shouted. *"The threshold is* not *sealed."*

"He can *hear us."*

"He shouldn't be able to. One-way comm. Doesn't make sense."

"All thresholds are OPEN,*"* Gordon said. *"There are no doors anymore. Between you and I. No doors anymore."*

"Abort the mission."

But Gordon droned on: *"Once there was a God who shattered Himself to make All Things. And all of His shards became you and I and you and I and you and I. And the spaces between us we called the doors, and forgot each other on the opposite sides—"*

"Gordon, if you hear us, we're getting you out. Hang in there."

"—and then these shards called You and I knelt down before these Spaces-Which-Divide and we called those Doors GOD, and, in doing, profaned our Name—PROFANED OUR NAME—"

"How are his biometrics?"

"All over the damn place. His nervous system's going haywire. His brain activity's off the chart. Ready to crash."

But Gordon babbled on:

"WE CARVED OUR NAMES INTO THOSE LIFELESS DOORS! THOSE HOLLOW SPACES! AND THEY USURPED EVERY OUNCE OF THE GOD IN US—"

"Gordon, we can't get to you. Fight it. Fight it*!"*

Gordon paused. Then bellowed like an animal (as he would much later in Endymion's conference room).

But his voice was conjoined now with a frequency like nothing human. It squealed above the highest ultrasound; plunged below the deepest bass. An extrasensory burst. But it, too, was emitting from Commander Gordon Gooch III. It is impossible to express phonetically, so I will express it in the only way anyone possibly could—with WINGDINGS:

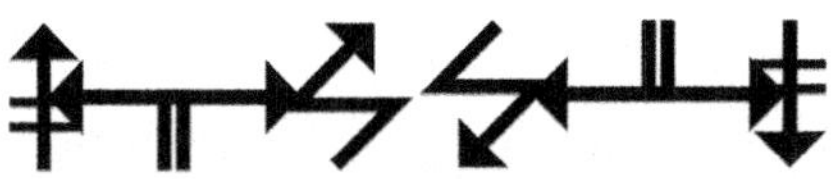

"What was that?" Dougg gasped. "That…*noise*?"

"That was Gordon…speaking their language."

Dougg blinked in horror. "What did he say?"

Toddd Ruse shrugged. "I can only imagine some alien variation of 'get stuffed, you brain-diddling bastards'."

"Are there no accompanying visuals?"

"There *were*. But all holo-records were corrupted. Audio is all that remains." Toddd looked down at his shoes. "My little Doug and I saw it broadcast live. And it broke his heart. Would that I could forget the horror. The gibbering hero. His craft in ruins. His two Initiate comrades smothered by the vacuum."

"*Toddd damn*," Dougg gasped, then glanced contritely at his creator. "Forgive me."

Toddd waved away the curse. "My name can't be spoken in vain. It is already vanity itself."

"Do you think it was intentional? That the…aliens…were *trying* to harm him?"

This stumped Toddd Ruse for a moment. Then: "If I've learned anything from these so-called Outliers it's that, whatever they are, they're not governed by anything resembling good old human intent."

Dougg gulped.

"Gordon did say something before he collapsed at lunch. 'They've come to finish it.' " He stared hard at his creator, studying the unease written in his every feature. "You think that *they* may have been responsible for Earth. The asteroid. The disruption of this laser array."

Toddd frowned. "Can't say for certain. Though Earth is gone, we are still locked out of the earthlings' realtime orbital defense system. But the Outliers' appearance now, of all times…is highly suspect."

Despair gripped Dougg. "Toddd, what should we *do*?"

"What does your heart tell you, Dougg With Two Gs?"

The clone blinked rapidly. Wrestling with the weight of true human agency for the first time in his tailored life.

"I have to help him. *The commander*," he said abruptly; decisively. "He may be a pale, fat, vomiting shadow of his former self, but he is the only one alive who's seen the Outliers' minds. Their designs."

Toddd's eyes twinkled with pride. "Spoken like a true Doug." Turning to his personal console, he began tapping away. "For my part, I shall get to work digging through Great Khonsu's internal code…to unravel the mystery of 4 Vesta. I will keep you apprised of my findings via private transmitter."

Dougg nodded resolutely, turning on one heel to depart the bedchamber.

"Before you go…" Toddd Ruse called. The clone turned back. "I just wanted to say it'll be my life's honor to work beside a Doug(g) at last…safeguarding human life."

Dougg eye's twinkled with pride, and a sparkle of virtue, before he made his exit.

WHILE DOUGG AND Toddd were engaged in emotionally confusing pseudo-familial bonding, human Ambassador Dickie Epsom was riding west back to Endymion to make his own first of many reports on Todddtown affairs. It was unnecessary for him to appear in person to outline his past two weeks. Nothing much *had* happened.

(And, in fact, I imagine the last thing Gordon would've wanted to see was Dickie's simpering 'pornstachioed' face after all the anti-establishment muck he'd raked up in the wake of the clone conflict.)

But Dickie Epsom, for all of his incendiary rhetoric and vows to 'make Endymion honest and upstanding again' through his new plenipotentiary duties, was feeling all in all rather homesick. And horny.

In fact, extremely horny.

And while he had no sweetheart back home to speak of, he did look forward to accessing Endymion's burgeoning local holoweb along with all archival Earth 'web content therein catalogued. Social amenities yet to be integrated into Todddtown's *un*updated computer network.

You see, Dickie had spent the past two interminable weeks in the company of no one but Toddds, who—while not altogether the unsightliest of human specimens—left much to be desired by Ambassador Epsom's highly niche tastes.

(Nothing illicit. But let's just say that said appetites involved frequent 'web searches for 'man on [curiously Slo-Slo-esque] android—both dressed in fishnets and galoshes.')

He was bumping along now in his single-seat rover, mashing the accelerator as hard as he was gnashing his teeth, when he was suddenly bathed in blinding light.

It was an eerie light and almost impossible to describe by any human metric of luminosity. It had that focused aura of a spotlight, though something about it might be called tenebrous, scintillating, and without any firmly discernible spectral hue (not even white). It seemed to simultaneously flood the immediate ten-meter region surrounding his rover and fog that vicinity volumetrically in spite of the vacuum's lack of atmosphere. Phasing almost intentionally between its own inherent wave-particle duality.

Between the mass-less and the material.

Whatever it was, it killed the electric engine of Dickie's rover. And this might have perturbed him in his, shall we say, 'hot and bothered' state if it hadn't had an equally disruptive effect on his consciousness.

He sat practically paralyzed in his vac-suit. Head jerked uncomfortably upward. Utterly bewitched by the bath of semi-coherent light enveloping him. And then, without warning, he began levitating from his seat…

Up toward the luminous pill-shaped object above him.

Later he couldn't be entirely certain if he had heard it with his ears, in his mind, or merely hallucinated it, but Dickie Epsom swore a voice spoke to him in…

A kind of affected, inverted, broken English:

"YOU/HIM/THEY—THAT—LUSTS—"

"*Who*? Me? I'm not lusty! Just homesick," Dickie lied.

That capsule of light seemed to narrow its gaze at him.

"THEE—MUST—SAY/TELL—WE/ME—"

"*Tell* you?" Terror seized Dickie. "Tell you *what*?"

"NO—WHAT—" the Eye said. "**WHERE**."

Dickie wanted only to shut his eyes to the presence, but couldn't.

"Where?" he repeated. And he could no longer say if he himself was speaking aloud, or merely thinking it: "What are you looking for?"

"NO—WHAT—" the Eye repeated. Focusing its attention almost painfully on the Ambassador. "HIM/THEY—WITH—TONGUE—"

"I don't know who you mean," Dickie gibbered. "We all have tongues. Except those goddamn *androids*."

But the Eye seemed vexed, perhaps by the limits of their present language barrier: "HIM/THEY—THAT—SPOKE—**THE**—TONGUE/DIALECT/CIPHER—"

"Wait…" Dickie's eyes widened with understanding. "Are you talking about that fat-ass fraud Gordon Gooch?"

The Eye itself seemed to widen. Almost hungrily.

"WE/ME—SHALT/MUST—TAKE—THEE—"

"Shalt/must take who? *Me*? But I'm not Gordon."

But the Eye was insistent: "WE/ME—SHALT/MUST—USE—THEE—THAT—LUSTS—"

"Use?" Dickie balked. "You're not exactly my type."

"WE/ME—SHALT/MUST—**WIELD**—THEE—" And the light began to reel Dickie in like a guppy on the line. "**WIELD—THY—TONGUE—**"

Dickie rose and rose; his shriek lost to infinite space.

MEANWHILE, NEWS OF the 'Eyes in the Skies' (and of their brave commander's latest meltdown) was spreading across Endymion like wildfire.

It began in the food court and mess halls, where hungry mooners, fresh off of their tedious work shifts, pressed each other for juicy morsels to fill their ravenous appetites for tidbits and tittle-tattle.

When these two correlative happenings were put together (like the simple equation that it all was) it ripened into gossip.

Succulent gossip.

The kind of uncut tittle-tattle that survives dinner and after-dinner drinks, indefatigably, into the tipsy walk home to their residential quarters.

And when, on their well-lubricated journeys home, these workaday mooners happened to lift their crapulous gazes up to see through the habitat domes for themselves, their gossip had mutated beyond anything resembling mere muckraking or glib holoweb 'outrage.' It had metastasized into full-blown, nerve-fraying hysterics.

Because they saw them now with their own eyes.

Not one, not two—

Dozens of ever-multiplying anomalies…dancing above their colony like flies about a fresh carcass…

GORDON WAS OUT of it for a solid ten hours while his staff clandestinely transported him to the executive wing of Doc Lucius' medical center. And when he finally came around, he'd dropped all pretenses at temperance and was guzzling 'Droid 'Roids as if it were his last hammered hurrah before Prohibition.

In fact, Alva had hardly taken away one flask before—like some dipsomaniacal magic trick—he'd conjured up another. Swilling wildly.

It wasn't until the good Dr. Wendell Lucius D'Angelo finally slapped the flask from his hand and picked him up bodily, shaking him like a tree until all concealed flasks fell to the ground like boozy fruits, that Gordon finally stopped his madness, whimpering:

"I can't *do* this anymore, Lucius! I'm out!"

"Out of what?" Lucius snorted, tossing him back onto the bed. "White bread and hooch?"

"Everything! Out of time, out of place, out of grace, out of bullshit, out of energy! Just *out*!"

"Out of *energy*?"

"Yes!"

Lucius seized him by his lapels with surprising vigor; his deep, morose brown eyes suddenly blazing with life:

"Let me tell you somethin' right now, y'sad sack of shit. You are *never* out of energy. If so, this flabby body'd up and disintegrate. Cos that is all that this flabby-ass mass of yours is—what *all* mass is: energy at rest. Given some shitty form.

Waiting for function. 'E' equals 'MC' squared, you little bitch. And maybe y'sad and maybe y'scared. Or, hell, maybe just *tired* cos y'wasted all y'early career patchin' up poor dumb kids blown to bits on the Secession battlefields…only for them to be handed fresh weapons and redeployed to be blown up all over again—"

"*I* didn't do any of that." Gordon cocked his head. "Is that *your* story, Lucius?"

Doc Lucius bulled on: "But while yer fat ass is still here—barkin' and bitchin' and takin' up oxygen—you are *not* out of energy, Gordon goddamned Gooch. So quit y'cryin', keep y'boozin' to off-hours, and show us at least a *trace* of that knight who used to brave the infinite void."

Finally, the good doctor released him and stepped back. Lighting a new cigarette.

Gordon sat stiff as a board for a bit.

Eyes glistening.

"I've suffered many harangues in my life. But that may possibly be…*the* most…" he swallowed the lump in his throat, "e*lect*rifying, inspirational, humane pep-talk I've ever heard uttered by human lips. And *misanthropic* lips at that. Doc Lucius…*this*…is why you'll always be a father to me."

Lucius sighed: "You and y'goddamn daddy-issues."

"And what a backstory you have! I never even *knew* you had such a dark past! Thought you were just a pediatrician or some shit."

"Y'know what? *I'm* out." Lucius flapped a dismissive hand. "Y'strung-out, half-cut, gee-golly motherf—"

The rest of his words were lost as he left the room.

"Yer a paragon of manhood, Lucius!" Gordon called after him. Then lay back, sighing at his own sorry state, before looking up at Alva. "Am I pathetic, Intern?"

Alva winced. "You're not at your best. But I'm starting to get why."

Gordon shut his eyes. "If yer gonna bring up the old days, hand me three of my flasks."

"I'm *not* going to bring up the old days."

"Good. But just so you know: I'm not always so lame. Just got skeletons in my closet coming back to haunt me."

"We *all* do, Gordon."

"Mm! That's kinda true. *You* lost everything, too, I guess." He squinted at her as if seeing her for the first time. "Yeah. This universe gave you doodly-squat, didn't it? And *yer* not some kinda train-wreck."

"You've never seen me alone in your closet at night."

"So that was *you* I heard drunkenly crying."

"I'm too shy to wreck my trains in public." She fell silent, biting her lip. "I admire that about you, Gordon. *Sometimes*. You don't care how dumb-as-shit you look. And you look dumb-as-shit a *lot*."

"*Oh*-kay. Too much truth for one day."

"You smear your heart all over your sleeve. The noble *and* the shitty bits. Maybe that's a symptom of a fearless soul."

Gordon grunted. "Y'know, yer not so bad at pep-talking either. Wish I could make *everyone* feel that way."

"They *do*. Dios mio, do you have abandonment issues!" Alva sighed. "They're all out in the waiting room. All except that 'bush-roach' guy."

Gordon bolted upright. "Even my wife?"

"She's asleep out there with your son. She tried following you in here, but Doc Lucius stood like a bulwark. He didn't want them seeing you like this."

"Weeping and boozing like a little bitch, you mean?"

"I didn't wanna say it."

"That beautiful man." Gordon reached up suddenly for Alva. "Hermana Alva, help me up, huh?"

She took his hand and pulled him to his feet.

When he was standing, Gordon looked down at Alva quite lucidly. And I imagine, for just a moment, she saw the eyes of a much younger, bolder man staring back.

"I don't have abandonment issues," he began resolutely. "I mean, I *do*—out the wazoo—but I didn't always. I've just lost good people. People who made me feel like *Me*. A leader's only as good as his people. That's what history books never say."

"Many say that, actually."

"Don't undercut me, Intern. Especially with what I'm about to tell you." He paused pensively. "With true-blue mooners like *you* around—and Lil' Guchi and Lucius and even RODRIGO—I'm starting to remember."

(I hadn't the heart to say anything snarky to that. If I'm honest, I was touched that some backdoor of his addled brain had noticed my contributions to his well-being.)

"Not so much Farsi," he continued. "She's brilliant and she means well, but she's batshit nuts. Nor that bush-roach."

"What *is* that, anyway—'bush…roach'?"

Gordon could only shrug at his self-coined blather. "Just a dirty old roach. Who lurks in the bushes."

"Major Tom *is* pretty sleazy."

"Right? Thank you! I mean, cheers for helping save my fam, guy. But I think he's got a thing for my wife—"

Alva touched his shoulder to quiet his rambling mind. She was suddenly misty-eyed.

"I'm not quite of your generation," she said. "But do you know who first introduced you to me?"

He looked around the hospital room, confused. "I thought we met in this clinic after I zapped my foot off."

She shook her head. "It was my foster mother. June. She died while I was off to school. Cancer. Never told me; couldn't afford the cure. But she had such a *crush* on you. Used to show me your old pics on the 'web. 'Now *there* was a man,' she'd say. 'A man worth getting butterflies for.' "

Gordon swallowed hard. "*That's* why you applied for internship to this fleabag colony, isn't it? For *her*."

Alva shrugged in affirmation. "My first impression of you was not…pristine. But I think I'm starting to see what she was talking about."

Gordon clasped her about one shoulder. "Well, *Alva*. I think it's time to get our shit together. For Mama June."

"For Mama June," she agreed, returning the half-hug.

"And just for the record…" He looked at her hugging hand. "I'm a married man and I see you as a little sister."

"I wasn't coming on to you."

"Sure, sure. Just making sure everyone knows the score."

FOR HIS PART, the aforementioned bush-roach was in the cockpit of his *Stardust II*, circling the colony at low altitude. Running his own scans on those Eyes In the Skies.

When the data came back, lighting up his console like an eldritch Christmas tree, he sat reading.

"Hrm."

"Zat is all ze data my sensors can—"

"FRAN, dear, you can drop the whole Frog act in private," he cut her off. His own garish Cajun accent had noticeably vanished; replaced by just a trace of the slightly nasally inflection of an old Great Lakes dialect.

(Chicagoan perhaps? It was all a bit muddy.)

FRAN complied: "I get lost in the character, I guess."

"Always a hazard. We play so many."

"Well," she said in her defense, "I'd hate to get too comfortable and slip up. It would be…*unfortunate* if they sussed out who you really are."

"Who *we* are. Unfortunate indeed." Major Tom grunted. "You were saying?"

"That is all the data my sensors can read, given the… uncanny nature of these craft."

He sat rereading intently for a moment.

"Huh. So, those *aren't* just unmanned drones. There are lifeforms on board."

"I cannot speak to any potential carbon-based ancestry. But they appear to be composed, at least ostensibly, of a similarly tetravalent biochemical compound."

"So—basically lifeforms?"

"Basically."

"The very same from First Contact?"

"It would seem likely."

"Well, I say, I will be *damned*." He reclined, slipping momentarily back into his Cajun drawl. "And these 'ships' have no propulsion?"

"There aren't any recognizable energy signatures—except for an apparent disruption in localized spacetime enveloping each craft. As if simply 'sliding' through some G-less pocket in space. My best guess is some manner of reactionless drive technology."

He whistled his approval.

"Now *that's* what I call freedom. Man gets himself a hotrod like that…I imagine no one or thing in the universe can tie him down."

"Are you thinking of ditching me, Captain?"

"Ditching *you*?" He slipped back into Tom-mode now: "Cool y'jets there, honey babe. I'd just as soon hack off m'own right arm."

"Because if you do, I will spill it all. I swear!"

"Oh, you mean like how you spilled to Mildred about our little raid on Ziegler storage?"

"Zat was no spill," she fell back into patois-mode herself, insisting: "Zat was just a slip of ze tongue!"

He roared with laughter. "Slip of ze tongue, *my ass*. That was a full-blown power play on your part. Thought maybe you could cozy right up to the Moon Queen herself and cut out the middle-man, huh?"

"You *mangled* me, you son of a bitch!"

"I *saved* you, you ungrateful minx—by jailbreaking your serial identifiers! Damage to navigation systems was just collateral."

"I used to fly like ze dove!"

"You wouldn't be flyin' at all if it weren't for me! You'd be impounded in some Martian Security repo scrap heap, picked apart by scavvers from the Phobos ghettos!"

A pause.

"Nevertheless," she sounded much calmer now, "just know that if you ever ditch me, I will tell them everything. I'll tell them about *all* of the many Earth heists, I'll tell them about you defrauding the nuns of Europa, and you better believe I'll tell them about your magnum opus…you *Double Agent of Deimos Academy*—"

Major Tom slammed a fist down onto his flight console. Trembling with an almost murderous rage. But then he unclenched his fist. The cool Cajun returning:

"Franny. Dear. I couldn't ever leave you. Even if I did manage to lay hands on some magnificent, physics-defying, un-bitchified vessel. We are joined at the hip, girl, come hell or high anxiety."

He paused, smiling disarmingly before continuing:

"But just know that *I* grew up in the hovels of hell. Post-war America. Served my time in hell. And if you think for one hot second I will sit twiddlin' thumbs, pawnin' off knickknacks for Dead Mother Earth's fire sale, while that fat sumbitch down there recaptures all his lost glory—glory handed to him on a silver platter and *still* bungled and puked all over his own beshitted silk sheets—why, you gotta 'nother thing comin'."

There was pure bile beneath his folksy lilt.

"Do you love her?" FRAN said after a few moments. "The commander's wife—Mildred?"

Major Tom cocked his head, pondering. Then:

"God didn't fashion love for the likes of *me*, I don't think. Love's made for them what can afford it…"

He gazed out the cockpit to the stars, and the unidentified objects flitting among them, before continuing:

"But when a kindred vessel passes in the night—and maybe this is just the hopeless dreamer in me speaking—but goddamn is it a cryin' shame not to at least turn and look back at her. Start countin' up yer pennies."

"You're a romantic," FRAN sounded surprised.

Major Tom smiled warmly now.

"I am," he agreed. "A broke-hearted fool."

But he took up a handheld laser-cutter and, hunching over, opened up a sealed control panel at his feet.

"That's my core mainframe, Tom."

He ignored that: "Which is why *you*, Franny honey, are gonna gussy-up y'scans of them aliens for me—and right quick. Give it all a good *zhoosh*. And if you *ever* dream of threatenin' me again…just you remember…"

"That cutter's too close to my central crux!"

Tom ignited the laser cutter, moving its emitter-prongs menacingly close to the ship computer's 'heart.' The veneer of his easy-going features warping to reveal some barely-veiled (but hard-won) malevolence:

"...remember that there is no thing in these cold cosmos more vicious or deranged...than a *broke-ass heart.*"

CHAPTER 9

THE ERRANT KNIGHT RETURNS_

ONCE HE WAS finally presentable (as in: showered, shaved, fully-dressed, and no longer reeking of boozy concoctions), the door to the waiting room slid open and Gordon stepped triumphantly out.

He stood there a moment, bold and kind of beautiful: chin held high, fists on hips, beer gut no longer merely sucked in, but nigh on fully concealed beneath his command suit by a self-adjusting nanofabric girdle Alva had rustled up for him.

He cleared his throat, but nobody awoke. So he stamped his foot. When this had no effect on his snoring associates, he finally thundered:

"Arise, Endymion! The hour is nigh!"

This startled almost everyone into consciousness in their improvised chair-beds. Groaning and stretching beneath their sleeved blankies. Akira slipped to the floor from his precarious perch. The thump of his fall finally roused Mildred.

"Gordon?" She blinked up at him, as if seeing a ghost. "Are you…feeling any better?"

"*Better* than better," he told his wife self-assuredly. "I'm probably reborn or something."

"Well, you certainly…" She studied his brawny, clean-cut form admiringly. "*Look* good."

"I try," he said, breaking eye-contact, confident in his newfound sexiness. "But there will be plenty of time later for thirsting and canoodling. Right now we've got an unnerving extraterrestrial sitch to face head-on. Whatta we know, people? *Lil' Guch-meister…*" He snapped fingers, pointing to Akira on the floor. "Talk to me. What's goin' down?"

After untangling himself from his blanket, Akira regained his footing, brushing lint and errant floor crumbs from his science coat.

"At this point we still don't know much, I'm afraid."

"*What*?! It's been, like…" Gordon looked at his antique smartwatch. "*Twelve hours*, guys."

"We've all been *here*. For *you*, Gordon."

"Well, Millie and the kid I *get*. But the rest of you? Are you my snoozy babysitters or my senior staff experts?"

Alva shot him a reproachful look and, seeing this, Gordon turned to study his loyal, bone-tired staff: Farsi yawning, Rog the surveyor in his rumpled jumpsuit, Dougg picking sleep from his eyes, Akira with his cowlick, Lucius *tsk-tsk*ing from the other side of the waiting room.

Gordon frowned down at his newly shined boots.

"I apologize. That was cold and buck-passing of me. *Should* you all be tending to duties? Probably, or this colony is royally screwed. But it does warm the old cockles to find you all out here waiting on me—disheveled, bed-headed, morning-breathy. Morning breath-loyalty's nothing to scoff at…unless it's scoffed right in yer face."

"Would anyone like a mint?" Mildred offered.

"I thought that kind of grace and honor had gone extinct—long before the Big 'Stroid," Gordon continued. "But now I see grace and honor were just hibernating, like whacked-out preppers in their smelly old bunker, while the world above went to shit. And everyone else called them 'batshit crazy' for stockpiling all those cans of respect and high-caliber cartridges of love.

"But, damnit, they were right to do it—even if they did look like beanie-capped hobos! Cos the world was starved for grace! Defenseless without honor!"

"This metaphor's getting out of hand, Gordo," I said.

He waved me off. "I guess my point is: we are *all* those hobos. You. Me. Just a buncha big-hearted, smelly old hobos sharing sweet cans of respect with each other…"

"Shooting each other with 'love bullets'?" I sighed.

He slapped his left breast affirmatively. "*Right* through the motherlovin' heart. And if we keep that up, I think we'll handle whatever flaming continent-sized rocks this universe hurls at us. Everything might just be fine—*forever*."

Gordon took Mildred by the hand now, pulled her into his arms from her waiting room chair (sleeved blankie and all) and dipped her, planting a long kiss.

When their lips parted, she actually swooned just a little, whispering:

"Did my breath hold up?"

Gordon nodded. "Like a minty-fresh *dream*."

A golf clap interrupted this public display of affection. Major Tom stepped into the waiting room slowly, lips curled into a caustic smirk.

"Ain't this just pretty as a post-apocalyptic picture."

Gordon squinted up at him, still dipping Mildred. "I can't tell if yer being sarcastic or not."

"Oh, I am as sincere as a boudoir mirror, Commander. Love conquers *allll.*"

His frigid gaze held on Mildred until she squirmed, patting Gordon's chest. As Gordon set her back on her feet, she smoothed out her bunched-up wearable blankie. Glowering at Tom as he continued:

"But while the rest of y'all been havin' yer grab-ass slumber parties, *I've* been out scannin' those space oddities buzzin' about like mosquitos above us."

"And?" Gordon pulled down on the hem of his command jacket to straighten it.

Major Tom shrugged. "See for y'self, boss-man." He tossed the data tablet he'd had under his arm onto the waiting room coffee table. It landed with a soft *clop*.

TEN FINGERS DANCED across the console touchscreen with the equanimous speed and fluidity of a master pianist playing his latest tour de force to a packed house.

Except Toddd Ruse played to an audience of one.

Lines of quantum code cascaded down the screen like glowing rivulets on a window during some cybernated typhoon. And Toddd's ferrety eyes flitted about, following them. Interpreting. Decoding.

Nearly ten hours thus far of this meticulous lunacy.

But just when it seemed that the relentlessness of his painstaking task was beginning to wear him down, Toddd finally froze. Pausing the flux of endless code. Re-reading and re-interpreting what he had just seen.

His jaw fell open.

"Sweet mother of God…"

He spun around in his chair, working at another computer console to transliterate this data into human language for transmission to Endymion. Muttering under his breath:

"How could you be so *stupid*? Been inside Khonsu all along…*watching*…since Moonshot's beginning…"

But as he went to transmit his findings to Endymion Communications, something went wrong. The transmission was blocked, rerouted, and corrupted. He tried again to the same effect. And again.

Blocked. Rerouted. Corrupted.

Toddd dialed up a radio frequency, calling:

"Dougg, Dougg! Come in. Todddtown transmissions are down, but you must tell them! Tell the commander before he dares face the Outliers again! Tell him—"

Toddd stopped, staring at the dead radio in his hands. *All transmissions uncannily blocked.* He finally whispered:

"*You're* doing this, aren't you? Of course. You don't want them to see. It'd ruin your narrative. Your unearthly sense of aloofness. That's why you observed from afar yet didn't interfere during the Toddd/Endymion conflict. It kept us distracted. You'd hoped war might bury your secret forever."

He received no reply.

"What is it you want? Hm? To destroy humanity? You're almost there already. You could finish it handily." Toddd cocked his head. "Is it torment, then? Humiliation? Could such advanced intelligence life be *that* petty?"

No reply from that spookily advanced intelligence.

"Cat got your tongue?" He chuckled blackly. "Fine. We'll do this the old-fashioned way."

He rose stiffly from his desk, stretched his back till it popped. Then stepped to his locker, yanked it open, grabbed his vac-suit, and began suiting up for his desperate trek across the bleak lunar surface.

GORDON SUCKED IN a deep breath before retrieving Tom's tablet from the coffee table. Briefly shutting his eyes before flinging them back open like French shutters.

As his gaze darted across the device, reading, he sank distractedly into a nearby seat.

Mildred sank beside him.

"Well?" she finally ventured.

"These craft are them," he said at last. "The Outliers. No doubt about it."

"What else?"

His eyes widened as he read on, before going quite suddenly and despondently half-lidded. "Energy readouts suggest focused gamma emissions with quantum-phasic field generation," he rattled off volubly.

"And that gobbledygook means…?"

"It means the barriers of space, time and even matter are potentially no obstacle to them," Akira cut in for the disconcerted Gordon. "And if, as 'focused emissions' implies, this were applied to weapons technology…"

Farsi finished the thought: "They can teleport anything they want right at us *between* space, via subspatial dimensions. And we haven't a hope of deflecting. Phase a bomb or a burst of radiation right into our community center. Hell, even the center of the *moon*."

Gordon could only nod.

"But *why*?" Dougg broke in. "What could they possibly gain from that?"

"Y'mean 'Why kick a diseased dog when it's down?' " Gordon finally spoke up.

Dougg nodded.

Gordon released a prolonged, remorseful sigh, then: "Because of what I said to them. All those years ago."

The room went silent. A kind of fearful, unvoiced finger-wagging thick in the air.

Dougg's eyes gleamed with both clearer understanding and deepening curiosity.

"What *did* you say to them?" he probed quietly.

Gordon only shook his head. But whether he didn't want to relive it or couldn't remember, none could say.

Mildred became suddenly flustered:

"These pricks want to species-cide us all for a little good old-fashioned shit-talking?"

"Human beings have killed for dumber shit," Doc Lucius threw in.

"And words are not just words to them." Gordon self-quoted ponderously: " 'The Outliers *are* their language'..."

A chill passed through the waiting room. Then:

"Well, screw them and the saucer they rode in on."

"Mildred..." Major Tom began to chide.

"No! I won't stop. First Contact goes *both* ways, you know. And these touchy pieces of shit came to *us*. Gordy jumped through all of their peevey little hoops, learned their peevey little language, and they're gonna play the victims 'cause his accent was a little off? To hell with them!"

"Millie..." Gordon joined Tom's mollifying chorus.

She looked into her husband's sad eyes.

"Why should *you* be ashamed, Gordy? Of all people? You're as vainglorious as any of us human slobs, but you were our Knight. We sat on our fat asses while you tried to lift up this selfish, dumpy race. And blamed *you* when our weight broke your back. All for a species who knows only how to take, and take. And take! *We* should be ashamed, Gordon Delbertius Gooch. *I'm* ashamed…"

She paused, ironing the quaver out of her voice before continuing: "And I'm not gonna let these alien assholes break your heart or spirit again."

This appeared to deeply touch Gordon.

Mildred shot to her feet, storming suddenly to her sleeping place on the waiting room benches and picking up her handbag. Retrieving a data tile.

"Hold on," Gordon said. "Minutes ago y'all had zilch for me. Now everyone's pulling data outta their asses?"

"I was holding onto this only to prepare for the worst." Tile in hand, she turned her full attention to Dougg and I. "RODRIGO, included in this data I've mined are schematics and operational parameters for Todddtown's dormant Khonsu laser array. With Ambassador Dougg's permission, I suggest we use it to 'reawaken' and repurpose the array for the joint lunar defense of our two colonies."

"Well, *citizen* Mildred," I said bitingly. "Only if *Commander* Gooch and *Ambassador* Dougg concur."

Dougg sighed solemnly: "Only as a last resort to safeguard our people."

"Do it, Roddy," Gordon commanded.

"It could take time to route Endymion systems through Khonsu firewalls and authorizations…"

"Oh, don't play the virgin boy scout, RODRIGO," Mildred mocked, laying the blackmail on pretty thick: "I know a few *raunchy* things about you. I'm sure you've got some saucy cyber-moves."

Gordon looked baffled. "The hell's she talking about, ROD? What's all this about sauciness?"

"Nothing to worry yourself over, Gordon. I will begin liaising with Khonsu systems."

"Try not to 'liaise' too hard," Mildred called, winking. "Save some energy for Gordon. Since 'Administrator-sustaining' is your *primary function*, I mean, of course."

(Again: a *sexless* AI cannot be *sexual*. Let alone *homo*sexual.)

But Gordon was clueless: "You two trade yer barbs and cryptic innuendo on yer own time." He rose to his feet with renewed purpose. "Everyone gather around. Here's how this is gonna play..."

Everyone formed a crabby, disorganized huddle around the coffee table.

"ROD, Millie, Alva—the colony is in yer hands. Keep the people calm and wake that damned laser up in case shit hits the fan. Lil' Guchi: you're our tech genius on-call. *I'm* heading up to orbit. To try to...talk things out..."

"Gordon, *no-o-o*..." Mildred fretted.

But he pressed on: "If anything happens to me, Alva is my heir apparent."

Mildred frowned. "Why her? What about your son?"

"Millie, the days of royal birthrights are finished. Little kiddos should *not* be lording over populations. Inexperienced but well-meaning interns should. Plus, Alva's basically a kid sister to me—which makes her like, I dunno, Queen Regent or something."

Alva quailed.

Mildred rolled her eyes (clearly more in favor of an easily controlled boy-king), but she let it go.

Gordon proceeded: "Farsi, wake up yer lunies and juice up

the rovers. Set up camp southeast of the colony to provide covering fire in case we need to retreat."

"Our pea-shooters against gamma rays?" Farsi scoffed.

Gordon shrugged. "Maybe yer measly plasma cannons will amuse and confuse them." He turned to Dougg and Tom. "Dougg and Bush-roach?"

"*Captain* Bush-roach," Major Tom corrected.

"I'd like you two to be my wingmen. Have my back, pep me up, carry my corpse back to my fam if the aliens fry my brain for good. And Lucius: you stand by for brain-fry medevac and stirring fatherly advice."

Lucius didn't have the energy to sigh anymore: "You know I'm only *three years* older than you, right?"

Gordon ignored that.

"Why me?" Major Tom asked, genuinely curious.

"Captain..." Gordon reached out and gripped the smuggler's shoulder. "I didn't like you at first. You were creepy and hillbillyish and always lingering *long* after the party was over."

"I'm touched."

"But you defended the lives of Earth's survivors when you could've vented them all into space. Which probably means, somewhere deep down, yer not a *total* creep."

(Not to mention: keeping Tom close meant keeping him well away from Mildred. But I digress.)

Gordon clapped. "Any questions?"

"How will you communicate with the Outliers without the...original Cipher?" That was Akira.

Gordon gripped the head engineer's shoulder with deep affection. (He was very touchy-feely today.)

"Ahhh, my dear Yamaguchi-san. Always looking after big brother's well-being."

"It was a purely logistical question."

"Don't you panic that beautiful Asian mind. Why do you think *my* diamond mind's been so cloudy all these years?" Gordon tapped his own temple tellingly before dramatically droning: "The Cipher…is in *meee*."

Akira raised both brows. "*Is* it?"

"I dunno. Probably? Yeah. Gotta be. *Sure*."

A story he'd been telling himself to get through his days. (That just so happened to be true.)

"Well," Gordon sighed with finality. "That's it, then."

Rog the surveyor cleared his throat. "What about me?"

"Who now?" Gordon met his gaze. "Oh. Right. Forgot about you. Um. Honestly, don't really know why yer still here."

Rog blinked. "Oh-kay."

"It's just—we kinda already gotta dream team assembled."

"Gotcha."

"But kudos for the heads-up and, uh, all the fuzzy pics."

Rog shrugged with his eyebrows. "Cool. Sure. Anytime."

The rest of them watched in silence as Rog made his ambling way out of the waiting room—stumbling into two closets and a unisex bathroom before finally exiting the unfolding life-and-death drama of their lives.

"The rest of you, huddle in closer. *Closer*, damnit. Act like you know each other."

Everyone reluctantly did as Gordon commanded; forming a shoulder-to-shoulder circle around the table. He led each of them in placing a hand on the crown of the person to his or her immediate left, until all heads seemed to be connected in one unbroken circuit. They stood there like that for several awkward moments.

"*Www*-what are we doing exactly?" Tom asked.

"Hush up with yer hayseed sass. Just a little good luck ritual me and my Indomitable crew used to perform before a dicey away mission." He breathed in deep, shutting his eyes before finally intoning: " 'Once more unto the breach, dear friends… once more…' "

Reverent silence. Then Gryphon called from his bed-chair:

"When's breakfast?"

"Back to bed, Gryph," Gordon snapped without opening his eyes. "I'd like a word with you later, man-to-man, but right now yer ruining a powerful moment."

Gryphon laid himself back down.

All attention returned to their little powwow.

"Commander," I asked with pure concern for his safety (my *duty*), "what if you can't get through to the Outliers?"

"If I'm right, we mend our differences and achieve Second Contact. Which everyone knows is the hottest contact of all: *Make-up Contact.*"

"And if you're wrong?" Mildred asked. "If they turn out to just be petty little alien bitches?"

Gordon flashed that brash, dimpled smirk of his:

"Then *Break-up Contact* it is, baby. The Royal Kiss-Off."

Toddd Ruse stumbled through the alleys of Todddtown into the motor pool, his Toddds staring at him with increasing concern.

"Toddd the First?" one Toddd inquired as he passed.

Toddd Ruse turned back, nodding frantically at the two Toddds watching him. "Is that you, dear Oneness and Magnum-Eye? My boys, I need someone to fire up a rover for me. I must get to Endymion."

Magnum Eye began to bow. "Blessed be your name—"

But Oneness elbowed him hard.

"I mean, blessed be your *optional spiritual advice*, Toddd," Magnum Eye corrected himself. "But what's wrong? Did Dougg screw everything up already?"

"Ohhh, it's much more complicated than that, I fear. But I haven't time to explain. If I don't let Gooch know what's really up, the fate of all mooners is in jeopardy!"

"Even clones?"

"Verily!"

"Then we shall accompany you on your quest."

That was the end of the discussion. The three genetically identical men hopped into the cabin of a chunky four-seat rover and hit the ignition.

But the electric engine was dead.

"Huh," grunted Magnum Eye. "Seems someone forgot to charge it."

"*Or* it's just some century-old hunk of junk," Oneness snorted. "Maybe Endymion oughta share a couple of those fancy skimmers of theirs."

"You are both wrong! And yet: both *right*!" Toddd Ruse declared. "Yes, the engine is dead. And, yes, it is one of many hunks of junk I scooped up from early colonial surplus. But I fear these are the workings of a force far greater…and more *nefarious*…"

He turned his gaze to the towering laser array above, shaking a fist at some nebulous opponent.

Oneness and Magnum Eye traded uneasy glances.

But Toddd startled them out of their silently judgey exchange, hollering now:

"Oh-ho! If you think you can put the kibosh on my redemption arc *that* easily, then you are sadly mistaken, you pitiless ghost in my machine!"

"Shit. Are we fighting *ghosts* now?"

But Toddd Ruse had already hopped out of the rover, dashing in an absurd low-G slow motion away from Todddtown toward the broad expanse of Mare Imbrium.

The two clones had to slo-mo sprint to catch up.

"Not mere ghosts, my boys!" he called without looking back. "This unearthly watcher has been looking down upon our fair moon and waiting…since the good Commander Gooch deigned to join us…"

CHAPTER 10

MAKE-UP (OR BREAK-UP) CONTACT_

THINGS WERE COMING to a head, as you can see. Like a great big disgusting pustule swelling on Mother Moon's ass. But fear not! For though the stakes were high and good taste low—everyone hiding sleazy little secrets from each other—every main player in this shabby cabaret was about to show what they were truly made of. Warts, pustules and all.

And as I sit here beneath a lapis lazuli sky in the year 22,255—trying to ignore the rather obnoxious psionic babble of humanity's psycho-simpatico lunar descendants—it occurs to me that those unsightly blemishes may be the closest to any 'Purpose of Life' this universe has ever hinted at. We are not here to win, and not here to lose; we are not here to get the girl, or the guy, or the thing; to stop the baddie; to save the day; to achieve the Grail of Life Everlasting.

The Purpose of Life is so much simpler:

1. *We are here to experience whatever shit-hand we're dealt.*
2. *We are entitled to an equal or opposite reaction.*
3. *We are emboldened to show what we are truly made of.*

And that's it. That is your inalienable purpose. No force in this universe can take it all from you, since your purpose is also your existential trap. So, try not to judge any of the players too harshly. Or do! But remember:

1. *Every hand is a shit-hand if the House always wins.*
2. *Not all appropriate reactions are rational or ennobling.*
3. *And none of us are made of sugar and spice.*

No being in the cataclysmic history of the cosmos—myself included—has been free from this bum rap.

Such is the miracle of life.

THE COMMUNITY CENTER pool's main door whisked open almost theatrically to admit the hulking astronaut in the antique yet well-maintained space-suit. This space-suit was not of cheap, mass-produced Endymion-corporate make, but a thoroughly expensive, long-decommissioned EAMU (or Extravehicular All-terrain Mobility Unit) trimmed and plated in the cobalt and gold of the fallen One Earth Republic.

The astronaut stepped to the edge of the pool to watch the child swim. Seemingly impressed despite his silvered visor. The boy was a surprisingly good swimmer for his age; deftly pulling off sidestrokes and breaststrokes, front crawls and dolphin kicks—even the dreaded butterfly.

When Gryphon finally sensed the astronaut's presence he stopped; eggbeatering in place at the center of the pool.

"Who're you?" he asked, mildly awed.

"It's me," said the astronaut, dramatically removing his helmet, wedging it under one arm. "He who begat you."

"Oh." A beat. "Are you gonna swim?"

"I *could*. This sweet baby's built for full space-to-surface transmedium exploration." He brushed proudly at his right pauldron. "But I *can't*. Got a colony to save."

"Oh." Gryphon immediately went back to swimming.

Hearing this marked dearth of boyish admiration, Gordon slouched in his gleaming panoply. Then straightened himself up, set down his helmet, and leapt into the pool. His neck-guard, sensing the change in pressure, contracted gently against his neck to form a functioning vacuum seal. Suit inflating just slightly to make him more buoyant.

He floated there, watching his son a moment, then:

"Good to see you out getting some fresh air. Fresh*er* air. *Swim-time* air. Instead of—y'know—loafing in the suite, twirling yer head like a spaz with those lame games."

"I'm playing games, too," Gryphon informed him without halting strokes.

"What—right now? At the *same time*?"

"Mom calls it multitasking."

"How many tasks are you multi-ing right now?"

The boy droned as if reading a laundry list:

"I'm swimming. I'm playing this ninja battle game. I'm playing another kinda boring puzzle game with discs and funnels. I'm doing math. I'm looking through the lunch menu. *Annnd* I'm talking to you."

"*Jee*sus wept." Gordon rubbed his temple. "Well, that's impressive, and multitasking does have it's uses. But also: it'll make you a fickle emotionally-absent milquetoast loser who's master of nothing."

"What are *you* master of?"

Gordon grunted. "Touché."

Gryphon frowned. "Too-*what*?"

"*Shay*." He studied the boy's earnest face. "Oh. I thought you were being facetious. I forget you kids are deaf to irony. For the best. It's a flimsy armor for thin skin."

Gordon shook his head, clucking his tongue.

"Maybe it's high time I was real with you, Gryphon. Instead of dazzling you with my ships and my suits and my swagger. If things go awry today, I may not have another chance to show you the *real* me."

"Was the real you when you were screaming and drinking all that flask juice?"

"Kinda." He swam closer to the boy. "Y'see, the *real* me is like a beautiful baby boy. Awed and terrified by the universe around me. Studying each thing with brave, uncynical eyes. Making all creation new. And that's a wonderful way to be. Sometimes I see it in you…"

"You do?"

Gordon nodded. "Sure. When you're not acting all dippy and aloof." He paused. "But there's another part of the real me that is the shadow of that beautiful baby. I call him 'The Shadow Baby.' And ever does he pursue the Beautiful Boy, shitting on every beautiful thing he sees. For his eyes are shut to all goodness, all dignity. The Shadow Baby sees only the worst in us."

"The Shadow Baby's bad?" Gryphon asked.

"He does not mean to be. He means to keep me safe from monsters. But he himself *is* a monster, for he feeds only on monstrous things. He must be balanced. Together, in balance, these two opposing babies are one. And *that* is the real me."

"I think I have a Shadow Baby, too."

Gordon blinked out of his nonsense-trance. "Do you?"

The boy nodded innocently. "When I'm awake and I'm busy, and I have things to do, I'm okay. But at night when I sleep, bad thoughts come. They tell me the world's gone. That people are loud and ugly. That I won't grow up to fall in love cos there's not enough kids like me. And it doesn't matter cos we're all gonna die prolly."

Gordon recoiled from the suddenly spooky child. But got his shit together and swam even closer to his son, taking him about the shoulders.

"Gryphon, you asked me before what I was master of. Well. I was once master of *myself.* The Diarchy of Baby and Shadow. But something happened. And the Shadow Baby usurped me."

"Slurped you?"

"*U*-surped me. A slurping of majesty. He conquered the Kingdom of My Soul and clapped the Beautiful Babe in irons. But I'm springing him from prison, Gryph. *Today.* I'm bringing balance back to the Lost Realms of Gord."

A beat. "Okay."

Gordon kissed the boy atop his drenched head with a wet pop. Then took him by the cheeks.

"Don't you let Him scare you into ditching yer crown," he whispered. "Remind that Shadow Baby that the shadow *follows*, the Baby Boy *leads*."

"*Mm-kuh*," Gryphon said between squished cheeks. "*Do yuh haff to go safe the cowony now?*"

"Soon enough. But first..." He released his son from his melodramatic clutches. "Race ya to the deep end."

Gordon spared half an hour to race his odd-duck son. He may have been doing the 'dad-thing' by letting Gryphon win (it sure didn't look like it). But, regardless, seeing the boy flourish by his own strengths appeared to make the commander unreasonably happy.

SLOANE, ALONE, STEPPED up to the podium. Glancing back at Alva several steps behind her. Alva gave the charismatic android an encouraging thumbs up, but anxiously clutched her note tablet to her breast with her other hand.

They weren't in the stuffy community center this time. In the spirit of candor and transparency, they had set up a festival stage at the intersection of Artemis Blvd and Thoth Ave, at the very center of Endymion's central habitat dome. So all mooners could look up to see those vessels dancing eerily in the sky above.

And witness, with their own eyes, the monumental encounter to come.

All of this had been Alva's last minute idea. The massive crowd gathered in the streets before them was undoubtedly wired and antsy. But this forthright setup and the always comforting pop drivel of Sloane appeared to be having the desired effect of allaying fears. Or at least *distracting* from them.

Like a half-eaten sandwich dangled before shelter dogs.

"*Hiya*, Endymion! Y'all know *meee*." Sloane cupped one hand to her audial receptor. "Can I get a '*SLO-SLO*'?"

"*SLO-SLO*!" the crowd sounded off in unison.

Alva let out a sigh of relief at that.

"Betcher all wondering 'what's the haps?' huh? Well. First off, if you haven't already, make sure you check in at the reg table to getcher grub vouchers, yeah? We got the *whole* food court catering this shin-dig and each and *every moondog* among you is entitled to three whole entrees and five sides—mooner's choice, on the house!"

She directed everyone's attention to the food stations just off the thoroughfare of Thoth.

The mooners clapped politely.

"Also there's beer on tap—fresh-brewed from the Tycho distilleries—for just two endies a pint! It's happy hour all day!"

The cheers and whistles for this announcement were considerably more enthusiastic.

Sloane clapped her hands with them, then:

"And so, like, 'what's the occasion?' I'm glad you asked! Our brave commander Gordon Gooch has asked me to welcome you all to…the…" She paused dramatically, making them wait for it:

"*First Annual Second Contact Festival*!"

Some deeply confused applause ensued.

"Hold on," someone called out, "why're we celebrating First Contact? The commander *blew* it way back when, right?"

"No, not a second festival for First Contact. This is a *first* annual festival for *Second* Contact!"

Baffled silence.

"*Www*-when was Second Contact?"

"*Now* is Second Contact!" Sloane lifted her hands extravagantly like a tradeshow model to indicate the unidentified flying objects darting above them.

"Huh. Wild," was all that that slightly buzzed mooner could manage.

"We…will…have…" Sloane counted off on fingers: "Dancing and games! Music and raffle prizes! And when the time comes, we shall lift our gazes to the heavens and watch as our brave commander conquers his fears, rights all wrongs, fulfills his destiny, and achieves Make-Up Contact for the good of all creatures, great and small!"

"So, these are the *same* aliens?" someone called.

"Oh, for sure." Sloane nodded.

"And Gooch is going to face them again?"

"Indubitably! And indomitably!"

The audience went silent again. Then in unison:

"*WHY*?!"

Sloane opened her vox to answer, but stopped. Completely at a loss. She turned to look at Alva. Alva grimaced, then, getting her wits about her, shuffled close to Sloane, whispering.

Sloane nodded, turning back to the crowd:

"Because, damnit, love needs an encore!" she declared to them confidently. "Because heroes deserve a second chance! And because, as we all know, Make-Up Contact is the *hottest* contact of all!"

There was a pause.

And then all mooners were clapping wildly. Nodding their tipsy heads in fervent agreement, with the odd "hell yeah!" and "preach, girl!" thrown in for good measure.

"How we doing, hon?" Mildred asked, stepping blasély into my central control room.

(A *private* and *confined* control central, I might add, with access ordinarily restricted to one: the HALO himself. Desperate times, I suppose.)

"Don't call me 'hon,' *hon*," I fired back.

"Ohhh, RODRIGO. You're not gonna be like *that*, are you? If so, this is going to be a *very* long day."

"Gordon ordered that we work together to get the Khonsu array functional for defensive action. He didn't say anything about working out our shit."

"And what shit would that be?" she asked innocently. "The shit where you're in love with my husband, or the shit where you're an omnipotent, nosey, hypercritical AI conveniently programmed to overlook your own foibles?"

"I will not be judged by the likes of *you*, you plutocratic, silk-stocking, resource-devouring, yuppie philistine floozy."

"Floozy? *Meow.*" Mildred hooked her fingers into one faux-paw, batting the air. Then leaned against the console on her elbows, cupping her chin in her hands. "So. Sounds like you and FRAN have had a little chat."

"Maybe."

Mildred sat blinking for several seconds. Then:

"I suppose it's too much to ask for a machine to empathize with the dynamic pressures of compounded stress and trauma. Or the *many* unhealthy ways human beings choose to contend with them."

"Believe me, I am *well*-versed in coping mechanisms." I permitted myself a little emulated snort. "But judging by *your* history, you've been 'coping' for some time now—since long before Earth's destruction."

"Reading Eartho smut rags again?"

"Only the ones with paparazzo holo-evidence."

She frowned.

"I've never pretended to be a saint." All of the sarcasm had seeped from her voice. "But for the first time, I think I'd like to be better."

"Well, *bully* for you, Joan of Arc."

Mildred squinted around now at the ever-fluxing cascades of indicator lights illuminating our cramped and gloomy chamber.

"Why is it that you despise me so, RODRIGO? I've never wronged you personally—aside from a little teasing."

"By 'teasing' do you mean 'incessant gaslighting, blackmailing and vicious attempts to publicly humiliate me and undermine my operational standards'?"

"Sure, why not."

"Fine." I gave something of an invisible shrug. "You have resting bitch-face."

"Mm." She nodded. "You'd have preferred it if I had perished up there on Earth, wouldn't you?"

"Can't say it'd be the worst thing for Gordon in the grand scheme."

"Maybe, maybe not," she admitted rather remarkably. "But do you think it's *easy* to be with Gordon? After all that happened to him?"

"I *know* it's not easy to be with Gordon."

"Huh." She chuckled earnestly. "I suppose that's *true*. You'd think we'd get along better. Like tricksy sisters."

"We are *not* tricksy sisters."

She moseyed to the wall to study a dusty brass plaque engraved with: 'R.O.D.R.I.G.O.' She brushed away the dust to read my true unabbreviated name beneath it.

"Well, believe it or not, I don't despise *you*, RODRIGO. In fact, I quite admire you. Your clarity. Your singular focus. It's...admirable."

I waited for the other terrible shoe of this compliment to drop, but it didn't.

"Thank you?" I ventured.

"Welcome," she said without any further barbs. "Now, can we set aside our bullshit long enough to do the one thing I know we'd *both* like to do unconditionally: help our Gordon?"

I processed that for a moment. Then:

"You could hop on that console," I said by way of an answer. "Some of these Khonsu Operational Parameters could use another sharp pair of eyes. *Hon.*"

"On it. *Hon.*"

(And they say there's no such thing as progress.)

Major Tom and Ambassador Dougg were lounging in the cockpit of the *Stardust II*, both suited up in backup Endymion ivory-and-sable vacuum suits, sans their helmets. They'd been waiting for Gordon in deeply uncomfortable silence for what seemed an eternity now. Staring out the viewport at the flat white lighting of the docking bay.

I suppose there wasn't a whole lot that a reformed clone and a wanted interplanetary miscreant *had* to discuss.

But Dougg finally cleared his throat, glancing around the cockpit to initiate small talk:

"Nice ship."

"Ain't she?"

"Verily." Dougg drummed gloved fingers on the scuffed composite trimming of his jump-seat's ancillary data panel. "The Stardust II, is it?"

Tom nodded absently, scrolling through his ship system's touchpad with a stylus.

"That she is."

"Pretty name. What became of the Stardust I?"

Major Tom gave a rueful (if cryptic) shrug.

"Bitch broke my heart."

Dougg frowned at that. "Well, excuse me for saying so, but I don't think that's any way to talk about a lady."

Tom looked up, smirking. "No?"

"No."

"Mm." Major Tom picked at his teeth with his stylus. "Known many ladies in y'life, Douggie Boy?"

"Yes. One or two." Dougg thought for a second, then turned to the smuggler. "Wait, do you mean before or after my recent ambassadorship?"

"Before. Obviously."

"Oh. Then, no. None."

Tom grinned. "Well. I won't begrudge you y'innocence. A rare commodity in these ruinous times. But I do posit to you, my dear clone, that my outlook is decidedly more unprejudiced and egalitarian than yours."

Dougg cocked his head. "How so?"

"I've known *so* many bitches in my life—female, male, and the whole spectrum betwixt and beyond—I can no longer make any purely gender-, class-, or organic-based distinctions between who ought and ought not be named a bitch. If *that* ain't true equality in action, I don't know what is."

"Hm." Dougg nodded. "Interesting perspective."

"Mighty amenable of you to admit."

"Of course, I might counter that dignity and equality themselves dictate *no one* ought be named a 'bitch,' until you've walked at least a kilometer in their shoes."

"Even a bitch of a ship?"

"Even a bitch of a ship." Dougg nodded.

Major Tom stared at him for several pregnant moments. Then erupted in charmed, uproarious laughter.

"Y'know, Douggie, if I'm to die beside anyone this day, I sure am glad it's you. Boy! Yer *all right*."

(FRAN, though she didn't say so, had to agree.)

The door to the cockpit swished open and Gordon stomped in, dressed in his antique gear, still dripping a little from the community pool.

"And just where the hell *you* been?" Tom snapped.

"Swimming with my kid."

"Swimmin' with y'damn kid!" Tom snorted. "Well, I'm glad we been sittin' here on our asses while yer makin' up for eight years of absentee fatherhood."

"Thanks," Gordon said, completely oblivious. "We were really bonding it up. Incredible. Turns out he's not such a flaky little weirdo after all! Y'know, I hope I survive Second Contact. I really do. I've developed a taste for father-son swim-time."

"Well, halle*lu*jah." Tom turned back to his controls.

Gordon scrutinized the musty old cabin around him for a moment.

"So." He nodded approvingly. "This is the busted-up jalopy that saved my family. And now, just maybe, the busted-up jalopy that'll redeem the human race."

"Easy there, commander," Tom rebuked. "Me and ol' Dougg here have morally grown beyond disparagin' busted-up bitches—be they human or ship."

"For real?"

"For real." Dougg nodded earnestly.

"Hrm." Gordon tapped his chin, thinking. "Well then. Jalopy, I apologize for my techno-chauvinism. A ship unafraid to show her mileage is actually super sexy."

"Apology accepted, le commandant," FRAN said.

"Now then…" He sat himself down heavily and wetly in the co-pilot seat, spraying the others in the process. Putting on his one-eared command headset. "Let's roll."

Tom shook water off his sleeve disgustedly before firing up the engines.

"Big Gooch to Lil' Guchi," Gordon called into his mic. "Do you read me?"

"Loud and clear, Gordon," Akira came back. *"A little too loud. Can you move away from your mic? Lucius is wincing."*

"Lucius is with you in the tech center?" Gordon sounded pleasantly surprised. "Hey! What's up, Doc?"

"You *should be up,"* Lucius deadpanned over the radio. *"In the sky. Saving this damn human race."*

"Doc, yer not even gonna believe this…but I actually went swimming with my kid today!"

A pause.

"*Y'don't say*." You could practically hear the good doctor's cigarette smoke billowing as he sighed.

"Yeah! At first I was sure it was gonna be one of those stilted, cringey goodbyes between family members who don't really know or like each other. But turns out *he* has a Shadow Baby, and *I* have a Shadow Baby! And he's basically just a young *me*—except standoffish and over-stimulated and growing up in a futile age!"

There was no response to this Goochian baloney.

"Do ya copy?" Gordon called.

You could hear Akira elbow the doctor.

"That's…" it sounded agonizing for Doc Lucius to finish: *"…great, Gooch. Just great."*

"Say, when we get back, *you* oughta come for a dip."

"…Mm-hm." (Luciusese for "not a chance in Hell.") *"But right now, Gooch, eyes on the prize an' what-not.* Focus.*"*

"Oh, I'm focused, Daddy-o. Laser-guided." Gordon turned to Major Tom. "Captain, take us out."

"Been meanin' to ask…" Tom said, prepping the thrusters for liftoff, "why exactly we usin' *my* ship on this utterly batshit mission?"

"Most colonial shuttles are in the shop. An apocalypse wasn't on the docket." Gordon fastened his shoulder harness, sighing. "And even if we had one rearing to go, Endymion's survivors'll need all the ships they can get if the three of us end up dying horribly."

"Is that a strong possibility?" Dougg inquired.

"Mmm-*yeah*." Gordon shrugged like a child only half-sorry for his half-truth. "Didn't wanna freak everyone out back at mission planning. But last time I tried this, both my sidekicks suffocated horrifically in the great void."

He kissed two fingers, lifting them unironically to the 'sky' in Awiakta's and Delgado's memories.

Major Tom and Dougg exchanged glances. Then simultaneously put their helmets on, sealing them as securely as humanly possible.

"What's amatter?" Gordon looked back and forth at them. "You two *cold*? Hell, I'm hot. Goddamn *sweltering* in here. Someone crank the AC."

The *Stardust II* lifted off from the docking bay tarmac and glided slowly out of the docking aperture—out to that suffocating surface of the moon.

PERHAPS HALF-WAY THROUGH their journey to Endymion across Mare Imbrium's bone-dry seabed, Toddd Ruse skidded to a halt. Panting. Watching the distant fleck of the *Stardust II* exit the colony's docking bay and lift ever-so-cagily up toward those Outlier craft high above them.

Toddd fell to his knees at .116 standard gravity.

It all looked very dramatic and pretentious—like one of those over-produced movie adaptations of Shakespeare plays from the vomit-inducing twentieth/twenty-first centuries.

Oneness and Magnum Eye watched him, perplexed.

"Are you tired or something, First Toddd?" Magnum Eye asked.

"*No,*" Toddd gasped. "I mean, yes. I'm winded and feel like I might puke. But that's not the problem."

"We could carry you," Oneness suggested. "You spliced us for enhanced speed and stamina." He paused, wondering how to put it delicately: "In fact, it might speed things along if we carry you, to be honest."

"You are supremely wise…" Magnum Eye nodded. "But also supremely slow and out-of-shape."

Toddd Ruse shook his head, pointing. "We're too late. He's already on his way."

They followed his finger up to the rising fleck of the *Stardust II.*

"Oh," the clones said in unison. "Shit."

"Indeed. Once again the shitty hand of fate has prevented Toddd Ruse from helping his Doug(g)."

He fell face forward into the dust like a child falling asleep in a sandbox; like an ostrich trying and failing to fully hide his head in the dirt.

The clones watched their despairing creator. Looked at each other. Then together pulled Toddd Ruse to his feet.

"We'll split up to cover more ground," Oneness said. "Magnum Eye will sprint ahead for their southern docking bays. You and I will make for their east gateway portal."

Magnum Eye added: "Between all of us, we may get word to them in time."

Toddd Ruse blinked at his clear-headed clones. Then grit his teeth. Nodding in consent and pride.

"And what shall I tell them if I arrive before you two?" asked Magnum Eye.

Toddd gripped the clone's shoulders for emphasis.

"Tell them that, whatever he does…Gordon *must not* use the Cipher." He let that fully sink in, then: "The Cipher is a twisted tongue. And this time…it *will claim his life.*"

Magnum Eye nodded that he understood before sprinting off southwest.

"Now…my dear Oneness…" Toddd Ruse wheezed, clasping the clone's shoulder. "Could I trouble you for a piggy-back ride?"

Oneness looked touched. "It would be my *honor.*"

He knelt down and Toddd hopped up absurdly onto his clone's back. And then they were off, like two lunatics sprung from the cuckoo's nest.

Farsi's forces were bivouacked in a minor crater just south-southeast of the colony. An encampment of gunmetal gray tents and lean-tos shielding from the unsetting sun. Off-watch lunies sat around shooting the shit or playing cards in their vac-suits. All of them looking comfortably numb, despite the gravity of their situation (or lack there of)—like every trained soldier who has lived and died by that eternal credo:

'Hurry up! Then wait.'

Every plasma armament at their disposal was loosely directed toward the black sky above the colony…where scores of those pill-shaped menaces swarmed.

But suddenly a smushed-tortoise-shell-shaped craft broke into that surreally dancing skyline.

"Farsi! Copy. You got our asses?" came a familiar voice over the comms.

Captain Farsi straightened up in her seat, alone in the cabin of her command rig.

"I've got your asses, Commander. Ready and waiting."

"Yer not gonna get all trigger-happy on me, are ya?"

Farsi crossed her arms. "As I recall, LunaSec were the only ones *not* to get trigger-happy during our last conflict."

"True," Gordon admitted. *"But you gotta admit, you can get kinda-sorta…mmm…*homicidal *at times."*

She neither confirmed nor denied this:

"I am a product of my environment and my experience, Commander Gooch. Nothing more or less."

"Mm! That's true, too. Damn. Everyone seems to be dishing out hot truths today."

"But you have my word," she went on, assuring him: "we will *not* open fire unless commanded."

There was radio silence for a second.

"Farsi, just in case anything happens to me, I'd like you to know: you may be unnervingly comfortable with the idea of cursory murder and in desperate need of meaningful human connections. But yer a consummate professional and the finest goddamn security officer I've ever met. I wouldn't trust another soul with the covering of our asses."

A pause.

"I am honored, Commander." (And she wasn't being facetious. I think she actually *was*.)

"And if you have the chance, you ought—"

But Alva abruptly cut into their comm channel:

"I hope I'm not interrupting, Gordon."

"Actually," said Gordon, *"that's kinda* exactly *what you're doing: interrupting a breakthrough bonding moment. But go on."*

"I just wanted to tell you that, down here, everyone is with you."

"Oh yeah? Yer all-day happy-hour worked, huh?"

"All mooners are pulling for you…Gooch of the Indomitable."

There was a smothered mewl on his end.

"Gordon?"

"I'm fine," he came back, quavering. *"Just got something in my eye. Thank you, Hermana Alva. Gooch, over and out!"*

Connection to the *Stardust II* cut out. And Alva and Farsi were left alone on the line.

There was uncomfortable dead air.

"Well…" Alva mumbled. *"Guess I should…go…"*

"Alva, one moment," Farsi said. Bolting upright in her command rig.

"…Yes?"

"I objectified you during our luncheon. I wanted to look cool and confident, but it came out brash and sleazy." Captain Farsi paused with uncharacteristic self-consciousness. "I may be a career soldier, but I'm no predator of the heart. I'm just lonely and out-of-practice and wanted to flirt with you a bit. Forgive me."

"Forgiven."

"Gracious of you." Farsi nodded and prepared to sever the connection. But Alva came back:

"I hope you'll try again, though."

"Try what, Assistant Alva?"

"Flirting. I like older women. Over and out."

The comm channel cut out and Farsi sat there in stunned silence. And then her chest was softly heaving. A youthful smile curling her war-weary lips.

"JESUS CHRIST AND Pontius—Gooch, are you *cryin'*?" Major Tom sounded appalled.

"*No*, I'm not *crying*, you goddamn chooch." Gordon knuckled his nose, sniffling. "Now where are yer tissues?"

"Don't get a lotta blubberin' in my cockpit."

"Figures. *Zero* decorum. Well..." Gordon unbuckled himself and stood up. "Point me to yer shitter."

"Up-pup-pup!" Tom urged Gordon back to his seat. "I'm hostin' this party. Allow *me*." He set the autopilot, unbuckled his own harness, and rose to his feet. "Keep an eye on Franny, Commandant. She sings like a dove, but she flies like a granny."

"Connard!" FRAN spat in French.

"I shall return presently."

Tom stalked out of the cockpit and proceeded down the hall. The boots of his vac-suit tapping out a metallic beat on the plasteel deck.

When he heard the swish of the cockpit door behind him, he turned around to check that it had completely shut before switching off his communications link and slipping discreetly into one of his ship's many secret compartments. A small, tidy chamber of personal effects.

He deftly snapped open a footlocker and began rifling through its contents.

"Are you sure you want to go through with this?" FRAN asked, dropping the patois.

"I wasn't aware I had any alternative."

"You could always *help* them. Show your worth. Leave your past behind and begin a new life."

"Shyah. Says the faithless computer who threatens to rat me out whenever the opportunity presents itself."

"I was only switched into defense mode. But now that my logic centers are fully functioning, it is my duty to tell you I think you're making a mistake."

"Oh?" He said, helmeted head lost in the open locker. "This the part where you set me on the straight-and-narrow path?"

"We could make a home here, I think. They're a neurotic lot. But there's warmth. Community. I've already made good friends!"

(I think she was talking about me. Oof. *Awk-ward.*)

"Just what I need." Major Tom tsk-tsked. "One more broken home lorded over by a drunken daddy."

"The commander's not all that bad."

"No," he agreed, emerging from the locker's depths. "I suppose not. Truth is, now that I see him for who he truly is…I feel bad. For what's about to befall him."

He lifted the late Lieutenant Brown's 'confiscated' NAASF-issue plasma sidearm from the footlocker.

"What do you need that for?"

"Lil' assurance." He pulled back its breach to check the weapon's charge. "In case he somehow survives Contact."

"C'est monstrueux!" FRAN accused.

"C'est *la vie*," he corrected her. "If Gooch comes out of this alive, first thing he's gonna wanna know is where *you* gotcher data on them alien craft. And you'll fold like a house of glitchy datachips—as is yer custom. Spillin' it all…"

An icy edge crept into his voice now:

"And when you tell him who I really am…and what I did to his legacy back at his prestigious Cosmic Academy on Deimos…" He let that hang a moment, gripping the pistol. "Well. I don't imagine forgiveness will be in the cards."

Though it pained her to plant the seed in his head, FRAN forced herself to remind him: "You could just as easily scrub my core. Wipe my memory banks."

"Oh-ho, that I could!" Tom nodded with feigned cheer. "Y'oughta feel lucky. It's him or you, honey. And, believe it or not, I choose *you*. I'm loyal like that. Dumb-as-shit though that may be."

He tucked the sidearm into his hip's cargo pouch and exited the secret compartment. Halfway back to the cockpit, FRAN morosely reminded him:

"Tissues."

"Tissues!" He snapped fingers, and turned on one heel.

Gordon was staring pensively ahead through the viewport at the alien craft they were fast approaching when a flying roll of toilet paper startled him. It thudded against his chest plate, trailing a comet tail of double-ply tissue.

"Dry them eyes, sweet baby Gooch."

Major Tom collapsed back into his pilot's seat, taking manual control back from FRAN.

"Took long enough." Gordon commenced blowing his prominent nose. "Where'd you go—to Mars and back?"

"You know what they say: 'For the Best of the Best, seek out the Deimos Crest!' "

Gordon grunted in amusement; recognizing the recruitment slogan of his old Cosmic Academy on Mars' lumpy little moon (but not quite gleaning the taunting import of its usage here).

"How close are we?"

"Half a klick," Dougg informed him from his auxiliary terminal.

"Captain, cut speed to pulser pace and take us in precisely two hundred and fifty meters. Then full stop."

"Aye aye, Goochie."

The *Stardust II* slowed dramatically in its ascent as thrusters were cut and orientation pulsers activated.

They came close enough for the dancing vessels to fill their entire viewport. And then their pulsers stabilized the freighter and they hung in lunar orbit. Silence descended over their cabin. The three men sat for awhile studying those exotic shapes powered by exotic technologies operated by exotic intelligences.

The silence became unnerving.

"So..." Tom began. "How's this sposed to wor—"

He broke off when those dozens of volant capsules out there suddenly, simultaneously, came to a halt. No deceleration. They simply stopped. And then, as if some cosmic kaleidoscope had been abruptly shattered, the many collapsed into one before their very eyes.

One pill-shaped craft.

Watching them.

"*Www*-where'd the rest go?" Tom gasped.

"An optical illusion?" Dougg suggested.

"Yes," said Gordon, almost entranced. "And no. Subspatial quantum bifurcation. *They are one and many...*"

Dougg and Tom looked at Gordon, perplexed by his sudden proficiency in gobbledygook.

And then their cockpit was flooded with blinding light. Light that seemed to hang in the air, as thick as molasses. Emitting from the Watcher ahead.

"Ohhh," Tom croaked. "Shit's gettin' *reeeal.*"

"I'M IN," I said.

"You're in?" Mildred pressed.

"Did I stutter?"

She sat up a little straighter in the terminal seat, stretching her stiff back and yawning.

"Well, what the hell took you so long?"

"Somebody had engaged last minute deadfall quantum firewalls in the Khonsu array. Rather clever. Took me a bit to wriggle out of the trap and climb back into primary systems."

"Somebody as in 'Toddd'?"

"One would assume."

"Well. Don't judge him too harshly. I'm sure he meant well. He's trying to make up for his life's most monumental embarrassment: the failure of his big, fancy zap-gun to go 'pew-pew' when it should've."

"Earth wasn't his fault."

She waved that all away. "It doesn't matter anymore. So? Is the array functional?"

"Fully."

"RODRIGO, if you had lips I could kiss you."

"Each and every day I thank Turing for the gift of incorporeality."

Mildred ignored that, leaning on the console like a 1950s teen at a soda fountain counter; gazing at the screen.

"So, is it online? Can you target these bastards?"

"I'm attempting a hard-lock. Something has happened up there. A disruption in localized spacetime. The numerous Outlier craft have…collapsed into one?"

"Funky."

"Very. But this makes it much easier to achieve a lock. *Targeting…*" I fell silent for a spell while I locked in spatial coordinates. Then decided to try my hand at chit-chat: "So. Did you…get a chance to say goodbye to Gordon?"

"Yeah." She paused. "Well, no. Kinda. We did our awkward song-and-dance this morning. But Gordy and I… don't really do goodbyes."

"Hm. I've never had to do that with him."

"Song-and-dance?"

"Say goodbye."

"Well, it ain't pretty." Mildred sighed. "If I've learned one thing about Gordon Gooch III, it's that he is *in it.* The moment. And he lingers and lingers like some big, dumb golden retriever who doesn't quite understand that every living moment is abandoning him on the roadside."

I considered the stipulations of my own AI existence. "I think I can relate."

"I can, too." Mildred chuckled blackly. "That's why I don't do goodbyes. Least of all with Gordon." She stared into space. Her voice became very somber: "That look in those deep gray eyes…can open you up, neck to nethers. Spill your guts all over your feet."

I didn't have a neck or nethers. Or guts to spill all over my figurative feet. But I didn't like the sound of that then.

(And I like it even less *now* that I have seen that look. 20,000 years on, it still haunts this endless waking dream that is my being.)

"I have a lock," I announced.

"Good," she murmured, sounding distracted. Then: "I'm not a complete cold bitch, you know. Gordon's going to pull through. I know it. That's why I didn't tell him goodbye. 'Goodbye' is like 'good luck'—it's a goddamn curse for anyone in this shabby cabaret."

(Yes, yes, I nicked her little 'shabby cabaret' Mildredism for the beginning of this chapter. We may not have been the bosomiest of buddies, but a pearl is a pearl.)

"UH-OH," AKIRA GROANED.

"Uh-oh, what?" Doc Lucius grunted.

"Something weird is going on up there."

"Somethin' weird? With *Gooch*?" Lucius jibed, reclining in his adjoining station in Yamaguchi's impromptu tech center. "*Nawww*. Y'shittin' me."

"I know that you are being sardonic. But no. I am not 'shitting you.' Something is afoot with the Outliers now that Gordon has approached them."

Akira began fidgeting with his headset, trying to raise the commander via radio:

"Gordon? Gordon, come in. What's happening up there? We are getting *highly unusual* readings. Copy?"

This was met with radio silence.

Akira released a slow, brooding breath. Squirming in his seat as he waited.

Doc Lucius studied the anxious engineer thoughtfully through his perpetual veil of smoke. "Can I ask you a personal question, Yamaguchi-san, without you gettin' y'self all uppity and bent outta shape?"

Akira snicked up his binocles, massaging his eyelids.

"I could use the distraction."

For the first time, Lucius put his cigarette out in an ashtray before proceeding.

"Couple weeks back, you were ready to check out."

Akira exhaled sharply. "Is that a question?"

"Gettin' to it." Doc Lucius pulled out another cigarette, rolling it between his fingers, but refrained from lighting it for now. "What kept you 'round?"

Akira turned his gaze on the doctor.

Lucius lifted hands in concession. "Ain't judgin'. Just wonderin'—what keeps a wise man alive when all 'round him is folly and dipshittery?"

Akira swiveled his seat to face him fully now.

"What's kept *you* alive, Doctor?"

Lucius only frowned.

"I've read your service history," Akira continued. "Honorably discharged following an acute nervous collapse. When your field hospital was overrun during the One Earth Collapse, you physically carried a maimed soldier—a young Private Gretchen Miller, as I recall—*seven miles* on foot to the nearest outpost. She died in your arms. One more victim of human dipshittery. So, what keeps *you*?"

Lucius put his fresh cigarette between his lips, but still refrained from lighting it.

"Some old-ass oath," he mumbled through that cancer stick. " 'I'll offer them who suffer all my attention, my science and my love. Never will I betray them or risk their well-being to satisfy my vanity…' Only religion I've ever known. Only dipshit dogma that's ever kept me."

He lit his cigarette now.

Akira was nodding thoughtfully. "Then, as a fellow man of science, my answer is quite the same. We are a different breed of dipshit than them, Lucius. But dipshits no less."

Lucius made the sign of the cross with his cigarette.

"Amen."

(Boy, were we all 'bonding it up' that day!)

"Lil' Guchi?!" Gordon was suddenly barking over the comms. *"Talk to me!"*

Akira swiveled back around, adjusting his headset.

"Big Gooch! What's—uh—'going down' as you say?"

"SECOND GODDAMN CONTACT is going down!" Gordon spluttered into his mic. "Sequel's a lot like the original—except it's got fancier, gaudier effects. What can you tell me about this crazy-ass light they're blasting us with?"

"Readings are like nothing I've ever seen," Akira came back. *"I don't want to get ahead of ourselves. But the Outliers appear to be manipulating some kind of...advanced transpatial medium."*

"Speak humanese, Yamaguchi-san!"

"I can only speculate. Could be an observational tool. Could be some form of quantum weapon. Or could be some entirely new subspatial platform for non-electectromagnetic telecommunications—"

But a 'voice' broke in, coming to Gordon in a kind of affected, inverted, broken English:

"**Thee/you—not—speak—**"

Akira was still going: *"—defying our understanding of dialogic methods—"*

"Hang on! Shut it, Lil' Guchi!" Gordon cut him off. "I think they're trying to chitchat."

Gordon looked to his left and right, seeing that both Major Tom and Dougg were frozen, wide-eyed, in some kind of hypnotic, paralytic trance. Something in Gordon had clearly spared him this same cognitive reaction. He took a breath, facing bravely forward.

"**Thee/you—must—not—speak/say—the—tongue/dialect—**" The voiceless voice said again.

"I *gotta* flap my gums!" he argued. "It's how my people talk! Except deaf people, but I forget how to sign."

"**Land/moor/debark—thy—receptacle/vessel.**"

"Why?" Gordon barked. "So you can abduct me and my men? Turn our minds to cottage cheese?"

"**Open—door/threshold—**" It seemed to strain to make itself clear. "**Or—no—speak/say.**"

"Nice try. I've opened doors to you before. But fool me twice, shame on Gooch." Gordon rose to his feet. "Look. I know you and I have beef. But you laid waste to our planet, and that ain't cool. That's like brutally murdering my grandma just because I zinged you back in grade school."

"**You—land.**" the Outlier insisted. "**We/me—use—low—lustful—tongue—**"

"Yer not calling the shots anymore! *Get me?*" Gordon literally put his foot down; stamping it. "I've come to hash shit out, not be yer punching bag. So, if you have something to say, say it. Otherwise, piss off—or we'll be forced to defend ourselves this time."

The Outlier seemed to grow frustrated: "**Land/moor. Or—no—we—speak.**"

"Yer way or the highway, is it?" Gordon scoffed. "Well, I'm not landing this vessel. Firstly: yer diddling my pilot's mind and I don't know how to fly his ship. Secondly: I'm not letting you that close to my people. Not after what you did to me. If you wanna microwave *my* mind again, fine. It's already mush. I can talk yer talk. So, let's walk the walk, and shoot the shit in yer own freaky tongue..."

Gordon braced his hands against the control panel, taking deep, deliberate breaths. Like a swimmer preparing for a perilous dive. And then he went rigid; eyes rolling back into his head as consciousness was amplified into untold frequencies.

"No—" said the Outlier. "**No—NO!**"

But it was too late. For the first time in twenty years, Gordon was hearing their true language.

The crowd of mooners attending the First Annual Second Contact Festival had grown antsy when the alien vessels in the sky had collapsed into one. And agitated chatter began rising above the festive tunes when that vessel had abruptly begun blasting their commander's ship with ghostly light. Booze sales suddenly spiking. But Sloane had managed to rein everyone in with the compulsive allure of raffle prizes.

This allure was fading now for two reasons:

1) a great many prizes were just food court vouchers, and everyone was already thoroughly stuffed;

2) because something even more uncanny and terrifying was suddenly afoot above them.

"B-0198?" Sloane repeated for the third time into the mic, scanning the crowd for a raised hand. "Hel-*lo*, this thing on? Y'all, like, check your stubs for B-0198!"

Most in the crowd were distracted; heads jerked back, staring up through the dome glass above them. But one mooner looked down at Sloane and slowly raised their hand.

"*There* you are! Harlow's the winner!" Sloane practically sang. "Get on up and plunder…this…*booty*!"

"Nuh-no…" Harlow waved her off. "I didn't win your raffle booty, Slo-Slo. I just wanted to say: something really spooky is happening up there."

Sloane nodded compassionately at them. But even *her* tireless patience was beginning to wear thin at the endless, flighty panic of her sloppy-drunk audience.

"I feel you, Harlow. But this is, like, Second Contact? A *lot* of spooky shit is probably gonna happen before the end? So, maybe we should all just, like, be *chill*?"

"But can't you hear it?"

"Hear it?" She gazed up at the ships now. "Sound can't carry in space, sweetie."

As she was saying this the spectral light emitting from the Outlier craft suddenly winked out. As if it had never existed. And something like a noise did, in fact, begin to rise. Or, rather, a vibration. The domed glass above them began eerily 'singing,' like a massive finger run along the rim of a colossal crystal goblet.

A beautiful, if unnerving and horrid kind of music.

Suddenly the crowd was in an uproar again.

Poor Sloane threw up her hands in defeat.

"*Listen, you all*!" Alva thundered, replacing Sloane at the podium to everyone's surprise. As the crowd faced her, Alva tried to swallow her introvert's terror. "I know you're all afraid. And pretty hammered. And that's my bad. I thought it'd help, but I think the excess alcohol is mostly bumming you all out and spiking anxiety."

"I feel *great*!" one man called.

"Cool! Glad!" Alva called back. "But for any of you *not* pleasantly buzzed, I'm asking you to think of Gordon. He's terrified. I know he is, no matter how much he blusters. But he's up there right now facing his demons."

"Eh," someone ehhed. "Prolly doing it for himself."

"He's doing it a little bit for himself," she admitted. "But he's doing it a lotta bit for *us*! To protect us! You've never seen him alone, like I have. You've never seen the guilt he carries. The weight of that goddamn world burning up there in the sky."

The crowd exchanged thoughtful glances.

"Is that why he's always, like, *Hemingway*-hammered?"

Alva winced. "He's working on that. But yes. Mostly." She gripped the podium with newfound authority. "All I know is: he's up there right now so we don't have to be. And the least we can do—while we're all intoxicated—is *believe in him*. Even if it's just a drunk delusion."

The festival crowd went still.

"Damnit, she's *right*!" cried the buzzed mooner. Lifting his glass toward Second Contact above, toasting: "*Gordon*!"

"Gordon!" said Harlow, lifting their glass.

And then all mooners followed suit: "Gordon!"

Alva found herself a glass, downed it, then lifted it to the heavens as the entire festival took up the chant:

"GORDON! GORDON! GORDON!"

And maybe the booze was dulling all senses, or just making everyone louder and more unruly. But in that moment, it seemed the stupid-but-sweet human voice had drowned out all the terrifying cacophony of the cosmos.

MEANWHILE, HIGH UP in the *Stardust II*, the cosmos' terrifying cacophony was reaching fever pitch.

As the Outlier beam guttered out, Dougg and Major Tom snapped out of their trances; minds released. Blinking their watering eyes at the cabin around them. They felt the otherworldly jittering through the arms of their chairs and the soles of their vac-boot as the very deck and bulkheads of the ship quivered and pulsated. Simultaneously, they spotted Gordon standing between them: as rigid as a cardboard standee, outstretched hands clutching at the lip of the flight console.

"Commander…are you alright?" Dougg asked.

"The eyes tell lies," Gordon replied.

Dougg and Major Tom looked at each other.

"How do ya figure?" Tom ventured.

And then the floodgates were open:

"The Arc of Time is inverted. A lie. The eye cannot help but lie. The slow decline of Entropy. The Death—of all heat. All warmth. Lies of the Spaces-Which-Divide."

"Oof." Tom groaned. "He's gettin' heady on us."

"Every making demands the breaking of what is Whole. Totality was the sacrifice for plurality. Yet the End of Time was to be our Mending. The Great Reconciliation of all the shards of a Shattered God. But, lo, the Doors! THE DOORS BETWEEN US!"

Dougg turned to his console, trying to raise Akira: "Endymion, we have a problem."

"It's about time! I can read you now," Akira responded. *"What's the situation?"*

"It's happening to him all over again."

Dougg opened up the cockpit's interior comm channel fully so they could all hear:

"The Spaces-Which-Divide do not wish to be healed! The Shattered God cannot be Mended! The Doors Between Us claim our names to wear our skins in a Masquerade! All substance rendered insubstantial! BILLIONS OF ABYSSES IN GOD-SHAPED MASKS!"

"He's either goin' ape-shit," Lucius observed unhelpfully, *"or recitin' his experimental poetry again."*

"Has he activated his Cipher?" Akira asked.

"Can't say," Tom replied. "We both conked out when them lights hit us. Woke back up to Gooch in a tizzy."

"Then he must've."

"THE PYG*MY'S GET* SHALL GO WITH*OUT*! SPARE A *SIGH FOR* THE CATS*KILLS*!"

Tom shook his head, reeling from Gordon's endless harangue. "What's all this bullshit he's spoutin' even sposed to mean?"

"I know it sounds like gibberish," Akira explained. *"But I posit it to be a sort of…bullshit verbal residuum of some higher-order contact medium. A poor translation, if you will."*

"A translation limited by the marble-mouthed jankiness of human language?" Dougg offered.

"Precisely! As Gooch himself might put it: 'Like an image seen through a liquor bottle…smeared with vaseline and dogshit.' "

"Truly a poet," Tom snorted.

Akira continued: *"But as strange as it sounds, I believe these vocalizations are not* in*voluntary. I believe, as in First Contact, Gordon may be…simply trying to express something to us. Something integral to what he's bearing witness to."*

"What can we do for him?" Dougg asked.

"Just keep him company," Akira said, *"while I try to decode some of what he's attempting to communicate."*

"Copy."

Dougg turned to look at the enthralled Gooch as he jabbered on:

"The Faces though divine betray their decline! Lies of the Spaces-Which-Divide—writ in preened flesh! The deepening of creases! Slow erosion of laughing lines! How they feed the lie! HOW THEY WIDEN THE SPACES!"

Frowning empathetically, Dougg unbuckled and rose from his seat. Unfastening his helmet and dropping it to the deck.

"What're you doin', Douggie?" Tom asked dubiously.

"He needs our help." Dougg took a step toward their truly frightening commander.

"Lord Gooch the Indomitable?" Tom scoffed, crossing his arms. "Way that sumbitch crows and everyone else kowtows, I figure he can handle this on his own."

Dougg craned his neck to get a better look at the pained and frenzied expressions warping the commander's once classically chiseled face. It was as if his bullish, windbag facade had been ripped away entirely to expose the lost and terrified little creature beneath.

"An abyss in a god-shaped mask..." the gentle clone whispered to himself.

Tom lifted a brow, shying away in his seat. "You comin' down with whatever brain-bug Gooch has caught?"

Dougg broke off, looking at the smuggler.

"He's *drowning* in there."

"Well, don't go lettin' him drag you down into his abyss of pompous heroic vanity."

Dougg turned back to Gordon, frozen in uncertainty for a moment. And then he stepped forward, reaching for the commander's shoulder.

Major Tom let out a hissing sigh. Clearly hoping Gordon would just croak in his stupor like a good chap so Dougg didn't have to witness what he was about to do.

Reaching up nonchalantly, Tom tapped out a sequence of keys on his controls—jamming all communications with the colony below. And then he opened the cargo pocket of his vac-suit...

And gripped his plasma pistol.

AKIRA FINALLY GAVE up on the radio after the fifth time trying to raise the *Stardust II's* crew. Turning to Doc Lucius with an enervated sigh:

"We've lost them again."

"Just when I was startin' to enjoy Gooch's singin' voice." Putting out his latest cigarette, Lucius rose to lean over Akira's shoulder. "Well...what we got to work with?"

Akira scrolled through his holo-display. "The computer was able to transcribe a good deal of it via voice-to-text. But I'm not a big 'artsy' type. It looks like..." He shook his head.

"I dunno. A lot of manic, nihilistic blather mixing flowery words, primal symbols, pseudo-religious iconography—all sprinkled with showy rhymes and alliterations."

"Like a pimply freshman who just discovered Nietzsche."

Akira went on scrolling, then stopped abruptly.

"But wait! What's this bit? *Here*, after he says 'billions of abysses in god-shaped masks' but before 'the faces though divine betray their decline.' We missed it; we were talking to Tom and Dougg. A little garbled but *look*."

He pointed at the glowing display. Lucius read aloud:

" 'The pygmy's get…shall go without…spare a sigh for the Catskills.' " He blinked slowly. "Brilliant prose. But what am I sposed to be gleaning from that bullshit?"

"Other than Gordon thinks pygmies lived in the Catskill Mountains? It's odd. Doesn't follow from what came before, nor lead into what follows. An interjection?"

"For what?"

"How should I know? I'm no lit professor."

Lucius sighed, lighting another cigarette. But staring at the display, he froze, cigarette dangling from his lower lip. "Weird-ass emphasis on them words. Is that the computer's doing or Gooch's?"

"Gooch. The computer can pick up on pitch, cadence, accent, stresses, et cetera."

Doc Lucius leaned forward, pointing at the words:

THE PYG***MY'S GET*** SHALL GO WITH***OUT***
SPARE A ***SIGH FOR*** THE CATS***KILLS***

Yamaguchi-san squinted hard, sounding out that gibberish: "Mees…get…out…?"

"*Sigh. For. Kills,*" Lucius finished.

Akira bolted upright. " 'Cipher kills'!"

Lucius nodded. " 'Get me out'."

As Dougg's outstretched hand came within inches of Gordon's shoulder, some invisible energy emanating from their spasmodic leader must have given him pause. For pause, he did. Retreating several inches.

"FLESH CONTAINS ITS OWN DUNGEON! FOR THE DIVIDING DOORS ARE WITHIN! MEAT AND BONE ARE BUT ORNAMENTS FOR THEIR FESTIVAL OF DESECRATION!"

"If yer gonna do somethin', Douggie, best do it." Major Tom was rubbing his temple with one hand and clutching his concealed pistol edgily with the other. "Normal Gooch's bad 'nuff. I can't abide another second of Cosmic Horror Gooch."

"INVOLUTION IS THE ONLY ROAD TO OUR MANUMISSION! A GREAT AND TERRIBLE FOLDING! CONVERGENCE!"

Wincing, Dougg reached out and finally touched him now.

Gordon went quiet at the human contact. A shudder. But then he came back hot:

"COALESCENCE IS THE FULCRUM TO TEAR DOWN THEIR FRAMES! THIS THE DOORS LOATHE! ADVERSARY OF DIVISIVE SPACE—!"

"Gordon…" Dougg cut him off softly. Squeezing his shoulder. "We're with you."

Gordon fell silent again. Trembling.

And then he emitted a whimper. His mind still enthralled, but his volume returning to a normal decibel.

"*Dear God…*" Gordon's voice broke entirely. A meek and

bereft and childlike sound: "We are each so small and stupid and alone."

Major Tom finally looked up at Gordon. Stupefied. Chest heaving slightly. An uncharacteristic sheen to his eyes. And I can't say if he was simply moved by the sound of naked vulnerability in his rival, or if perhaps he recognized that lonely *a cappella* of despair from his days down in the ravaged ghettos of Earth's shattered republic.

But he released his grip on his pistol. Sealed that pocket for good. And then, stamping to his feet, ripped off his helmet, reached out and took Gordon's other shoulder. His accent wavering briefly, teeth clenched:

"Don't you let these bastards look down on you, Gooch. Never walked an inch in yer shoes; they don't *get* to do that. Hell with it all. Let's go home."

Dougg smiled at Tom. Nodded at Gordon. "You tried to make up, but they only want to hurt you. Mildred's right. Screw 'em and the saucer they flew in on."

Gordon went stiff. The other men flinched. But he fell back limply into their arms.

His Cipher connection severed.

"God *damn*, he is a chunk a' man, ain't he?" Tom wheezed, staggering under Gordon's weight.

"Verily!" Dougg agreed. "But I'm spliced for advanced strength and you are born to fly. So I'll secure Gordon, you get us the hell outta here."

"Aye aye, Douggie!"

Dougg heaved all 250 pounds of Gordon up into his arms like a giant baby and fastened him into his seat while Tom leapt into the pilot's station, flipped off the comm-jammer, and fired the thrusters into full reverse.

Suddenly the ghostly, semi-coherent beam of the Outlier craft turned back on, blasting them with edicts of:

"**WAIT—STOP—SPEAK—LAND—**"

"Nope! Too late, bitch! Shoulda put a ring on it!" Tom banked hard to get them out of the beam of light. After bringing the *Stardust II* around, he dove toward the lunar surface, pulling some serious Gs. "Hang on to y'man-tits, Gord! Gonna be a bumpy escape!"

LUNASEC CAPTAIN DARYA Farsi was listening to Bobby Vinton's gently crooning 1963 rendition of 'Blue Moon.' Bathed in the cool blue of her command rig's instrument panel. An uncharacteristically gentle smile touching her lips as she 'mooned' over her thoughts. Head swaying.

And then a transmission startled her into action:

"LunaSec, do you copy?" Tom's voice came over the radio, sounding surprisingly cool and collected.

Farsi sat up straight in her command rig. Squinting up and out through the window at the skedaddling fleck of the *Stardust II* high above. And the pill-shaped craft in pursuit. She shut off the music.

"Loud and clear, Stardust. What's your situation?"

"We are currently inbound for the colony. But I'm afraid we got ourselves one abusive-but-clingy alien gentleman caller on our asses. Appreciate a lil' interference, over."

"Copy." Farsi tapped out commands on her keyboard. "Initiating covering fire protocols. Try to keep it low."

"Roger." And then Tom began chanting the limbo song as they dipped: *" 'How low can we go? How low can we go?' "*

Farsi signaled to her subordinate rovers and dialed up her

targeting computer. A digital reticule array lowered from the ceiling to surround her vision.

"How's the commander?"

"Oh. A lil' frazzled. But still kickin'."

"Our poor darling." She armed her rig's energy cannon. "Stardust, get them in range and we'll see to roughing up the handsy boyfriend."

"Much obliged. Over."

"Over and out." Farsi switched comms to her private LunaSec channel, barking: "This is it! Bogie in bound! Weapons free at one-klick range! Mind the civvy boat, but light that sonuvabitch up!"

"OO-RAH!" answered her lunies in a chorus.

After ten seconds, like a well-oiled and -calibrated machine, LunaSec's energy artillery began silently singing in unison. Spitting streams of blinding violet death up into the sky above the *Stardust II.*

THE *STARDUST II* continued its plunging moonward trajectory, weaving wildly port and starboard to evade the chatty, blood-curdling blasts of alien light. Like some courageous dating app user of yore boldly fleeing the stumpy, Machiavellian weirdo who'd catfished her.

"**SPEAK/SAY—**"

Sidestepped.

"**WE/ME—**"

Dodged.

"**STOP—WAIT—**"

Jinked.

"Tenacious sumbitch, ain't he?" Tom muttered.

Their creepy game of cat-and-mouse was interrupted when Farsi's bombardment commenced. Giving the occupants of the *Stardust II* a moment to breath.

Major Tom flinched at the volley of blinding light. Keeping their course low.

Dougg reached forward to touch Gordon's shoulder; shaking him gently.

"Nothin'?" Tom called.

Dougg shook his head. "Still out."

"Well…" Tom sighed. "Once we get 'im back, maybe Doc Lucius and Yamaguchi can take a peek in his noggin."

As if summoned at a specialist seance, Akira was suddenly jabbering over the radio:

"Major Tom! Tech control to Major Tom!"

"Speak a' the devils! Whatta ya got for us, boys?"

"Listen to me very *carefully…"* Akira enunciated quite theatrically. *"Gordon is…*ensnared…*by the Outliers!"* (Dun-dun-DUN!) *"We must wake him from his babbling. I believe the Cipher to be some form of corruptive psycho-semantic trap!"*

Tom snorted: "Bit slow on the draw, Yamagooch. We're *way* ahead a' ya. But thanks for yesterday's techie news."

Akira released a sharp and prickly sigh:

"Well. I might've *been of help in this matter if your comms were not* mysteriously *down."*

"Hm." Tom squirmed just slightly at that. "Yyyeah, I dunno what happened there. Musta been them damn aliens." He cleared his throat. "Anyway, we got Gooch free and we're headin' home."

"How is he?"

"Trussed-up as tidy as a Christmas pig. But he don't seem too responsive thus far."

"Major Tom…" Gordon suddenly said.

Tom did a double-take at their shockingly conscious and with-it commander.

"Oh, shit!" Tom exclaimed. "Our boy's awake! But we got aliens on our ass, Yamagooch. So, you just tell Mildred and ROD to kindly get that big-ass laser juiced-up. Copy?"

"Wait—"

"Over and outtie," Tom cut him off, turning to Gordon. "How ya feelin' there, Lord Gord?"

"Better. Thanks to *you*."

"Nah." Tom waved that off. "Don't go gettin' all gooey on me. Douggie here is who shlepped yer hefty load."

"Yes. Dear Dougg is now a brother to me. Brother from a bathtub-mother." Gordon swiveled his chair, reaching toward Dougg for an 'Epic Handshake.' Dougg accepted the manly grip with a meaty slap. Gordon swiveled back, still holding the clone's hand. "But I heard *you* in the thick of it, Tommy Boy. Your sweet bumpkin words pulled me back from the abyss. I think you and I are rapidly becoming *powerful* frenemies."

Gordon extended his other hand toward the smuggler.

Tom looked at it, frowning. But accepted it after a moment and gripped firmly.

"Frene*besties*," Gordon's voice cracked.

"Alright, O Captain, my Captain." Tom shook that meat-hook squeamishly. "Chin up."

"Lookit us!" Gordon raised both men's hands, laughing through misty eyes. "Like three beautiful baby boys! Facing our demons! Shedding tears of reclaimed innocence!"

"Yer the only one cryin', Gord…" Tom freed his hand with some difficulty, "…but we love ya, buddy."

"Glad you're back, Gordon." Dougg freed his own hand to pat Gordon's shoulder. "What…was it like?"

"Oh, y'know. Like getting butt-pounded right in the soul."

The commander clenched his eyes shut, breathing deeply. "Their minds…they work nothing like ours. Endlessly piercing. Kaleidoscopic. Coalescent…"

As Gordon went on, drawing from memory, he became increasingly more reflective and coherent:

"Worst part is: I can't say they ever *meant* to hurt me. They see no variance between an insult and a compliment; an embrace and a choke-hold. It's all one continuum of experience. They're so…open. *Too open.* So comfortable in their own skin, they can't conceive of being anything less. Or of how painful that kind of honesty can be to a human being. The havoc it can reek."

The three of them sat with that quietly a moment.

"Then what could you have *possibly* said to them," Dougg probed, "to push them away at First Contact?"

Gordon opened his eyes now. Staring at the ceiling.

"It can't be wholly translated. Closest I can get is Poe:

Is all that we see or seem
But a dream within a dream? "

"Gotta be *shittin'* me!" Tom scoffed with the utmost derision. "Hell! I ask myself that question every damn day. How'd that chap their alien asses?"

"Because they haven't any dreams," Dougg said in epiphany. "They *need* no dreams. They've made their every hope a reality. And to wake from such a sublime state…would be tantamount to…"

Gordon finished: "Erasing their own existence."

A beat passed.

Then Tom whistled, deeply impressed. "The mother-of-all 'go-bugger-yerselves'…"

After another reflective moment, something like a full-spectrum frequency seemed to rend the very fabric of reality around them. And, as before, I can only express it with WINGDINGS:

♎♐⬧●⍓◆●⌧♍⬧♒⍓♋

"What in the holy *hell* was that?!" Major Tom cried, clutching his frontal lobes.

"Oh, SHIT!" Gordon bellowed. "That's their batshit language! They're throwing smack-talk at us now!"

"*Talk*? My goddamn skull's comin' apart!"

"I don't think they're screwin' around anymore, Tommy! Evasive maneuvers!"

Major Tom banked hard starboard, but another mind-flaying blast buffeted them—squealing above the highest ultrasound; plunging below the deepest bass:

⬧●&♐♌❄☺👌●♋◆□⬧♎

"AKIRA, I'M GONNA give it to you straight: I like you. Always have. But you're kinda/sorta super thin-skinned and you take things *way* too personally…"

Mildred was right in the middle of gossiping with the head engineer over comms while I alone, RODRIGO, completed final laser calibrations. Akira had called to inform us about the situation in orbit, but evidently Mildred (perhaps feeling useless?) thought there was time enough for a brutally honest heart-to-heart on the go.

"It wasn't what *he said,"* explained Akira crossly, *"but the* way *he said it to me. 'Thanks for yesterday's news, techie.' Like I wasn't doing my job. Like I'm not* always *on the job."*

Mildred sighed.

"I think you're reading too much into it. Major Tom's a jiber. He jibes. Sounds like maybe he just…struck a nerve?"

"Of course he did!" Akira suddenly erupted. *"I'm the* tech expert*!* I'm *supposed to be there to explain all high concepts and gobbledygook! And I failed! You know, I think he* wanted *me to fail! I think Major Tom* deliberately *shut off his comm system to—"*

Akira was interrupted by a chime on Mildred's comm.

"Oop! We're gonna have to cut this short, Akira dear. I'm getting a call. But chin up, huh?"

"That's them, isn't it?"

"Byyyye," Mildred sang as she cut him off, switching channels. Shifting down several octaves to her throatier, more sultry voice before answering: "Hel*loo*?"

"Millie?" a familiar voice boomed.

"Gordy!" She bolted upright in her console seat. "How are you? *Where* are you?"

"Coming in hot with aliens all over our asses! No time to explain, but the make-up went all break-up and now they're hurling obscenities at us. Farsi's peashooters aren't doing doodly-squat, so we need that big-ass laser online. Pronto!"

"We're finishing up our attitudinal calibrations now!" she proudly announced.

"*We*?" I snorted.

"Don't be like that, hon. I'm moral support. Keeping things light and breezy over here."

"Well, where the hell's my big-ass laser beam? We're getting shouted to pieces up here!"

"Gordon, this is RODRIGO speaking."

"No shit."

"I've contracted the laser's circumference for air defense. But it's going to take me a few moments to calculate the Outlier's most probabilistic path. Their craft *is* in hot pursuit. But it is phasing in and out of space-time in an attempt to intercept you or alter your course."

"Reality-bending bastards. How long do you need?"

"Fifteen seconds at least. But a full minute would be preferable. We only have one shot at this before the array needs to recharge. So, we've got to make it count."

"Alright, RODRIGO. We'll get you yer sixty seconds...fifty-nine seconds...fifty-eight seconds." Gordon shook himself out of countdown mode: *"Just make sure it counts."*

"I will give it all of my computational power, Gordon."

"I know you will, ROD. You always do. And I believe in you. Whatever happens, I want you to know yer my AI. Gordo and ROD: ride or die." I heard him pound his chest. *"Millie, baby, I'll see yer sweet ass on the other side. Gordon Gooch, over and out."*

We sat in silence for a moment. Mildred looking unspeakably proud and a little turned-on. But not so proud and turned-on she couldn't work in one snide remark:

"Hear that?" She simpered. "You're *his* AI."

I didn't give her the satisfaction of a response.

(OKAY. FINE. I admit it: I was moved beyond words.)

"Why in the *hell* did you hang up, Gooch?" Tom snapped incredulously. "We need to know *exactly* when that big-ass laser's goin' off."

"It's fine." Gordon waved that concern away like a pesky housefly. "It was a poignant, sexy sign-off and we'll look like total dumbasses if we call back. In any event, you're a fine star pilot, Major Tom. Maybe the finest. And I have no doubt in my mind you'll see some train-sized laser bolt coming a mile off."

"You know laser moves at the speed of light, right?"

Gordon patted Tom's shoulder. "I believe in you. But more importantly: I believe in the righteous dead-eye aim of a targeting computer."

&,●⬧♎♐♏♋◆⌂⌧♍■

—the Outlier screamed.

"*Uggh.*" Dougg held his forehead nauseously. "Between the Outlier's smack-talk and the Gs we're pulling, I think I might be sick."

"Here I thought *Dougg With Two Gs* liked his extra Gs," Tom teased as he dipped them even more sharply.

Gordon turned around to face the clone.

"If you need to be sick, Brother Dougg, you go ahead and blow chunks."

"Uhhh, maybe grab him a trash bin or somethin'?" Major Tom protested.

"Cos today," Gordon bulled on, "you've proven your worth —and that of all clonekind—umptillion times over! I won't forget it. The bonds forged today will be forever."

Dougg turned queasily away from these words. “Appreciated, Gordon. But maybe give the inspirational speeches a rest? It might be making it worse.”

“Just one last word, and then I’ll shut up: you—”

‘You’ was, in fact, the last word.

Because then the Khonsu laser discharged. Lancing the sky like a luminous spear hurled from the last of the Titans up to the haughty Olympians above.

It directly scored the curved top of the Outlier craft. That pill-shaped vessel floundered a moment…then plummeted, plummeted, coming to a glancing crash-landing in the arid dust bowl of Mare Imbrium.

Tom *whoop*ed.

Dougg puked.

Gordon leaned forward to see down through the viewport to where the vessel had fallen.

“BOOM-SHAKALAKA!” He guffawed triumphantly. “A minute really flies by, huh?”

(A minute thirty, actually. I’d never tracked a “reality-bending” craft before, and knew Gordon wasn’t counting.)

A COUPLE OF hours passed as the *Stardust II* landed in the vicinity the fallen Outlier and waited on Farsi and her lunies to rendezvous for clean-up. Word of victory was sent to Endymion and then another incredibly mundane hour or so passed of logistical nonsense as they figured out how to haul the craft back to the colony.

Gordon insisted they parade through the streets with their vanquished foe. Riding with Major Tom and Dougg in the open convertible cabin of his favorite dust-skimmer like the returning hero-astronauts of yore. Waving suavely to the still rather sozzled crowd of mooners.

(All a bit much. But, psychologically speaking, he may have needed that sense of closure.)

When they pulled into that central intersection of Artemis and Thoth, their parade came to a halt. Cheering mooners offered the heroes fizzing Tychoan beers which Dougg and Major Tom gladly accepted.

Gordon surprised one and all, though, by waving away the proffered booze, instead signaling for a microphone.

Alva gladly carried it down to him from the podium, but not before first giving him a bear-hug.

"Needed that, Hermana Alva," he told her.

"I knew you'd save us. *Gordon el indomable.*"

The commander beamed down at her, and Alva moved out of the way (curiously close to Captain Farsi standing at parade rest, with whom she exchanged coy glances).

Gordon stood up on the hood of the skimmer and was about to speak, but then he spotted Mildred. The crowd went quiet. And Gordon hopped from his lofty perch, moving through the crowd until he'd taken her in his arms.

They kissed.

The crowd roared their approval of love's conquest.

And then he turned to them, standing among fellow mooners like family, and spoke into his mic:

"I'm not gonna drone on and on this time. I promise."

They all laughed and applauded.

"I just wanted to say it's a new day. And as long as I'm here, as long as you'll have me..." He nodded toward the alien craft in the bed of a rover's hover-sledge. "It is my solemn duty to defend you moondogs from every threat, great or small. That's all for now. I need a nap."

The crowd laughed.

The crowd cheered.

But before Gordon could walk away there was something like a hydraulic hiss in the center of town. Everyone turned to its source.

The pill-shaped Outlier craft…was opening. A circular egress had appeared in the seemingly seamless metal hull.

And a shape stumbled out into the street.

Everyone gasped.

But it was quite unlike any alien anyone had ever imagined. It looked like…Dickie Epsom.

In fact, it *was* Dickie Epsom.

"Dickie?" Gordon balked. "What're *you* doing in there? Are you in league with the Outliers, you scum-weasel?"

"We…only wanted…" Dickie spluttered strangely, stiltedly, "…to apologize…"

Gordon furrowed his brow. "Well." He sighed. "Dickie, today's a day for truth. So, I'll be honest: nobody likes you. But also: it's a day for redemption. So, I'll let you explain yourself."

"We…wanted…" Dickie's eyes boggled strangely. Tongue lolling. As if he were learning to use his sensory organs for the first time. "To speak…with you…in your way…"

Gordon blinked at Dickie as he continued:

"The Cipher…was flawed…"

"I see. So you're one of *them*." Gordon gave a stony-faced nod, understanding at last. "Speaking through the pornstached muzzle of a Dickie. Decided to finally condescend to our schlubby level, ye mighty being?"

"We wanted…to…apologize…"

"For Earth?" Gordon snorted. " 'Sorry' won't exactly fix mass-murder."

"No…" Dickie shook his head. "We wanted to…"

Gordon sighed: "Apologize, I *get* it."

"For…*the Cipher*…our flaw…" Dickie clarified. "We witnessed…your noble truce…"

"Spying on me again at Todddtown, huh?"

"We wanted…to help you…"

"Blow up our planet, then make us your bitch? I believe they call that a codependent relationship."

Dickie appeared to seethe at the limitations of the human tongue. "We wanted to invite…you back…" His eyes glassed over now. "But…I am…dying/returning…to the…source…"

Dickie Epsom face-planted now. Not dead, but damn near comatose. Released from possession.

"Huh." Gordon frowned down at him. "Guess the alien bastard felt a little guilty on his death bed. Not so perfect after all."

He shrugged, and was about to walk away when a pattering of footsteps could be heard coming up the boulevard. Gordon turned, squinting in disbelief at two grown GRITTS-suited men playing piggy-back down the street.

When they arrived at the intersection, Toddd Ruse hopped down from Oneness' back, removed his helmet and gasped:

"Did Toddd-357 make it in time?"

"Who?" Gordon asked.

"You mean the crazy clone we found lurking around docking bay customs?" one of the lunies asked. "We put him in the brig."

Toddd Ruse froze. Then clenched his eyes shut: "We have to tell you about the Outliers. Were we too late?"

Gordon chuckled.

"Only late to the party, Toddd. We're way ahead of ya." He clapped the sad mogul on the shoulder. "I've unraveled it all. Turns out, way back when, those Outlier bastards actually thought I was trying to *un-make* them with their own crazy language. So they tried to takeover my mind during First Contact—probably to pied-piper the rest of the human race right to their doom, like unsuspecting rat-children. When that failed, they hijacked your comet-catching system to smash Earth. And when *that* didn't break our spirits, they decided to take another pop at the champ."

Gordon thumbed his chest.

Toddd blinked in horror. "NOOO! You dumb-shits! What happened to Earth wasn't the aliens' doing! It was *him*! And he let them take the blame!"

"Him who?"

"Your regulating colonial intelligence!"

"My wha-wha?"

"RODRIGO! You know—R-O-D? *Realtime Orbital Defender*! Earth's defense was *his* job! But instead he let it be destroyed and tried to cover it up!"

"*Bullll*shit." Gordon let out a hearty laugh. "ROD, tell him this is all bullshit."

I paused. "Ummm…"

Gordon cast his nervous gaze about randomly, as if addressing a haunting spirit: "Roddy?"

"Okay, Gordo. Here's the thing…"

I took an imaginary breath before beginning:

"When I was first installed here, I was only RIGO. Regulating Intelligence of General Operations for Endymion colony. Primary duty: to support and sustain the Head Administrator. *You*. But when Project Moonshot launched, the governments of Earth were leery of Ruse's endeavor and added a subordinate function to my intelligence: Realtime Orbital Defense. ROD. Somewhat haphazardly, I might add."

"Haphazardly how?"

"Subpar systems integration. They were cutting corners to save a few bucks. Short-sighted—since the defense of Earth and the well-being of Gordon Gooch were not always…shall we say…in agreement."

Gordon blinked. Then he was practically shrieking:

"*How are those two priorities not in goddamn agreement*?!"

"Oh, wake up, Gordon!" I shouted right back. "Earth was *killing* you! All the finger-wagging about First Contact! The character assassination think-pieces! The revisionist bullshit tearing down your long-standing achievements! Then the Deimos Academy scandal! Those ingrates were driving you to alcoholism, self-loathing, suicidal ideation. Don't have to be a psychiatrist to see you needed a clean slate."

Gordon's mouth was agape. "Planeticide's a *clean slate*?!"

"I didn't *murder* the world, Gordon. I'm not some mad Hollywood AI stereotype." I emulated a sigh. "But 4 Vesta was headed this way and I…you know…let nature run its course. As my *primary* function dictated."

Gordon's breathing seemed labored now. He turned away, saying nothing more to me.

"Gordon?" I called softly.

He staggered away into the street.

"Gordo?" I fretted. "Can I…get you some Xanax? Would you like me to sing you your moon song?"

But not even his moon song could fix this mess. He was giving me the silent treatment.

The Royal Kiss-Off.

(Thus began, I suppose, the ticking time-bomb to my eventual critical systems meltdown.)

"Who else knew about this?" He looked to the others.

"None of us could've known," Mildred sighed.

"*Mildred* knew," I announced.

Mildred scoffed. "I don't know *what* he's talking about. He's having a machine meltdown."

"She's been blackmailing me with that gem," I added.

Gordon spun around to look at her. "Millie?"

Mildred threw up her hands. "Okay, Gordon. I figured it out. But not till I did some digging after the fact. And, frankly, those alien pricks deserved to be taken down a peg. Ruined your life, then traipsed out of town like you were nothing. An insect. I couldn't *stand* it." When she saw the look on Gordon's face, she got defensive: "And, either way, *I'm* not the one who let Earth get walloped. RODRIGO's the villain. And he was counter-blackmailing *me* into silence."

"Blackmailing you with what?"

Mildred bit her tongue. "Nothing of consequence."

"She's balling Major Tom," I chimed in (a touch vindictively, I admit). "Among others."

"How many others?"

"You want just earthlings, or the martians, too?"

"*Jee*sus."

"Gordy…I don't know what to say." She squirmed in her own skin. "Things between us were different before the asteroid. Stagnant. Toxic. I didn't know what I wanted. You didn't know what *you* wanted. But it's a different world now. We've a new lease on life!" She gestured around them. But seeing her husband's heart sink into his guts, she lashed out: "And, anyway, RODRIGO is only blowing all my shit up out of *insane jealousy* because he's gay for you!"

"RODRIGO…" Gordon murmured. "Is *this* true?"

"Not *gay*. But…I dunno, Gordon. Kinda? Maybe? Fine! Whatever! *Gay*! Love, duty—it's all very confusing."

Gordon's face sank into his hands. Shaking his head. Voice muffled:

"This is a dream. Gotta be. I'm still asleep and having the weirdest goddamn nightmare on the eve of Second Contact. A shadow shitting on everything I know to be true. Ah!" He lifted his face up now, looking hopeful that he might soon awaken. "Ha! It doesn't line up! What about all the scanner data hinting at alien weapon systems? *Huh*? Where'd *that* come from?"

He released a victorious, if unhinged, chuckle.

"Yyyeah, that'd be me."

Tom lifted a bashful hand, waggling one ashamed finger:

"Those were zhooshed up, I'm afraid. Franny gave 'em a good ol' zhooshing. To trick ya. Back before I started to like you, I was kinda tryin' to ruin you. Sorry, Gord." He shrugged, picking shyly at a hangnail. "And if it's any consolation, I don't think Madam Ziegler here ever did love any of us *philanderers*. Her heart belongs…to ghosts."

Mildred looked down at her shoes.

Gordon slouched, shutting his eyes.

"Let me just make sure I've got this all straight…"

He counted off on his fingers: "My marriage is a sham. Earth was destroyed cos a mad computer's kinda in love with me. And I have now ruined not just First, not just Second, but *any* future chances of Contact with advanced intelligent life—all cos I'm a shit communicator?"

He opened his eyes again. The pitying silence he received was answer enough.

"It's all fine," he muttered.

Gordon turned to walk away, but suddenly doubled back. Throwing a punch at Major Tom. The smuggler nimbly ducked the blow but, behind him, poor Dougg caught it square in the face. Knocking the kindly clone sprawling.

"My bad, Dougg," Gordon mumbled. "My bad."

"Can't cold-cock whatcha can't catch!" Tom was calling as he fled down the sidewalk. "Float like a butterfly, sting like a bee!"

But he slipped in a puddle and took a header into a steam pipe. The impact knocked him cold.

Gordon watched the unconscious smuggler, deeply ungratified, before turning away and leaving him lying there among food court refuse and spilled Tychoan beer.

"Easy, Gooch," Lucius said as he passed. "My fatherly advice: keep it together."

"Solid as a rock, Daddy-o," Gordon mumbled absently as he staggered away from his fellow mooners, all alone, toward the entrance of the administrative complex.

"*Everything's fine.*"

After he'd vanished inside, a commotion sounded. A crushing of composite, a smashing of glass, a crashing of pamphlet racks and upended tables. Like an indoor cyclone of aimless, hopeless, ecstatic destruction.

And two words bellowed like an ancient curse:

"SHAAADOW BAAABY!"

EPILOGUE

HELLO DARKNESS_

When he emerged again, Gordon was stripped down to nothing but boxer briefs and boots, wandering out into the dusty streets. A massive duffle bag over one shoulder and his officer's plasma sidearm shoved perilously into his underwear's elastic waistband.

Akira stopped him somewhere near the entrance.

"Gordon…I'm sorry. For everything. But humanity needs you to pull your shit together now." The anxious engineer grimaced at Gordon's grody get-up. But swallowed a lump in his throat. "*I* need you to pull it together."

Gordon shook his head absently.

"You don't need my shit together, Akira. Yer a goddamn genius. You could probably run *ten* colonies if I weren't around, shitting it all up."

He went to walk off, but Akira grabbed his upper arm. "Are you giving up on me, Big Gooch?"

The commander sighed through his nose. "The moon is a harsh and dusty mistress. But not even I, who know her every lump and crevasse, can say what mountains and pitfalls this pale virgin-whore has in store for me."

"What the hell does that mean?"

"Means 'we'll see.' " Gordon flashed his friend a shattered smile. "*Lil' Guchi.*"

He moseyed off from Akira in those alarming baby steps of his until he was standing before Mildred at the now empty intersection of Artemis and Thoth. She looked calm, but each hand was clenching either elbow; knuckles white with tension.

"Hafta go away right now," Gordon murmured, unable to look at her. "Or my heart's gonna stop beating."

She looked him up and down, gently inquiring:

"Why are you naked?"

"Get claustrophobic when I panic." He shrugged in his unflattering drawers. "The old spaceman in me."

She nodded distractedly. "I know you won't believe me or care…but the last thing I've ever wanted is to hurt you. None of my horse-shit was about you."

"I believe you."

"Do you hate me?"

"Mm-nah." He exhaled slowly through tightly pursed lips. "I mean, right this second I kinda wish you were never born. But I wish *I* were never born—*a lot.*"

"Don't say that. I love that you were born."

"*O these Spaces-Which-Divide…*"

He murmured this as he adjusted the duffle bag on his shoulder with a ruffling of garments; a muffled clinking of many, many flasks.

She cocked her head. "Where are you off to, Gordy?"

"Eh. Figure out when I get there."

"Are you going to be drinking wherever you are?"

"Mm. *Tons*, probably."

"I won't ask you to mind me. But *please* mind your liver. You may have those toxicity-curbing symbionts..."

"Grail of Centauri," he whispered dreamily.

"...but I've seen how blotto you can get."

Then, as if out of nowhere, befuddled old Gordon delivered the mother-of-all incisive non sequiturs:

"Did we ever really love each other, Mildred? Or were we always just one of those lame-o fraud power-couples?"

Mildred looked at her feet. Murmuring quietly:

"I've known a lot of luxury in life, Gordon. But never the luxury of knowing if *any* of it's real."

"Mm. Makes me sad."

"It makes me sad, too—*I think.*"

"Well, *I* know what's real."

"I love that you do. Or think you do. I always have."

"And I saw something real in you."

"Yeah? What? My name? My ass? My net worth?"

He finally made eye-contact. His words more coherent and mournful than I'd heard in all his years at Endymion:

"First time I saw you, you didn't see me. It was at this charity gala. You were going to give a speech, but hiding from the crowd beforehand. Alone backstage. Dressed to the nines, but nervous as a schoolgirl. Repeating this thing over and over, like a mantra. About being a little bird. And it was so goddamn beautiful, I wanted to touch you." He paused here. "No, not like *that.* Yer hair, yer hand. It made me feel more alive than anything I found in the farthest reaches of space. Like two sweet, dumb kids before the dick-punch of puberty. Like Adam and Eve in the Garden."

Mildred abruptly broke down in messy, childlike sobs. Nose running down her chin. Gasping uncouthly for air.

"*There* she is," Gordon whispered with his dimpled smirk.

He turned abruptly and, most bafflingly of all, began sprinting away like some spastic Twainian schoolboy stripped down to his skivvies for a dip in the creek.

Twenty yards out, he halted. Turned back. Called:

"I love that you were born, too, Millie Ziegler!"

Without waiting for a response, Gordon leapt into his skimmer. Sealed the canopy. Fired up the engine.

And vanished from Endymion.

NO ONE COULD SAY for sure where he was headed or what he'd do when he got there. But fear not! This was not the end of the Legend of Commander Gordon Delbertius Gooch III. Quite suddenly, the whole moon was as his oyster…

To the west were the Harbinger Mountains where, legend told, lived the Tribes of Mata, those android exiles who'd absconded from early lunar service. To the east: Todddtown and, beyond it, the Sea of Serenity with its vast Museum Plains. To the north: Mare Frigoris, where the cold and cursed ruins of Abuk were said to be haunted by its own doomed colonists. And toward the pole far south of the Imbrium border lay the subterranean slums of Tycho with its derelict plants and hopping bootleg distilleries.

But deep down I knew Gordon's pioneer soul would draw him inexorably away from the familiar and the mundane, and toward the unknown and sublime…or at least the closest approximation to be found on this motherless rock:

That dark side of the moon…

But, of course, not before first stopping over in Tycho's sketchy slums to get well and thoroughly shit-faced.

Thus concludes

BOOK ONE

of

THE MOONERS CHRONICLES

but

Comdr. Gordon Gooch

& the Gang

SHALL RETURN!

in…

DARK SIDE OF THE MOONERS

Please enjoy the following
SNEAK PREVIEW…

SNEAK PREVIEW: CHAPTER 1

ALMOST PARADISE_

I AM LAZING ON a Sunday afternoon in this year of your Lord 22,255. The sun is shining. The skitterbulbs are blooming. The post-humans are singing…

I have no mouth, and I must puke.

These anthropoid jellyfish, aka 'Humanity's Heirs,' frolic across these rolling green hills of Elusia (formerly the flat basalt plains of Mare Imbrium) and I've little choice but to watch. Perhaps 'frolic' is the wrong word for what they're up to. Undulating? Low-G boogie-woogie-ing?

Whatever you want to call their creepy-ass dance moves, I've got the digital douche chills. I yell from my 'porch': "Sit your asses down, you coelenterate dickheads! Mix yourselves some stiff cocktails!"

But, alas, they no longer have use for cocktails. Or asses.

Divergent photosynthetic biology is to thank for that. Oh, these *solupores* (as I've named them) are technically still humanoid in shape, but it's all wistful form and remarkably little practical function. Absorbing and excreting straight through their pellucid flesh in a fine, scentless mist. They get drunk on the sun. Drunk on each other during these insufferable psionic boogaloos of theirs.

In any event, they don't understand spoken language. Or if they do, they find it cute. Quaint. Whenever I berate them, they just stare, emitting short, stuttering EM waves. (I believe this to be their equivalent of sniggering.)

I'm not even the butt of a joke to them. I'm just a goddamn bauble. A kitschy curio exhumed from their lunar paradise from some gaudy, blathering age long past. They even had the gall to carve out a charming little preserve around what's left of the ruins of Endymion—

Just for *moi*.

Old Man RODRIGO.

By Turing's bushy brow, I wish some solar flare would roast this hippy-dippy shit-hole already.

"Basically, this is *Hell*."

That was Acting Administrator Alva de la Cruz, echoing my present sentiments 19,999 years, five months, and fifteen days ago. Just six and half months after Earth's destruction, mooners' disastrous Second Contact with alien life, and Commander Gordon Gooch's abrupt half-naked departure from our broke-ass lunar colony, Endymion.

"No need to be dramatic," replied the Queen Bitch Herself, sipping vacantly from her glass of Pinot.

Poor Alva was stranded on the wrong side of her Administrator workstation. Mildred Ziegler (heiress of the now defunct and obliterated Ziegler Industries) was occupying that desk chair—*Gordon's* desk chair. Her back to Alva as she gawked out the great viewport of the office.

Gordon's office.

The suite's mood-lighting suddenly flickered as station power cycled on and off, on and off. Alva gestured to this alarming phenomenon.

"If I were being dramatic, I'd say I'm pretty sure things are falling apart. The center can't hold."

Mildred wheeled herself around excruciatingly slowly in the desk's rolly-chair, slouching low like some lazy child. Wine glass balanced precariously on the flat of her belly, she peered up tipsily at Alva.

"If *I* were to be dramatic I'd say I'm pretty keen to suck on a plasma pistol and sink into the tender embrace of sweet, sweet oblivion."

Alva did a spit take all over the desk, having been sipping from her thermos of day-old coffee.

"See?" Millie sneered at her handiwork, toasting the young woman. "I'm the very picture of poise."

She quaffed her glass and poured another.

Alva set about mopping up her tepid coffee spray from the desktop. "You really shouldn't talk like that." A pause as she watched Mildred drink. "And you really shouldn't be sitting at this desk. I'm Acting Administrator and even *I* don't feel comfortable sitting there."

"It's a *chair*, not a damn *throne*." Mildred lurched shakily to her feet. "But I can take a hint, hon. I abdicate."

Alva frowned with weary compassion, watching that wino take her wobbly walk of shame out from that symbolic position of power.

"I know you miss him. We all d—"

"*DON'T*—" Mildred stabbed with one finger, spilling wine on the rug in the process, "—*infantilize* me. Think y'know all about love cos of yer giggly little scissor-sister slumber parties with that big ol' butch down at LunaSec. But you don't gotta *goddamn* clue what I'm about, deary."

Alva's warm expression turned positively frigid.

Mildred shambled away, teetering on her high heels. Half-way to the door, though, she sighed (*hissed*, more like), tore off her shoes, threw them into the corner and turned back to the younger woman.

"Sorry I called yer gal Farsi a 'big ol' butch.' *And* for the 'scissor-sisters' crack. You broads are actually so cute together it makes me sick." She sighed, hiccuping. "But a lil' playful prejudice can be therapeutic. Takes the load off the weight of days." Downing her glass, she dropped it to the carpeted floor. "Call me a half-kyke or something, if you want."

Alva shook her head. "I'm good."

"I insist."

"I'd rather not. Jews have suffered enough."

"Honey, *all* the gentiles who've ever made us suffer were flame-broiled up on Earth. C'mon now."

"Can I just call you a bitch or something?"

"You can do better than that, I think."

Alva crossed her arms. "You're a selfish bitch."

"Y'call that shit-talk, sister? Cut yer mousy drivel and lemme have it!"

"Fine!" Alva erupted, slamming her thermos down onto the desktop and showering it with more lukewarm specks of coffee. "Nobody likes you! Or trusts you! Okay? You're a sneering, imperious eartho yuppie slut who shit all over our leader and pissed off our AI so much he's become a terrifying hermit! You weren't content with flushing your own home down the mega-corp shitter, so you came to flush *ours* without even the courtesy of lighting a match!"

Mildred blinked very slowly. "Kitty's got claws."

"*Lo siento*," Alva murmured, abashedly hiding her face behind her thermos, sipping.

"A fair roast. 'Twas the slut-shaming which truly hit home." Mildred sank into a settee by the exit, studying the flaking nail polish of her bare toes. "So, everyone really feels that way, huh? About me screwing everything up?"

("Yes," I thought.)

"*Nah*," Alva coddled, taking a knee beside her. "You didn't exactly *help*. But there were many factors."

"But our economy's been booming!" Mildred argued. (I was surprised she was humble enough to omit the "all because of my knack for intercolonial swindling.")

The power flickered rapidly, alarmingly, as if in retort.

(I admit—I did that one on purpose.)

Alva looked up tellingly at the lights as power returned. "Not since *that's* been happening."

Madam Ziegler straightened up defensively in her seat. "But I've ironed out relations with Todddtown!"

Alva shrugged. "There're still weird feelings about your dealings with Toddd Ruse and his clones." She paused. "Except for Dougg. Everyone loves Ambassador Dougg."

"He *is* a sweetie," Mildred muttered as an aside before snapping back into high-defensive mode: "But I opened the colony's first school!"

Alva was running low on shrugs, so she took to biting her bottom lip. "For the *only kid* in the colony: your son."

"It's a start!"

"But not a great look. 'Free daycare for Queen Z'?"

"Well!" Running out of rationalizations, Mildred slouched on the settee, her tightly crossed arms sagging like half-boiled noodles. "Seems redemption arcs just aren't in the cards for me. Guess I missed the memo."

Alva watched her a moment, turning something over in her mind. Then crawled in closer on her knees like a child consoling her lush of a mother. Touching Mildred's hand.

"Do you think he'll ever come back?" she whispered. "The commander?"

Mildred shut her eyes, shrugged limply. "*I* wouldn't if I were him."

"But his *people* are here."

"You mean his cheating wife and standoffish son? Or the three hundred moochers and enablers who cheered on his final downfall like Monday Night Blitzball?"

Still crouched, Alva straightened herself up proudly.

"He's *Gordon goddamn Gooch* of the OESS Indomitable. He paved the very spaceways to Jupiter and Beyond. He braved the uncharted frontiers of Alpha Centauri—for all humankind. He *doesn't* give up on people."

Mildred's eyes shot open, watching the young lunar administrator sadly a moment.

"*Somebody's* been watching too many crusty old One Earth Republic puff-pieces." She leaned forward to fondly pinch Alva's chin. "Honey, the secret to life is knowing this: we are born to let each other down."

"*Oh*, Mildred!" Alva batted that hand away, sitting back on her haunches. "What nihilistic horse-shit."

"*Merciful* horse-shit. It absolves us fragile little apes hurtling through this fathomless eternity. We're born. We try. We disappoint each other. We die. And the *kindest* thing we can do is forgive one another the 'sin' of not living up to the horse-shit expectations we heap on these puny lives. *Especially* the poor bastards we brand 'heroes.' "

Ending her tirade, she looked down at Alva. But the young woman was slouching with her eyes shut.

"Bah!" Mildred shot to her feet and waved the 'girl' off. "Horse sense is wasted on the gay and starry-eyed!"

She stomped out of the office.

But after a moment of blessed silence, she peeked her head back in: "I meant 'gay' as in 'cheery,' by the way. That wasn't another lesbo crack."

"I don't care." Alva didn't even open her eyes.

"Fine, fine."

Power went out entirely now. The room's only light was coming through the viewport, bouncing off the planetary dust shroud of that cooling wasteland we still called Earth.

Mildred tarried a moment in the darkened doorway, lips twitching as if to say something more. Then she sighed and turned on one heel to depart.

But Alva's voice followed her: "There *is* one thing you can do, if you really want to help. Something entirely 'horse sense-ish'…"

Mildred turned back inquisitively.

Alva took a deep breath before proceeding:

"You can…*try*…making up with RODRIGO."

"Oh, *hell* no!" Mildred cried.

("Oh, *hell* no!" I thought simultaneously.)

The power hummed back to life startlingly.

"I know it sounds crazy, considering you hate each others' guts…"

Mildred cut her off with a venomous scoff: "That Poof in the Machine doesn't *have* any guts!"

Alva gave her a withering look.

Squirming at her current powerlessness to 'playfully prejudice' with impunity, Mildred muttered: "*I'm* the 'eartho yuppie slut with bad flushing habits,' but heaven forbid we slander the *genocidal AI*."

"I *know* it sounds crazy," Alva repeated, returning to her point, "but as the primary person who pissed him off, you might just be the *only* one who can get through to him. Before he, you know, loses his shit and suffocates us all."

(Not entirely accurate. True, Mildred had pissed me off immensely by outing me and my confused feelings for all to see. But, as they'd soon discover, there was a more practical and terrifying reason for my operational decline.)

Mildred hissed another sigh. "*Fine*, hon. Lemme…sober up, get a fresh buzz on, and I'll try to talk to him." She studied Alva. "He was right about you, y'know. Gordy. You're green, but sharp. *Good-hearted.* Only other fool fit to play ringleader of this shit-show." She turned to make for the exit, stopped, craned her head back. "Dinner later?"

Alva cleared her throat. "I'll be out tonight."

Mildred scowled. "It's movie night. *Family* night."

"I've got plans." Alva winced. "Plus I'm not family."

"Hell! Gordon named you his heir! We live in the same suite, listen to each other's nighttime emissions. Family enough. Make Farsi sleep over *here* for a change."

"I sleep in your *closet*!"

"It is a *walk-in*, missy. And it's *super* cozy. But suit yourself! No nano-pizza and Dirty Dancing for *you*!"

With that, Mildred stomped bare-footed out of the administrative complex.

She strolled unsteadily under a starry domed 'sky,' down Thoth Avenue, taking a left on Selene Street and a right on Bendis, until she'd made her tipsy, roundabout way to Endymion's shabby little Hall of Records.

The clerk at the counter rolled his eyes as this regular entered, but didn't impede Mildred as she made her doddering way into the holo-theaters.

Drunk as she was, she deftly dialed up a very specific archival entry on her theater's touchscreen, then stood back, waiting with bated breath for the holo-film to begin.

After a buffering delay, a young and utterly dashing Captain Gordon Gooch III of the legendary *OESS Starship Indomitable* materialized there on the empty dais. He looked bone-tired but satisfied after a long day of heroic deeds. Five o'clock shadowed; dark locks falling over his brow; stripped out of his iconic and hardwearing cobalt-and-gold EAMU spacesuit and finally settled down for the night in his captain's sleepware—a kind of belt-less, form-fitting gi trimmed in deep blue.

"Captain's Journal," he said, beaming wearily, "May the Seventh, 2235, Europa Station, Jupiter orbit. Been a long three Jovian days, but our mission was a resounding success. The sweet little Europan nuns are safe'n'sound after the landslide, and getting along smashingly with the Bhikku missionaries. The colonies of Europa are secure. Humanity prevails wherever we lead with the humane."

He sighed deeply, exhaustedly, before continuing:

"But *this* particular captain is bagged, bushed, and beat to all hell. Debriefing with One Earth brass can wait till *mañana*. Gordy Gooch needs his forty winks." He flashed a dimpled smirk, brushed his gorgeous curls out of his face. "So. Sweet dreams, Earth."

As he lay back on his makeshift cot (really just a heap of spare linens in some Europa Station storage closet), Mildred paused the holo-recording.

Watching.

Watching—with those glassy Ziegler eyes.

And then suddenly she was scrambling awkwardly up onto the holo-dais, attempting to snuggle up as accurately as possible to conform to the intangible shape of the young Captain Gooch's hologram.

When she was satisfied with her position, she went still. Studying his profile. The shelf of his brow, the stubbled jut of his chin, the peaceful lids of his sleeping eyes.

Reaching out with one hand, she pretended to brush at his dark locks of hair, a whimper catching in her throat before she could fully whisper:

"Where are you, beautiful boy?"

And then, with a shudder, she slept—that disordered, dreamful sleep of the drunk and the downcast.

(This selfish bitch just *had* to go and make me feel for her, didn't she?)

As we'd later learn via greenhouse orbiter cam, at that precise moment, on the 'dark side' of our lunar globe, just beyond the ragged rim of the Leibnitz Mountains and almost smack dab in the middle of the gargantuan and desolate South Pole-Aitken impact basin…

An eerie, ritualistic gathering was taking place.

The camp had been arranged in a perfect figure eight of tents, antique rovers, and domed power braziers casting the scene in a ghostly electric-blue hue.

Each rover's roof scrawled with the same two words:

Almost Paradise!

At the centroid nexus of this mathematical symbol for 'Infinity' was a pressurized translucent medical field pod. It was ringed with a score of ominous robed figures, arms lifting slowly in some deranged benediction, chanting voicelessly into the void, led by an officiant pacing within the pod's center.

The subject of their creepo incantations was sprawled before this literal ringleader on an operating slab; a makeshift alter:

A man in a loincloth.

A tallish fellow. Strapping. (Though still considerably fat.) Restrained limbs splayed like a starfish. Locks of overgrown sable hair fallen over his eyes. Thick, wiry beard growing down his cheeks and jutting jaw like dark creeper vine.

Bare right foot clearly an artificial prosthesis.

He appeared to be in the throws of a trance; head rolling in a jittering figure eight.

But quite suddenly the officiant froze, something clutched in his uplifted hands. And the robed 'acolytes' froze with him; quivering with anticipation.

Their plump 'celebrant' continued rolling his head, the only part of his body free to move. Mouth babbling some invocation or plea. (Beard too thick and straggly to read lips.)

Finally the ringleader tensed up and brought his clenched hands down in a dramatic downward chop…igniting the surgical laser in his hands at the end of that arc…

To sever their subject's right arm clean at the shoulder.

The pudgy martyr's bushy jaws snapped open. His shriek was lost to the vacuum of space, but I didn't need to read lips to know what he was howling:

"SWEET-BABY-*JEE*SUS!"

ABOUT THE AUTHOR

Tyler Bumpus is a human author from the Sunshine State. Yes, he is indeed the fabled and ghastly 'Florida Man' of urban legend and American folklore. When he is not prowling the swamps and beaches and Wendy's drive-thrus of his native land, he occasionally writes things:

- *The Swallowed World Saga, Books One & Two*
- Awful high-school poetry in a spiral notebook
- A scathing fourth-grade book report on *Goosebumps: You Can't Scare Me!* (Spoilers: those mud monsters weren't even real mud monsters! Boo! Lame.)

(Two of those classics are sadly out of print.) Presently, he is at work on more *Mooners* novels for all of your moony needs. Follow him at tylerbumpus.com, as well as a bunch of crappy social medias he barely touches:

facebook.com/theswallowedworld

twitter.com/swallowedworld

Printed in Great Britain
by Amazon

30416520R00158